UNBRIDLED

This Large Print Book carries the
Seal of Approval of N.A.V.H.

UNBRIDLED

DIANA PALMER

THORNDIKE PRESS
A part of Gale, a Cengage Company

Farmington Hills, Mich • San Francisco • New York • Waterville, Maine
Meriden, Conn • Mason, Ohio • Chicago

Copyright © 2018 by Diana Palmer.
Long, Tall Texans.
Thorndike Press, a part of Gale, a Cengage Company.

Thorndike Press® Large Print Romance.
The text of this Large Print edition is unabridged.
Other aspects of the book may vary from the original edition.
Set in 16 pt. Plantin.

LIBRARY OF CONGRESS CIP DATA ON FILE.
CATALOGUING IN PUBLICATION FOR THIS BOOK
IS AVAILABLE FROM THE LIBRARY OF CONGRESS.

ISBN-13: 978-1-4328-5491-1 (hardcover)

Published in 2018 by arrangement with Harlequin Books S.A.

Printed in Mexico
1 2 3 4 5 6 7 22 21 20 19 18

To Margaret and her sister, Carol,
who take such wonderful care of my
two Amazon parrots.
Thanks for all the wonderful years of
friendship. Love you both.

Dear Reader,

I never get tired of writing books about Jacobsville and Comanche Wells, my fictional homes in Texas. This is no exception. Every time I revisit the area, I connect with old friends (Cash Grier just won't go away, and he turns up everywhere!) and catch up on news about characters from many books ago. It probably shows that I love Texas!

I grew up in southwest Georgia, where a Texan would feel at home. We had much the same sort of scenery, but I grew up on a farm, not a ranch. We had mules and hogs, and my grandfather looked after a small herd of cattle for the landowner — we even had Jack Russell terriers who were trained to round up the big animals if they got loose. I was a child, but everybody worked. Granny made me a little shoulder bag of canvas that I used to pick cotton in. I

7

remember Grandaddy working beside me in the blazing heat, singing "Amazing Grace" off-key. Hard times. Wonderful times. No money, but an abundance of love. I was so happy that I never realized we were poor.

The heroine in this book is a nurse. My mother was, also. She trained at Grady Hospital in Atlanta and worked at many hospitals in the metro area while my sister and I were growing up. I have a special place in my heart for the profession. The hero is a Texas Ranger, one of the most unique law enforcement jobs in existence. There's also a kindhearted young man of eleven who has serious problems of his own. Neither the hero nor the heroine knows about the other's involvement in his life as they work to protect him from a dangerous gang of teens. His identity threatens their growing attraction. I had a wonderful time telling this story. I hope you enjoy reading it.

As always, I am your biggest fan.

Diana Palmer

ONE

It was two weeks until Christmas. Suna Wesley, whom her coworkers called Sunny, was standing by herself at the edge of the makeshift dance floor in the boardroom at the San Antonio Hal Marshall Memorial Children's Hospital, watching as her colleagues in the hospital laughed and performed to the music on the loudspeakers. A disc jockey from a local radio station, related to one of the nurses, had been persuaded to provide commentary. There was plenty of punch and refreshments. Doctors and nurses, orderlies and dieticians, mingled around the buffet table. It was a holiday-themed party, the Saturday after Thanksgiving. One of the favorite staff doctors had taken a job back east, so it was mostly a going-away party.

Christmas decorations were draped around the room, marking the start of the holiday season. Holly and mistletoe and golden bells mingled with red bows. It made the holidays come to life in the red and green decor. But the whole holiday season was sad for Sunny. It brought back haunting memories of the season with her father and mother and little brother. Those days were long gone.

As she watched a nurse flirt with one of the interns, Sunny wished it was over. She'd been persuaded to stay after her shift and join in the fun. But it was the same as always. She was alone, because she was too shy to push herself into one of the many small groups and engage in conversation. She lived alone, stayed alone, was resigned to being alone for the rest of her life.

She pushed back her long, platinum blond hair and wished she were beautiful. Her hair was her one good quality. It was straight and pretty when she left it long, and it fell to her waist in back. She had big brown eyes that reflected her loneliness when she was alone and didn't have to hide it from others.

It was sad that she had no partner. Her mother and father had loved to dance. Her father had taught her all the exotic Latin dances that at least three couples were mutilating on the dance floor. Her feet itched to try it. But she avoided men. It was useless to become involved with anyone, considering her limitations. No, better to stand all alone with a glass of punch that she hadn't even touched and feel sorry for herself, decked out in a floral nurse's tunic and droopy slacks, not a smidgeon of lipstick or powder on her soft features. Her brown eyes were dull with memories that hurt. Holidays were the worst . . .

"Hey, Ruiz, you going to show us how to do that samba?" somebody called to a tall man in a shepherd's coat and wide-brimmed creamy felt hat with a feather decoration. It reminded Sunny that even in San Antonio, autumn was cold.

Her eyes went to the newcomer. Her heart skipped a beat just at the sight of him. He was gorgeous! Tall, olive-complexioned, elegant, with powerful long legs and a face that would have graced a magazine cover. He had a very masculine face, with a chiseled, sensuous mouth. Black eyes danced under a rakishly tilted cream-colored Stetson, white teeth flashed at the questioner.

"Hey, do I look like I got time to give you pilgrims dance lessons?" he called back in a deep voice just faintly accented. "I'm a working stiff!"

"Lies!" the physician called back. "Get

11

over here and have some fun. You're too serious!"

"If I wasn't serious, you guys would have to pay people to let you operate on them," he scoffed.

"One dance," the physician dared. "Come on, you spineless coward!"

"Ah, now, that's fighting words." He chuckled, looking around for a victim. His eyes fell on Sunny's long, beautiful hair and narrowed on her exquisite complexion.

No, she thought. *Oh, no, no . . . !*

While she was thinking it, he took her drink, put it on the table, caught her around the waist and riveted her to his tall, powerful body as he drew her onto the dance floor. He was very strong, and he looked taller in the shepherd's coat he was wearing with jeans and boots. He even smelled nice.

"Hey, *rubia,*" he teased, using the Spanish word for a blonde female. "You dance with me, okay?"

"I . . . can't . . ." she faltered and blushed.

"Not true. Everybody can dance. Some people just do it with more natural rhythm and grace than others!" He chuckled and pulled her closer as he made quick turns. He was incredible on the dance floor. But she was afraid of the effect he had on her, and it was a very public sort of dance.

12

Everyone was looking at them and smiling, and she was painfully shy.

The contact was electric. She tingled all over from being so close to his long-legged, powerful body, so close and warm against her flowered top and pants, warming her body, making her feel things she'd never felt. She'd never been so close to a man in her adult life, and it shocked her, how much she liked it.

But she knew that she had no hope of sustaining a relationship with a man, and she was too honest to start something she couldn't finish. The stranger appealed to her in every single way there was. She couldn't afford to indulge this weakness. She froze, embarrassed at the physical ache that welled up in her so suddenly. She caught her breath, biting her lower lip. "Please," she faltered, looking up at him with tragic dark brown eyes. "I don't . . . dance well . . ." She tugged against his arms, frightened of sensations she'd never felt in her life as she was held far too close to a man she didn't even know. She could barely force her eyes up to his handsome face as the contact made her stammer. He was the stuff of dreams, but not for a shy, innocent woman with too many secrets.

Something flashed in his black eyes, but

the smile only faded a little. He let her go abruptly. "Forgive me," he said softly, giving her a mock bow. "Obviously you prefer a paler dance partner, yes?"

He turned and walked off, throwing up a hand at the doctor. "Okay, I danced, now I'm going to work, you slacker!"

There was a gale of laughter, following him out the door.

Sunny went back to her place on the sidelines, embarrassed at being made conspicuous. She was even more embarrassed at the opinion he seemed to have formed, that she didn't want to dance with him because he was Latino. She could have told him that was a misconception. He was the most gorgeous man she'd ever seen in her life, and when he'd put his arms around her, something inside her woke up and wept at the sense of loss she felt. Because she could never encourage a man, be intimate with a man. Not ever.

She drew in a long breath, ignored the glass of punch that he'd taken away from her and left it sitting on the table. She went toward the elevator, in a fog.

"You aren't leaving already?" Merrie York exclaimed. "Sunny, the party is just starting!"

They worked together on the pediatric

14

ward, on the night shift. Merrie was a wonderful nurse, patient and kind. She and her brother lived south of San Antonio on a huge ranch. They were absolutely loaded, but Stuart and Merrie both still worked.

"I have to go," Sunny said, forcing a smile. "You know I'm no party animal, I'll just put a damper on things."

"You were dancing with Ruiz," Merrie said with a wicked grin. "Isn't he beautiful? You should have cut loose, girl. You can out-dance anybody else here."

"He's so gorgeous," she confessed. "It shocked me, a man like that wanting to dance with somebody as plain as me."

Merrie grinned. "He is handsome, isn't he? You wouldn't believe the women who chase him. He just walks right by them. You should have kept dancing, Sunny," she added.

"I don't like dancing in front of people," she faltered.

"I can't remember the last time I saw Ruiz look twice at a woman, much less ask her to dance," Merrie began.

"I feel terrible," Sunny said huskily. "He thought I didn't want to dance with him, because he was Hispanic. That wasn't it at all. I didn't believe someone like him, who could have had any woman in the room,

15

would even want to dance with me. It . . . shocked me."

"You undervalue yourself," Merrie said softly. "You aren't plain, Sunny. You're unique, in so many ways."

She smiled at the compliment. "Thanks." She hesitated. "Merrie, that man I danced with . . . who is he?" Sunny asked helplessly, hungry for more information about the man who'd chosen her from a roomful of beautiful nurses to dance with.

"He's . . . Oh, darn, I have to go, Motts is waving frantically. I promised him a dance, and he's being stalked by Sylvia," she said with mock horror. "She's so nice. He's afraid of her, so I'm his security blanket."

"He's afraid of her?" she asked, diverted.

"Sylvia wants to get married and have kids, and Motts wants to sample at least one woman of every name in the baby book," Merrie said with a chuckle. "And no, he hasn't sampled me. My brother would have him for lunch, and my sister-in-law would help put catsup on him."

"You and your family," Sunny laughed. "Your brother is really good-looking," she added, because she'd seen Stuart York on rare occasions when he came to hospital functions with his wife, Ivy. Merrie and Stuart were rich beyond imagining, owning

16

thousands of acres of ranch land in three states. They ran purebred cattle. Neither of them had to work for a living, but Merrie loved nursing and couldn't contend with a life of leisure, any more than Stuart could sit at a desk.

Merrie looked very much like her only sibling; she had long, jet-black hair and pale, steely blue eyes. She didn't really date anyone seriously, although she'd had a crush on a divorced doctor who'd just gone back to his wife. Like Sunny, Merrie didn't really move with the times. She wasn't into multiple relationships.

"My sister-in-law would totally agree, that my brother is gorgeous," came the amused reply.

"Are they ever going to have kids?" Sunny wondered.

"I keep hoping. So far, they're making the rounds of all the historic places on earth. I think they're down to the last thousand now." She grimaced as she glanced toward the refreshment table. "Got to run. Motts is turning purple. Don't go," she pleaded. "You stay too much by yourself."

"I like my own company," she said gently. "But thanks. See you. I'm off until Monday!"

"Lucky devil. I wish I was. Be careful going home."

"I always am," Sunny said, and shivered inwardly. She usually took cabs that she couldn't afford, even though her apartment was only two blocks away. She was too afraid to walk through neighborhoods with gang activity. But sometimes money was really tight, and she had to make the perilous journey.

She'd lived in the neighborhood since she was thirteen. She'd shared it with her mother and little brother until the tragedy that left her alone. Now she hated the very sight of the gang that had taken over the once peaceful block of apartments, who were called *Los Diablos Lobitos* — the Little Devil Wolves. They ranged in age from early teens to early twenties and they terrified everyone, but especially Sunny. She had more reason than most to hate and fear them.

The cabdriver let her out at her front door. She paid him and he flashed her a smile as he drove off. She walked inside, unlocked her door and looked around her meager surroundings.

It was a ground-floor, one-bedroom apartment. No frills, no luxuries. There was a small stove that she used for cooking and a fridge that had some age on it but still functioned. Her twin bed had a bedspread that her mother had painstakingly crocheted, and of which Sunny was very fond. It was multicolored, beautiful. It brightened the dull room.

The back window bothered her, because it had a loose screen and she couldn't lock it. She'd asked the maintenance man to fix it times without number, and he always promised. But somehow, he never seemed to get around to it. So far, nobody had tried to break in. Probably they knew she had nothing worth stealing.

She had a very small television that had been given to her, secondhand, by one of the other nurses. The apartment's rent covered cable, so she had access to the local news and weather and a few programs that were free. She could never have afforded a package that offered prime movies and things. Not that she missed them. Her shift left her drained and ready for bed. She slept, if fitfully. She did have Wi-Fi, courtesy of the landlord, as well as all utilities. The apartments were occupied mostly by people in the services industry, predominantly medical personnel. Marcus Carrera might have been a mobster at one time, but he was a man with a huge heart. Sunny never failed to send him birthday cards and

Christmas cards, always with thanks. He'd done a lot for her in the past. He was married to a very nice Jacobsville woman and they had a little son.

Lying in bed, in her soft white cotton gown, she thought about the gorgeous man who'd tugged her onto the dance floor at work. What had they called him, Ruiz? Was that his first name or last name, she wondered. Surely a man that handsome was married. He looked to be in his early thirties, another reason he was probably spoken for.

She wished she could have explained why she was nervous about dancing with him. She was sorry she'd given him the idea she didn't like him because his skin was just a little darker than hers. She loved Latin men. Her favorite music was Latin, and she loved the dances her dad had taught her.

But she was shy around men she didn't know. Sunny had only dated once in high school, and the date had been a disaster. She still shivered with misery, thinking about what had happened. The experience had taught her that it was better to be alone than to try her luck with a man. She knew that she was repulsive to them. Hadn't her date told her so, graphically? It had been a painful experience. But perhaps it had been a good one. It taught her that she would be alone for the rest of her life, and that she must make the most of it.

She'd done her nurses' training at the Hal Marshall Memorial Hospital, but when this new adjacent children's hospital opened, she'd opted to apply there, along with a few nurses she already knew, like Merrie York. It was a wonderful place to work. People were friendly, even the administrator, and the rooms were like children's rooms at home, stocked with toys and pictures on the wall and things that made the environment less traumatic for them while they recovered from illnesses and surgeries. Sunny loved her job. But she was lonely.

Several of her coworkers kept trying to set her up with men. She didn't know what she was missing, one laughed, a girl who had two lovers. Sunny needed to get rid of her hang-ups and dive into the dating scene. Wasn't she unhappy, going without sex?

Sunny had replied that she couldn't very well miss something she'd never had, which caused the girl to give her a shocked, pitying look and get back to work. It wasn't something she advertised, but the comment had disturbed her. She went to church, although fitfully. She only had a couple of Sundays off in a month. But she loved her congregation and was welcomed on the days she could participate in the services. Faith had carried her through many storms. She didn't advertise that, though. It was better to never discuss religion or politics with strangers, her mother had once said. It was the best way in the world to start a fight. Sunny, who'd noticed some very hot arguments in the latest political climate, couldn't help but agree.

She had an emergency a few days later. One of the children in her ward, a toddler, Bess, had been showing signs of abdominal distress. The little girl had suddenly started screaming, and Sunny had called for a doctor. The examination disclosed a blockage in the child's colon, which led to immediate surgery.

It depressed Sunny, who'd become attached to Bess. She had bright yellow curls and big blue eyes, and Sunny spent a little more time with her than with the other children when she was on duty. Bess had only one parent, a mother who was working two jobs to support her four children. The father had just walked away from the big family he'd said he wanted, when he became involved with another woman. So Bess's poor mother struggled just to feed them.

Bess had been in the hospital for a week already, confined for vague symptoms that didn't seem to clear up and which had been difficult to diagnose until today. At least, after the surgery, the child would improve and could go home. It was a charity case, one of many the children's hospital took on without argument. So many people still couldn't afford even basic medical insurance, despite the government's attempts to provide it to those most in need.

She worked her shift, making up reports, checking vitals, providing comfort and care to all her little patients. She was looking forward to seeing Bess out of surgery. She frowned as she looked at the clock. Surely the surgery was over by now? It had been several hours. She hadn't noticed because she'd been so busy.

As she started to go off duty, she saw the surgeon who had performed the operation on Bess. She smiled as she asked him how the child was. The smile faded when she saw his expression. He looked devastated.

He explained, tight-lipped, that the child had gone into cardiac arrest during the surgery, and none of their efforts had been successful in bringing her back. They'd lost her due to an undiagnosed heart condition that nobody had even suspected she had.

He walked away, his expression betraying his sorrow. Surgeons sometimes went off by themselves for hours after they lost a patient, Sunny knew. They took it hard when they couldn't save one.

Sunny gave her report to the next shift, tidied up her things and left the hospital in a daze. Bess was gone. Sweet little Bess, who'd always been smiling and happy. She fought tears. Nurses were taught not to get too close to their patients. It interfered with duty, one of the senior nurses had told her, because attachment led to grief when a patient was lost. But Sunny had never learned how to separate her heart from her job, and she mourned.

The apartment was lonely. It was her second Sunday off in two weeks, a lucky break, and she was off the next day as well. Nurses worked long shifts during a very long week before days off, but they were fulfilling ones. Usually. Not today.

She had plenty to do. There was laundry to sort, cabinets to clean out. She could vacuum. She could bake a pie. But none of those mundane tasks helped the hurt.

In the end, she did what she always did when she was depressed and unable to cope with life. She took a cab to the San Fernando Cathedral and went inside to light a candle for her late father, who had been Catholic.

She smiled sadly at the memory. He'd been driving a cattle truck for a rancher down near Jacobsville when a dog had run into the road and he'd swerved to avoid hitting it. The truck had overturned and killed him instantly.

Sunny and her mother, Sandra, and her little brother, Mark, had been devastated. Like now, it was the holiday season, which just amplified the loss as families gathered around Christmas trees to sing carols.

Her father, Ryan Wesley, had been a lifelong Catholic. Her mother had been a staunch Methodist. But the differences in faith hadn't dulled the feeling her parents had for each other. It was truly a love match. They'd met in grammar school. They'd always known that they'd marry one day and have kids.

Sunny smiled at the memory. Her mother had loved to take out the family album and sit around the apartment with Sunny and Mark and tell them the stories that went with the wealth of photographs going back to Sandra's own childhood, and Ryan's. They'd been very close after the accident, so it had hurt terribly when Sunny lost her mother and brother in a tragedy that still had the power to bring tears to her eyes six years afterward.

She walked slowly to the front of the church and lit candles for all three of them. She looked up at the pulpit. She'd come with her father to Mass from time to time, just as she attended services with her mother at the local Methodist church. It had been faith that kept her going when she was ready to throw up her hands and just sit and give up. She truly believed that everything had a purpose, even tragedies that seemed without one.

She stood in front of the candles. She'd left her hair loose, since she wasn't at work. It flowed down her back in a thick, pale curtain around the black dress and coat she was wearing off duty. Most women wore pantsuits when they attended services, but Sunny had stayed with her grandmother after school every day when Ryan and Sandra were working. After Mark came along, he stayed with her as well. Their grandmother had always worn dresses to church and funeral homes, and she instilled that custom in Sunny from childhood.

It had been a blow when the old lady fell suddenly to the floor with a stroke and nothing known to medical science could save her. She'd died in the Hal Marshall Medical Center, in fact, next door to the children's hospital with the same name where Sunny worked. The woman had been a fixture in San Antonio society, the widow of one of the city's best loved police officers who'd died on the job. Her funeral had been attended by dozens of people, and the flowers had covered the area around the pulpit. It had made her family proud, to see how much people loved and respected her.

In fact, Sunny's family had been some of the first settlers in south Texas, immigrating from Georgia in the aftermath of the Civil War. The Wesleys were a founding family.

All those thoughts buzzed in her mind, all those memories tugged at her heart, while she watched the candles burn bright in the darkness of the great cathedral, the oldest in the city. It was founded in 1731 by Canary Islanders, although construction of the great edifice only began in 1749. It had an amazing history.

She heard the heavy front door open, but she didn't turn. Many people who weren't even Catholic came to light candles in memory of lost loved ones. It was rare for anyone to be alone for long in the church.

She heard a deep, melodic voice calling to a priest, and deep laughter following as the men conversed. Sunny couldn't hear what they were talking about. Her mind was drifting into the past, into happier days, happier times, when the holidays had meant shopping for a special Christmas tree and cooking cakes and pies and turkey in the little house outside the city where her family had lived before her father's death.

She said a silent prayer as she stood at the altar, her brown eyes sad and quiet.

Footsteps sounded just behind her, echoing in the cavernous depths of the church. She knew the sound of footwear. Those were boots. She smiled to herself. A cowboy, probably, stopping to light a candle for someone . . .

"A strange place to find you, *rubia,*" came a familiar laughing voice. It was oddly soft, almost affectionate.

She turned and looked up, her breath catching. It was the man in the shepherd's coat, the gorgeous man who'd taken her onto the dance floor at the Christmas party.

"Oh," she stammered, flushing. "Hello."

He studied her for a moment before he replied. "Hello." He glanced at the candles. "I come here every Christmas season to light them, for my people," he said quietly. "You, too?"

She turned her attention back to the

candles, nodding. "Yes. My mother and father. And my little brother," she said softly.

He scowled. "All of them?"

"Yes," she said quietly. "My whole family." She forced a smile. "My father went here all his life. My mother was Methodist. They were both stubborn, so I went to services at both places when I was little. I learned the Mass in Spanish, because that's how *la Santa Misa* is said here."

"My father brought me here when I was a boy, too," he replied. He didn't add that he'd once brought his own son, Antonio, who was eleven. But now, the boy didn't want any part of religion. He wasn't keen on his father, either. Since the death of Ruiz's wife, three years ago, the relationship between him and his son was difficult, to say the least.

"It wasn't because you're, well, because you're Latin," she stammered. "The dance, I mean. I . . . I . . . ."

He looked down at her with an oddly affectionate expression. "I know. It was because you didn't think such a gorgeous man would want to dance with somebody like you, is what you told one of the nurses," he said outrageously.

Her face went scarlet. She turned, her only thought to escape, but he was in front of her, towering over her.

"No, don't run away," he said softly. "I'm not embarrassed, so why should you be?"

She looked up, her eyes wide and turbulent.

"And there's nothing wrong with you," he added in a deep, tender tone.

She bit her lip. "The room was full of pretty women . . ."

"They all look alike to me," he said, suddenly serious. "Young men look at what's on the outside. I look deeper."

She could smell the cologne he wore. It was as attractive as he was. She kept her eyes down, nervous and uncertain.

"You work at a children's hospital," he said, by way of explanation.

"Yes. The night shift, on the pediatric ward."

"That's why I haven't seen you before," he mused. "I spend most of my time at the hospital in the emergency room, either there or at the general hospital next door." His face hardened. "We see a lot of children injured by gangs and parents."

That brought her eyes up, wide and questioning on his handsome face. "Gangs?" she blurted out.

He pursed his sensual lips and pulled back the shepherd's coat over his broad chest to reveal a silver star.

"Oh," she stammered. "You're a Texas Ranger!"

"For six years," he said, smiling. "Didn't you notice the gun, when we danced?" he teased, nodding toward the .45 automatic in a holster on his wide, hand-tooled belt.

"Well, no," she said. She was lost in his black eyes. They shimmered like onyx in the light of the candles.

"Who are you?" he asked gently.

"I'm Suna," she said. "Suna Wesley. But I'm called Sunny."

He smiled slowly. "Sunny. It suits you."

She laughed self-consciously. "You're Ruiz," she said, recalling what one of the physicians had called him.

He nodded. "John Ruiz," he said.

She studied his face, seeing the lines and hardness of it. It was a face that smiled through adversity. It had character as much as male beauty. "Your job must be hard sometimes."

"Like yours," he agreed. "You lost a patient on your ward yesterday."

She fought tears. She managed to nod.

"I have a cousin who works in the hospital," he said, not adding that his son spent a lot of afternoons after school in the cafeteria until his cousin-by-marriage got off work

31

and could drive him down to Ruiz's ranch in Jacobsville. The cousin, Rosa, lived in a boarding house in nearby Comanche Wells. She, like John, commuted to San Antonio to work. "She said that the whole nursing staff was in mourning. It's sad to lose a child."

She twisted her purse in her hands. "We're supposed to stand apart from emotion on the job," she said.

"Yeah. Me, too. But you get involved, when people are grieving. I've got a widow right now who's hoping for an arrest in her case. Some wild-eyed fool shot her husband outside a convenience store for ten dollars and change. She's got two little boys." His face was grim. "I'll find the man who did it," he added quietly, his black eyes flashing. "And he'll go up for a long time."

"I hope you catch him."

"Didn't you hear?" he asked, his mood lightening. "We always get our man."

She frowned. "I thought that was the Canadian Mounties."

He shrugged. "We're all on the same side of the law," he said, his black eyes twinkling. "So we can borrow catchphrases from them."

She laughed softly. "I guess so."

There was a loud buzz. He grimaced and

pulled his cell phone out of a leather holder on his belt. He noted the caller and answered it. "Ruiz," he said, suddenly all business. "Yeah. When? Right now? Give me five minutes." He paused and laughed. "I'll make sure I hit all the lights green. No more tickets. Honest. Sure." He hung up. "A new case. I gotta go. See you, *rubia.*"

She smiled shyly. Her heart felt lighter than air. "See you."

He cocked his head. "Go home and find something to watch on TV. There's a rerun of *Scrooged,*" he added, referring to a Bill Murray movie that had become something of a cult classic around the holidays.

She laughed. "I think I have it memorized already."

"Me, too. It's a great film."

"Yes, it is."

He searched her eyes slowly, watching her flush. She acted like a green girl. Why hadn't he noticed that at the party? She was shy. It made him feel oddly protective. She drew him, when he hadn't paid attention to women in years, not since he'd lost Maria. He wondered what it was about her that made him feel hungry. She wasn't beautiful. She was small breasted and tall, almost elegant. But that hair, that gorgeous, beautiful, sexy hair, made her far more attractive than she realized.

"Well, see you," he said, and forced himself to smile and walk away.

Before she could reply, he was headed out the door onto the street.

She thought about him when she got home and turned on the television. What a strange coincidence, running into him in a church unexpectedly. Someone had told him what she said about him. She flushed and then laughed, self-consciously. It had been a little embarrassing, but he was so uninhibited. It hadn't bothered him at all. She ground her teeth at the memory of how he'd taken her shy withdrawal. It was probably just as well that he knew the truth, even if it made her squirm. She'd found him devastating. And she didn't prefer men with a paler complexion, she mused. He was perfect. Absolutely perfect.

Was he married? She wanted to know more about him. But if she started asking questions, it would get back to him, just as her embarrassing disclosure had. Maybe someone who knew him would talk about him and she could eavesdrop. Or maybe, she thought, and her heart raced, she might see him again.

That possibility made her warm all over.

He was strong and handsome and he made her feel things she'd never felt.

She hoped that he wasn't married. But as she thought it, she withdrew mentally from any hope of romance. She couldn't tell him why she spent her life alone, why she discouraged men from even asking her out.

She couldn't tell him that she wasn't what she seemed to be at all. The humiliation would be too much to bear.

No. Better to be alone than to have him back away from her. She could never tell him the truth. It broke her heart to realize that the attraction she felt had no future. She didn't dare get involved with anyone.

She got ready for bed and thought again of little Bess and the tragedy that had sent her to the cathedral for comfort. Poor Bess. Her poor mother. Tears trailed down her cheeks as she closed her eyes and tried to sleep.

Two

"What have we got?" John asked the San Antonio policeman he knew who'd phoned him for assistance. John was a specialist in gang warfare.

"A mess," the patrolman sighed as he indicated the body of a boy. "Looks like it might be the beginning of a gang war."

John went down on one knee beside the body and narrowed his eyes. He noted the tattoos on both arms and the neck of the dead male, who'd been shot neatly through the chest, twice.

"Tats," he murmured, noting the cobra's head on both arms and a small one on his neck.

"Yes. And you know who those belong to," the officer said with a resigned sigh.

"Los Serpientes." John nodded, his black eyes flashing. "They're recruiting them younger and younger. This kid looks no older than twelve. Maybe thirteen." It set him off, because his own son, Tonio, was eleven, not much younger than the victim.

John's keen eyes noted a small chalk drawing just at the top of the boy's head, on the pavement. It was a wolf's head.

"Los Diablos Lobitos," he murmured. "A warning to the rival gang not to trespass." He looked up. "Los Lobitos are trying to take over Los Serpientes' territory." He knew that Los Lobitos operated in the alternative school where Tonio was a student, near the hospital where his cousin worked.

"They're getting bolder. Going against Los Serpientes with a vengeance. This is simple retribution, warning Los Serpientes to back off from the territory, I'd bet my badge on it. They're making an example of this kid to show that they mean business." He looked at John. "This is not going to end well, if we wind up with a gang war."

"Tell me about it." John's keen eyes were scanning the body for anything out of place, for any clue that might indicate the assailant. "He isn't wearing a coat. Not even a hoodie."

"I noticed that." The officer stood up. "It's damned cold out here. I'd say he couldn't afford a coat, but he's wearing about a thousand dollars' worth of gold. Maybe a coat wasn't a priority."

He was, indeed, wearing his wealth, in the form of rings and a watch and layers of thick gold chains around his neck. The pattern was recognizable, and they were eighteen-karat gold. Some were twenty-four karat. Very expensive. John didn't mention that to the officer. He wasn't comfortable telling anyone how he could recognize high-ticket items. He kept his private life quiet.

"Los Diablos Lobitos," John muttered. "Little wolf devils. They are, too. This is just their latest victim. Your department nabbed one of them last month for the rape and murder of an eighty-year-old woman." His face mirrored his distaste. "An initiation. The would-be gang member responsible will do time. A lot of time."

"He sure will. He took the woman out of her own home and transported her to a deserted parking lot. That's kidnapping. Federal charges. And they tried him as an adult, because of the nature of the crime."

"I have to confess that I was glad the feds took over the case. I understand that Senior FBI Agent Jon Blackhawk taught the crime unit guys some brand-new words when he saw the victim."

"His mother is elderly," John replied. "The crime would have outraged him on that basis alone."

"The crime unit should have already been here," the officer remarked, looking around. He looked down at the body again. "I hate having to leave DBs out here like this," he added. "It seems vaguely indecent."

"But if we cover them up before the crime unit does its job, we contaminate the crime scene. And then some brilliant defense attorney puts us through a sausage grinder on the stand and saves his poor, sad client from the criminal justice system."

The officer made a sound deep in his throat. "If you ask me, it's the honest citizens who need saving from the poor, oppressed criminals."

"Shhh," John said with twinkling eyes. "The thought police will come and arrest you for hate speech."

That brought a smile from the younger man. "I hate political correctness."

"I do, as well, but we can't turn back time. We have to live in the society that's being warped around us." He shook his head. "I asked my son how he liked studying about the second world war in his history section. His teacher's course of study was so broad that he couldn't name me a single individual European general who commanded an army."

"Santayana said that those who don't study history and learn the lessons it teaches will be condemned to repeat it," the officer said quietly, loosely quoting a philosopher from the past.

"And those of us who only serve will suffer right along with the people who make the big decisions," John chuckled. "But by then, we may be hit by a giant asteroid or a comet or an EMP, or a coronal mass ejection . . ."

"Stop!" the officer groaned. "I get enough anxiety just watching the national news."

"I stopped years ago," John confessed. "I get so much stress on the job that I couldn't handle any more. It helps to remember that the news is news because what they report is the exception, not the rule. Dog bites man, who cares. But man bites dog, then you have a story."

"I see what you mean."

"And there they are," John remarked, standing to watch a white van pull up in the parking lot beside them.

A tall brunette with short hair and blue eyes gave them a wry look. "And here we are again, Ruiz," Alice Mayfield Jones Fowler teased. "We were just together last week on another homicide. We really have to stop meeting like this. My husband thinks

I have a secret yen for you."

"You tell gang members to stop killing other gang members in my jurisdiction, and I'll be happy to wave you goodbye," John chuckled.

"That's never going to happen." She slipped on latex gloves and put booties over her shoes. She went to kneel by the victim.

"How long dead?" John asked.

She was examining his eyelids, neck and jaw, as she listened. "Rigor's just now setting in. I can't give you an exact time, you know that. But rigor usually presents two to six hours after death, first in the areas I'm checking." She looked up at them with pursed lips. "As many autopsies as you Texas Rangers have attended, Ruiz, I expect you already knew that."

John gave her a Latin shrug and a smile.

"An approximate time of death will help us retrace his steps," the officer interjected.

"Double tap," she noted after inspecting the wounds, both of which had penetrated the boy's heart. "Execution?" she asked, looking up at the men.

"That would be my call," John replied. "He made someone very angry, apparently. Note the tats as well."

"Los Serpientes," she muttered, grimacing. "And unless my eyes are going, that little wolf's head in chalk means that the little devil wolves are responsible for the DB. If there's a hell on earth, that gang of teenage imbeciles created it."

"They're trying to take over some gang territory that's owned by Los Serpientes," John noted. "And I'll tell you frankly that Los Serpientes is a better class of gang. They operate mostly in Houston. They don't require initiates to shoot people and they actually do some good in low-rent areas where crime is rampant. They never hurt children or old people. And they go after people who do."

"A gang is a gang, Ruiz," she said heavily. "Why do we still have gangs in the twenty-first century?"

"I was going to ask you that," he chuckled. "I don't know. I guess we've got Mom and Dad both working to keep the bills paid, or just Mom or Dad trying to support several children. The kids get left in daycare or on their own too much. Gangs offer lonely kids a family and emotional support and affection . . . Things they sometimes lack at home. It gets them a lot of traffic."

"If I ever have kids, they'll never have time to join a gang," she murmured as she worked bagging the victim's hands. "We have a ranch. It's small by Texas standards, but it's a ranch. We never run out of work. Of course, it's not as big as Cy Parks's spread, or yours."

"You and Harley have a nice ranch," John said, and smiled. "I buy stock from your husband's boss. Cy Parks has some of the finest young Santa Gertrudis bulls in Texas."

"I keep forgetting that your ranch is outside Jacobsville." She made a face. "Not that we'll ever be any threat to you. My gosh, your place is almost as big as Jason Pendleton's ranch!"

"Ah, but he built his from the ground up. Mine is an old Spanish land grant," he replied, making light of it. "I inherited it from my grandfather. All I had to do was let his people do their jobs. I'm still doing that, while I work at my own."

"Cattle baron," she teased.

He chuckled. "Hardly that. A cattle ranch is a money pit."

"Tell me about it." She stood up. "After the floods this year brought on by that stupid hurricane, half the ranchers in south Texas had to buy hay to feed their herds."

"Most of them. But I'm totally organic, like Parks and J.D. Langley and Jason Pendleton. We never use pesticides or pack-aged fertilizer, and that helped us recuperate faster than ranchers who do," John replied.

"Not you, too," she groaned. "Honestly, even my own husband is starting to go the organic route. I can't even use spray on my roses to keep bugs from eating them!"

"Research prey species that feed on your bugs," he said with a grin.

She shook her head. "I guess I'll have to." She sighed. "The worst of the hurricane was the displaced people, though," she added softly. "It broke my heart, to see so many homeless."

"Mine, as well," he agreed. "We've got several families in Jacobsville, living with relatives. It's so small that we can hardly house our own population," he chuckled. "But we managed to secure housing for an elderly couple from Houston."

"Cy Parks had an empty cabin on his place. He's letting a big family from the coast live in it, and they're working for him." She laughed. "He says they're not sure they want to go home. There are six kids, and they all love working on the ranch around the animals."

"I hate cities," John said. "Well, I like San Antonio," he amended. "But, then, I don't live here. I live in Jacobs County."

"How's your boy?" she asked.

His face hardened. "Not so good. He hates going to school up here."

"Why doesn't he go to school in Jacobsville?" she asked.

"We had a few problems there," he said, and turned his attention back to the body. He didn't add that he had to pay a fee for Tonio to go to school near the hospital where his cousin worked. It was a special school, San Felipe Academy, one for boys who were disciplinary problems.

Sadly, Tonio had discovered Los Diablos Lobitos in San Antonio just a few weeks after the change of schools and joined them before John found him. That had been a year ago, after John brought a woman home for dinner. It was the first time he'd even dated since the death of his wife. It was a colleague from work, not a romantic interest, just a woman he liked who was very attractive. But Tonio had hated her on sight. He'd gone crazy. He'd run away from home the very next day, while he was in the canteen at the children's hospital in San Antonio, where he waited every afternoon for John's cousin to get off work to take him home. Unknown to John, Tonio had met some member of the gang around town, who befriended him when he ran away. He ended up staying with the boy, who lived

45

with his prostitute sister. The boy was in the gang and he'd introduced him to Rado, who led the wolves. Rado had welcomed Tonio like a long-lost relative.

John had tracked him down through the same boy who was Tonio's friend at San Felipe. Tonio had said that the boy knew the leader of the gang, though, not that he was a member of it. It had been hard work getting Tonio to go home with him. He'd had to promise that he wouldn't bring any more women home. John was willing to go that far, to ensure his son's safety. He felt guilty enough already, because his job ate up every waking minute of his time. There was little left for his only child.

But it had been before that when the trouble had started. Tonio had already gotten himself expelled from Jacobsville Middle School by punching a teacher. Since it was the only middle school in the small county, and the principal had recommended expulsion at the hearing shortly thereafter, John had no choice but to enroll him in San Antonio. And because of Tonio's issues, it needed to be an alternative school. It had the other advantage that if there were problems, either John or his cousin Rosa was nearby during the day.

46

The principal at San Felipe also kept an eye on Tonio, as did the school police officer, who was a former colleague of John's. Sadly, neither of them knew about David Lopez's Los Diablos Lobitos connection, or his sister's. David was the only real friend Tonio had besides Jake. But Tonio rarely saw Jake these days. San Felipe was a religious school, but it offered an excellent academic program as well as a soaring soccer program with a winning team. Tonio loved soccer. But he refused to play, because his father had suggested it. Anything John mentioned to his rebellious son was instantly shot down.

So far, there had been no real issues at San Felipe, except Tonio's bad attitude and lack of respect for authority figures. Not that he learned that at home. He had discipline as well as love, but he was completely out of hand. Apparently having his father even attempt to date a woman was enough to turn him wild.

It was so worrying that John had him in the care of a psychologist. But half the time Tonio would sit in the man's office and refuse to speak for an hour. It was rough.

"I said, are you coming to the autopsy?" Alice asked.

"What? Sorry," he apologized. "My mind

47

drifted off to Tahiti for a brief vacation." He smiled. "Sure. When?"

"I'll have them call your office."

"I hate autopsies," he said, staring down at the boy. "Especially on children."

"No more than we do, at the crime unit," Alice agreed. "I wish kids would stop killing kids."

"I wish parents were less distracted by work and the world, and had time to be with their kids more." John sighed.

"I take mine camping and fishing and to church every Sunday," the police officer said with a smile. "So far, we're doing okay."

John nodded. "That's how it's done. I used to take my boy fishing, but he lost his taste for it when his mother died."

"That's sad."

"She was a good woman," John replied. "We started dating in high school." He sighed. "Well, I'll get back to work. Let me know, about the autopsy."

"Sure thing," Alice said, as she motioned to a colleague to help her put the corpse into a body bag and get it into the van for transport to the crime lab.

John was depressed for the rest of the day. There would almost certainly be a reprisal from Los Serpientes for the slaying of their young gang member. It would be expected. Kids killing kids. Anyone would be depressed.

It was after dark when he drove down to Jacobsville. The demands of his job kept him away from the ranch a good deal of the time. He had days off, which he tried to spend with Tonio. But his son refused any offers of shared pastimes, staying shut up in his room playing video games. The only good thing about the games were their value in discipline. When Tonio stepped badly out of line, he lost his gaming privileges for a week. He also lost the privilege to visit Jake, his only local friend in Comanche Wells — because Jake had every video game known to man. Not that Tonio saw much of Jake anymore.

John walked in the door, savoring the smell of chicken *à l'orange* and roasted potatoes. His housekeeper, Adele, was married to his foreman, and she was a mistress of gourmet cooking.

"My favorite," he exclaimed, grinning as he hung up his shepherd's coat and hat and walked into the dining room.

"I didn't know!" Adele said with mock surprise.

"Where's Tonio?"

She made a face and indicated the hallway

that led back to the bedrooms, one of which was Tonio's. The house was huge. It had four bedrooms, two bathrooms, a living room, dining room, kitchen, indoor swimming pool, recreation room and even a set of rooms that were designated for servants in the early days of the twentieth century. San Benito Ranch was over three hundred years old. The present structure had been largely remodeled in the 1990s, while John's grandfather was still alive. The old gentleman had raised him after the death of his parents in Argentina, where the family raised thoroughbred racehorses. John had lived there until his tenth birthday. After the tragedy, his grandfather assumed responsibility for him and had him brought to America.

Very few people knew about the great wealth that the Ruiz family had in Argentina, about the yacht that sailed the Atlantic or the incredible herds of cattle that dotted pastures and were overseen by gauchos in the pampas on the sprawling family ranch. A cousin was responsible for the day-to-day operation of it, but it belonged by right of inheritance to John. He and the cousin were best friends, and John had given him a large share in the property — more wealth than the older man would have imagined only years before. It was to the cousin's credit that he wasn't greedy. He loved his cousin John and the feeling was mutual.

Tonio wasn't privy to that information, about the wealth of the Ruiz family. John had decided just after his birth to keep his family background secret. He didn't want his son to grow up with a distorted sense of values, least of all in a small community where most people with his Hispanic background had far less. John wanted him to grow up valuing all people, having less respect for things than for other human beings.

So far, it had worked well. Tonio, while rebellious, had friends who were mostly below the national average in financial wealth. That was when he was in school in Jacobsville, the county seat of Jacobs County. As Tonio's behavioral problems in school had accelerated, his list of friends dwindled to just Jake. It disturbed John to see the ongoing deterioration of his son's attitude. He knew that his job was part of the problem; it required him to be away from home often in the course of his duties. But he loved the work he did. He felt that it contributed to the protection of the community he loved. The life of a rich ranchero had never appealed to him. He left the yacht and the aristocracy to his cousin, who loved it. John devoted his time to being a Texas Ranger.

He tapped on Tonio's door and opened it. The boy was sitting in front of a wide-screen TV with a gaming controller in his hands. There was a battle going on, in his favorite game, *Destiny 2*.

"Supper," John said curtly.

"Aw, Dad, I'm in the middle of a —"

"Damn, Tony, watch what the hell you're doing! You let that bast—"

"Hey!" John said shortly.

There was a sharp pause. Tonio looked at his parent with flushed cheeks. There was a small voice coming from the television. "Hey, Tony, I think I better go now. See you!"

There was a click. Tonio grimaced and turned off the game.

"Who the hell was that other boy?" John demanded, black eyes flashing.

Tonio swallowed. He could cross tongues with the meanest of other students, even teachers, but he quailed in the sight of his father's muffled fury. "Uh, that was, that was David," he began.

"Who's David?" came the softer, more dangerous question.

Tonio got up. "You said supper?" he

asked, trying to soothe his father.

It didn't work. "I said, who's David."

Tonio grimaced. "Okay. He's a guy from school. We play online together. He's in my clan."

"Your what?"

"We have clans in Destiny," Tonio explained. "It's like guilds in other games. Groups of us play together."

"You still haven't answered the question."

"He's in eighth grade," he said finally. That was two grades above Tonio. "He plays Destiny with me, and we talk back and forth."

John's eyes narrowed. "I cuss. You don't," he said. "And I don't want you around kids who do."

Tonio laughed.

"What's funny?"

"I'm in an alternative school, Dad," the boy said. "Not exactly church, is it?"

"You're in alternative school because you attacked a teacher at Jacobsville Middle School," came the sharp reply. "And you're lucky Sheriff Hayes Carson didn't arrest you. The teacher saved your neck, even though you were expelled."

"He pushed me," Tonio said, repeating what he'd told his father before, but he kept his head down when he said it.

"We've been through this before," John said quietly. "He was trying to get you away from the other boy, who was hitting you. You thought the teacher was attacking you, so you punched him in the stomach. That's assault," he added curtly.

"Then why didn't they arrest Teddy? He was hitting me!"

"Doesn't work the same way between students as between students and teachers," he replied. "The world is changing. You have to change with it."

Tonio bit his lower lip. "I don't like the new school."

"So? You didn't like the old one, either."

"Jake goes to school in Jacobsville," he said. "I only have David in San Antonio."

David. The boy who cursed like a sailor. For not the first time, John worried that he'd made a mistake taking his son to San Antonio for his education. But he hadn't had a great deal of choice.

"That fancy chicken again." Tonio sighed, making a face as he and his father sat down at the table.

"It's elegant chicken," Adele chided, "and you like it."

He made the face at her, too, but he smiled. He loved Adele. "I'll eat it. Go ahead. Use me for a guinea pig for all your recipes."

"I will." She dropped a kiss on his head and finished serving the meal. She pulled off her apron. "Leave the dishes, I'll be back when I feed my brood!"

John chuckled. "Thanks, Adele."

"No problem."

"I miss Mama," Tonio said suddenly.

"Yeah. Me, too," John replied tersely.

Tonio's cell phone rang. They could both hear it coming from his room.

"Leave it," John said. "No electronic devices at the table." That had been the psychologist's advice. It did seem to be working, a bit. At least the two talked, although not much.

"How was school?" John asked.

Tonio grimaced as he picked at his food. "Older kids just love to torment us."

"That's life. Get used to it. There's a pecking order everywhere you go. I have a lieutenant who tells me what to do, he has a captain who tells him what to do. That's life," he repeated.

"David's sister went to the school and raised . . . she raised the devil," Tonio said, "when an older kid picked on him."

"I don't interfere unless I have to," he was reminded. "Listen, son, you won't learn to stand on your own two feet if I fight all your battles for you."

"Sure." His dad never fought any. The first time he'd even been to Tonio's school in Jacobsville was after the fight. Other kids had both parents, and they took an interest in what their children were doing. Tonio's parent was rarely even home. His job took up almost all his time. Tonio got what little was left. At least at the supper table they could exchange one or two sentences. Not that it would last long. He sighed. Any minute now . . .

Sure enough, the pager on John's belt buzzed. He pulled it out and looked at it. He didn't even glance at his son as he went to retrieve his cell phone from the pocket of his shepherd's coat. He punched in a number.

"Ruiz," he said.

"It's Alice. Autopsy's in an hour. You coming?"

"I'll be right there."

He hung up and swung on his coat. "I have to go back to the city. I'll be late. Finish your supper, do your homework and get to bed early. Adele will make sure you do."

"Okay."

John swung on his coat, grabbed his keys from the holder beside the front door and

56

went out to climb into the black SUV he drove to work.

Tonio sat at the table all alone, thinking about how miserable his life had become. His father hardly noticed him, except when he was acting out. He had only one friend in the world, and now Jake was involved in soccer at his school in Jacobsville, as well as being an active member of the school's agriculture club, and he hardly ever had time for Tonio after school or on weekends.

That left David. His father didn't know who David really was. He didn't realize that Tonio's new friend was actually the same boy who'd helped him run away from home last year. David was a member of Los Diablos Lobitos. He and his brother, Harry, had lived with their grown sister, Tina, who was a call girl. The older brother had been killed three years earlier. There were rumors that Rado Sanchez had done it.

Tonio was afraid of Rado. But Tina always looked so nice, and she smelled sweet. She'd been kind to Tonio the two days he'd lived with them. She'd teased him and picked at him and ruffled his hair. He liked her a lot. He knew what she did for a living. David said she hated it, but Rado made her. He said Rado was always around. Tina got along with him. Probably because she did what he told her to. She loved her little brother. David never talked about the brother who'd died. Not ever.

Tonio's father almost never talked to him. He hardly ever touched him. He was never here. Tonio was growing up all alone. He had no brothers or sisters and he didn't want a substitute mother. That was the problem. Ever since he'd objected so violently to his father's woman friend, there had been a wall between them.

John said that life went on, that you lost people but you couldn't climb into the grave with them. John had loved little Maria, his wife. But it had never been the sort of passionate love they showed in movies. It had been more a relationship between good friends.

Tonio had loved his mother, so much. She'd been his anchor. She was always making things for him, hugging him, telling him how much she loved him, making him feel part of her life. She'd worked in the emergency room of one of the other hospitals in San Antonio, not the one where Rosa was a clerk. Maria had once told Tonio that she felt she did a worthwhile job, a noble thing, helping to save lives. It made her feel good inside. His cousin Rosa, his mother's first cousin, worked at the Hal Marshall Memorial Children's Hospital as a clerk. He liked Rosa, but she was in her late twenties, unmarried, and she didn't know a lot about kids. She worked in the office, not as a nurse. She'd been a policewoman before she changed jobs. She liked Tonio. But it wasn't the same as when his mother had been alive. Rosa was tough. Well, people in law enforcement usually were. His dad was a prime example.

He poked at the potato dish that went with the chicken, but he barely tasted it. There was a cake on the table, in a plastic carrier. He never touched sweets. His father liked them occasionally, but neither of them cared much for dessert. Just as well. This cake was one Adele had baked for the family of a person who'd just died. She was always doing things for other people. Like Tonio's mother had.

He got up from the table and went into the living room. There was a painting of his mother on the wall, one his father had commissioned when Tonio was just a year old. His mother had been lovely. She had long, thick black hair and a sweet, pretty face with big black eyes and thick eyelashes and a light olive complexion. Her hands, in the painting, were as they'd been in life, long-fingered and elegant, with pink nails. She was smiling, the way she always smiled in life. In her lap was a small boy with touseled brown hair and big brown eyes, looking toward the artist. The subjects were so realistic that they could have walked out of the painting.

It had cost a lot of money. His father never spoke of finances, but there were checks now and then from Argentina. There were letters from someone who lived there. And once, Tonio had seen a website that his father visited in Argentina, which showed a ranch with thoroughbred horses, many at stud or for sale.

Tonio had asked why his father was looking at a ranch that specialized in racehorses. John had just shrugged and said he chanced upon it during a search and was curious about the name of the horse ranch, because it was Ruiz, like his own name. Not that he was interested in buying any fancy horses, he'd added. The quarter horses they had on the ranch were quite good enough for him.

The answer had satisfied Tonio, who never could keep his mind on anything for very long. That psychologist he went to see said he had attention deficit disorder. Tonio had drifted off into daydreams while the man droned on, explaining the problem to him. He imagined that his father had also drifted off, listening to the long-winded explanation, because they'd never discussed it again. Tonio wondered if his father had been affronted because the problem might be inherited from him. His dad was touchy about such things.

His dad's profession had caused him some issues in Jacobsville. The older kids had made fun of Tonio because his dad was a Texas Ranger. A few sharp words from one of the teachers had stopped some of it, but teachers couldn't be everywhere. The student he'd gotten in the fight with had said that all cops were crooked and since Tonio's dad was a Latino, he was probably even more crooked than the rest. Tonio's blood had boiled. He wasn't ashamed of his blood, and he didn't like hate speech, so he'd plowed into the other student.

He'd tried to explain the insult to his father, but there had been a phone call, another crime scene that his dad had to go to. It seemed that any time he tried to tell his father anything important, to talk to him, that cell phone was always in the way. He couldn't even have one uninterrupted meal with his only remaining parent.

Adele came back. He said the food was good, when she groaned at the lack of empty plates, but his dad had to leave and he'd eaten too much at lunch. He went back into his room and picked up the game controller. As an afterthought, he called David back on Skype.

"Hey, man, watch your language when you hear my dad come in, okay?" Tonio asked. "He's a Texas Ranger."

"Yeah. I know," came the sarcastic reply. "You poor kid. But, okay, I'll watch my mouth when the heat's around. Now, where were we?"

THREE

David liked Tonio. But there were other, older members of Los Diablos Lobitos who didn't. One of them was Rado Sanchez. Nobody knew what the nickname meant or where it came from, but he was cold, dangerous, and he'd taken over leadership of the gang several years ago when its former leader went to prison for murder. Rado was the sort who wouldn't balk at murder. He sent initiates out to do some pretty bad things. One of them had just been sent to jail for the rape and murder of an old lady. That had shocked and frightened Tonio. He wasn't in the gang and he wasn't trying to be in it anymore. But that didn't stop Rado from trying to pressure him into joining it.

Rado was tall and thin, with a face like a rat and a smoking cigarette in his hand constantly. He stopped Tonio just off the grounds of the children's hospital where his cousin worked, late one afternoon.

"You coming into the gang or what?" Rado asked.

"Not yet," Tonio said, trying to look cool as he hid his secret dislike for the older boy.

"Why not? You scared of your daddy?" Rado drawled sarcastically.

Tonio straightened. "No."

"Sure you are. That's why you won't join. You're scared of the heat."

"I can do what I want," he began.

"Oh, right," he said, making a choked sort of laugh as he exchanged amused glances with his three companions, all of whom looked as ratty as he did. "That's why you're up here in an alternative school."

"I punched a teacher," Tonio said, trying to make himself look good.

"I put a teacher in the hospital," the older boy countered. "Beat him almost to death. He was one of my dealers and he got cold feet." His face tautened. "That's what we do to people who cross us. If he'd tried to report us, or if he talked about me, to anybody, he'd be dead."

Tonio fought down the fear. "I gotta go," he said.

They moved around him, encircling him. "Oh, yeah? And what if we don't want you to go, Tony boy?" Rado drawled. "What if we got a little job we want you to do for us?"

Tonio felt real fear, but he tried not to show it. "I don't have time."

"Lots of kids in that hospital. Scared kids. Sick kids. We got drugs you can give them."

One of the boys went backward, tugged by the back of his jacket. A woman with long, blond hair in a long black coat moved right into the circle with her cell phone out. "Yes, is this 911?" she asked and glared right at Rado. "I want to report —"

"Let's go!"

Rado and his friends scattered. Rado looked back, furious. "I'll get you! I missed once. I won't miss again!"

Before she could speak, he and his gang ran into the parking lot and disappeared past the surrounding buildings.

The blonde put the phone, which she hadn't even activated, back into her pocket. She kept her hands in her pockets, so that the boy wouldn't notice that they were shaking. It took nerve to stand up to Rado, and she had more reason than most to fear him. But seeing the boy being tormented brought back memories of bullying that she'd had to survive when she was in school. She hated bullies.

Tonio was barely able to get his breath.

His heart was hammering in his chest. He looked up into the soft, brown eyes of the woman who'd saved him. She looked like an angel to him when she smiled.

"You okay?" she asked softly. She took her hand out of her pocket long enough to push back a lock of thick, black hair that had fallen into Tonio's eyes. Her touch was as gentle as her manner.

"Yeah." He swallowed. "Thanks," he whispered, grimacing.

"Those boys are big trouble," she said, glaring after them. "We get victims of Los Diablos Lobitos in the hospital from time to time. Yesterday we got one of Los Serpientes. They're pretty sure that Lobitos killed him." She cocked her head. "You know about the little devil wolves? They like to recruit boys for their gang, because juvies don't go to prison for things that would put them away for years."

"I know about them," he said in a quiet tone. "Los Diablos Lobitos keeps after me. I don't want to join them."

"That Rado is bad news," she continued. "He's killed men. The police here keep trying to put him away, but he's as slippery as a fresh-caught fish."

He managed a smile. "How do you know about Rado?"

"I live in the Alamo Trace apartments, there," she said, indicating an older building in the distance. "Rado's been around here for many years." She didn't add that she knew him very well because of what he'd done to her family. They were old enemies. She'd have given anything to see him go up for murder, but he couldn't be caught.

"You work around here?" he asked.

She smiled. "I work there." She indicated the children's hospital.

"You do?" he asked. "I don't recognize you."

Her eyebrows lifted.

He laughed. "I stay here in the cafeteria after school. My cousin works here, too. She gives me a ride home."

"Well! Small world," she teased.

"Do you work in the office?" he asked.

She shook her head. "I'm a nurse."

So had his mother been. He loved nurses. "You like nursing?"

"More than anything." She pulled her coat closer. "If you're going my way, you can walk with me and protect me from evil gang members," she teased.

He chuckled. "That was sort of the other way around."

"I was bluffing. The phone wasn't even turned on. I should take up poker," she said, frowning, as they walked together toward the main entrance. "Apparently, I bluff pretty good."

He laughed out loud. "Yes, you do."

"Want to have a snack with me?" she asked. "I'm not on duty for another thirty minutes. I don't usually come in this early, but I set my clock wrong." She sighed. "I'm a born klutz. I unplugged it to clean, and then when I finally plugged it back in, I forgot to reset it."

He grinned. His dad was the same way. "I'd love to have a snack. I have money left over from lunch," he added quickly, to make sure she knew he wasn't going to mooch off her. He knew that nursing didn't create millionaires. Most nurses weren't in it for the money, anyway.

She grinned back. "Okay."

She went with him to the canteen on the first floor, the one used by visitors. There were always members of the staff around, and security, so it was safe for a young boy to sit there while his cousin finished her shift.

"I'm Tonio," he said, not volunteering his last name. He didn't advertise his dad's profession. He knew that his dad was around emergency rooms a lot. She might recognize the name, and he didn't want her to. Not yet.

She smiled. "I'm Sunny. What would you like?"

He pulled out a dollar bill. "I always have money for the machines," he explained. "I eat at school, but mostly it's healthy stuff. I like junk food."

She laughed. "Me, too," she confessed.

She got a cup of black coffee for herself and a sweet roll, something to keep her blood sugar up. She was forever running on the job. She only slowed down when she went off shift.

Tonio got a pack of potato chips and a cup of hot chocolate.

"I like the hot chocolate, too," she remarked. "I don't usually like it out of machines, but this one seems to be a fairly decent crafter of hot beverages."

He grinned. She smiled and the sun came out.

"Do you go to school around here?"

"Yeah. At San Felipe," he added and then watched for her reaction.

"Is it a middle school or a high school?" she asked. She made a face as she sipped hot chocolate. "Sorry, I don't know much about education these days. I'm not married."

"Wow, really? I'm not married, either!"

She gave him a wide-eyed look and then burst into laughter.

He laughed, too. He hadn't laughed so much in a long time.

"This is a really nice place," he commented.

"It is. I've worked here ever since it opened. I'd just graduated from nursing school."

"What did you mean, about somebody in Serpientes being killed?" he asked.

She frowned. "I shouldn't talk about things like that to someone your age," she said gently.

He was going to tell her that he knew all about murder, because his dad was in law enforcement. But he didn't want her to know. He didn't want to tell her about his dad. He wasn't even sure why.

"Okay," he said. "If you want to stunt my educational growth. But I'm eleven, going on twelve. And I do watch the local news on TV," he added.

She wrinkled her nose. "I guess you're old enough. He was found shot to death on the street, with a wolf's head drawn in chalk near the body."

"Los Diablos Lobitos want their territory, so they killed a Serpiente as a warning, I guess, to try and scare them off." He fished in the package for the last of the potato chips. "I don't want to be in a gang," he added heavily. "Lobitos make you kill somebody in order to join. I did a dumb thing once. I ran away from home and I got to know this boy who belongs to the gang. I said I'd like to be part of it, but I was real upset and I didn't know what I was doing. Except that they told Rado, and now he's on my case." He grimaced. "He makes these threats. Like today." He lifted angry brown eyes to hers. "He said that he wanted somebody to take drugs into the hospital. Into a children's hospital! He's crazy!"

She searched the boy's eyes. "You have a heart. You don't seem at all like the sort of person who'd deal drugs to little children." She smiled.

His heart jumped. He felt the praise go right to his own heart. She made him feel . . . different. Good and useful. She made him feel as his mother had, when she was alive.

"I never would," he replied. "That Rado, though, he would," he added with a heavy sigh.

She glanced at her watch with the second hand and sighed. "Time to go to work."

"Is it hard, working here?" he asked. "I

mean, my cousin works in one of the offices. But you have to be with the kids when they . . . well . . ."

Her face was sad. "Yes. We lost a child a few days ago. I cried and cried. We're not supposed to get involved with patients, but she was so sweet . . ." She swallowed, hard, and fought tears.

He never touched people. Not even his dad. But he reached out a hand and grasped hers in it, tight. "My mother always said that God picked all sorts of people for the bouquets He made, little ones and big ones alike. She said . . ." he tried to remember ". . . that we have to accept that the days of our lives are numbered, and that we have to make the best of every single one we have."

"Your mother must be a very special person," she said, returning the pressure of his hand for a second before she released it to pick up her coat and purse.

"She was," Tonio said with a sad smile. "She was a nurse, too, but she didn't work here."

She hesitated, seeing the sorrow in his big, brown eyes. "I'm so sorry," Sunny replied. "I know what it is, to lose a mother." Her brown eyes were sadder than his. "I lost my whole family."

He grimaced. "I'm sorry, too."

"Life compensates us, my mother used to say. She was a good person, too." She glanced at her watch. "I'd better get moving before my new supervisor hangs me out the window from a sheet. Nice to have met you, Tonio. Maybe I'll see you again."

"Same here. And I hope I see you again."

She grinned. "Bye."

"Bye."

He watched her go and felt as if the sun had just gone down. He'd never met anybody like her. How odd, to have a stranger come into your life and feel like part of your family.

He wondered which one of the wolves had killed the Serpiente. He wouldn't have put it past Rado. He was grateful to Sunny for protecting him, but troubled that Rado had sworn revenge. He hoped his new friend wasn't going to get hurt because of him. But, then, Rado often threatened people. It had been nice, having somebody stand up for him. She could see that he had Hispanic blood, too, and that hadn't stopped her from defending him. He liked that. She wasn't beautiful, but he thought she was pretty, with her long blond hair and big brown eyes and sweet smile. He really hoped that he'd see her again.

He sat back and sipped his hot chocolate,

forcing Rado and the gang to the back of his mind.

The autopsy was routine, and John had grown used to them, after a fashion. But he never quite got used to seeing the damage one human being could do to another. This young boy, nude on the table, with cobra head tattoos all over him, had a mother and father somewhere. How would he feel, if that was his Tonio on that table? It made it far more personal than he liked to admit.

The attending coroner was speaking into a microphone, detailing the damage and extracting material that might help point to the perpetrator. John was pretty sure that it was one of the wolves, but he had to have evidence to find out which one had killed the boy.

Besides John, there was a representative from the San Antonio Police Department's violent crime unit, a detective named Bronson. He was about John's age and had apparently seen his own share of autopsies. He didn't seem to be overly emotional, like the brand-new detective who'd shown up at the autopsy and had to absent himself to throw up.

John looked over the body at the detective with that thought in his head and a faintly quizzical look in his black eyes.

The detective glowered at him. "I don't throw up at autopsies."

John smothered a laugh, turning it into a cough.

The coroner glanced up, rolled his eyes and went back to the body.

"Cavitation," he murmured, sighing. "Catastrophic damage to the heart." He looked up, angry. "Just a kid, and they killed him over drug territory. This is unspeakably sick."

"Tell me about it," John said quietly. "He wasn't even into his teens, by the look of him."

"Your boy's about this age, isn't he, Ruiz?" the coroner asked gently.

John grimaced. "Tonio's eleven," he agreed. He scowled. "These autopsies get harder when you've got a kid the same age as the victim."

"That's why we do what we do," the detective interjected. "To keep more kids from dying like this."

John smiled at him. "Good point."

Just as he spoke, the coroner extracted a bullet. "Exhibit number one," he said proudly as he dropped it into a dish.

"Hopefully, it has something to connect it to the killer," John agreed, studying it. "Not too much damage, that will help. Looks like a .22 slug."

"Damned Saturday Night Specials," the detective muttered. "More dangerous than a higher caliber gun, because the bullets fragment and cause more damage."

"Exactly," John agreed.

"Well, if the bullet kills you, the caliber isn't all that relevant, now, is it?" the coroner asked them.

They conceded the point.

John was home late. He searched in the fridge for sandwich meat and got mustard and bread down from the cabinet.

Tonio poked his head out the door of his room. "You home for good?"

"Well, for the night, I hope," John said. "You hungry?"

Tonio grinned. "Always. What you got?"

"Bologna and mustard."

"Okay."

They sat down at the table to eat.

Tonio was still happy about his new friend, although it was a secret he didn't want to share with his father.

He noticed the hard lines in his dad's face. Harder than usual. "Something bothering you?" he asked. It was unusual, because he didn't notice his father much these days.

John nodded. "I had to attend an autopsy. A gang shooting victim. The kid wasn't even into his teens."

Tonio pretended ignorance. "A gang victim?"

John nodded, not paying much attention to Tonio's expression. It was a shame.

"Los Lobitos?" Tonio probed.

"No," John replied after a bite of sandwich and a sip of black coffee. "One of Los Serpientes."

"Los Lobitos kill him, you think?" Tonio asked.

He looked up, black eyes narrowed. "You aren't hanging around with that gang?" he asked suspiciously.

He gave his parent his best surprised expression. "Not me!" He wasn't about to let on that he already knew about the shooting, from his new friend. "Isn't Los Serpientes a Houston gang?" he asked. "They were on the news . . ." He trailed off, letting his dad think that was how he knew about the serpents.

It seemed to work. His father's face relaxed. "They used to be a Houston gang. Now they're in a lot of places. They've been in San Antonio for several years, that I know of. It seems that the serpents are encroaching more heavily on the wolves' lucrative drug territory, so they're setting an example," came the sad reply. John shook his head. "God, I'm tired of dead kids!"

Tonio was certain that Rado knew about the shooting. He wondered what David knew about it. Or if he knew anything.

"You stay out of gangs," John said shortly. "I'm not going to any more autopsies on boys. You hear me?"

Tonio forced a smile. "I don't do gangs. Really, Dad," he added, because they both remembered that he'd been willing to join a gang when he ran away from home.

John searched the eyes that were so much like his own. He smiled gently. "Okay."

"You're gonna get whoever killed him, right?"

John chuckled. "I always get my man. Or boy. Or woman." He shrugged. "Whatever." He finished the sandwich. "How's school?" he asked.

"You know, it's not so bad," Tonio said surprisingly. "They have a really good soccer program. I thought . . . I might go out for it?"

John was hesitant. Tonio had been militant about joining before. It was an olive branch. "Tell you what. You bring your grades up and keep out of trouble until spring, and I'll make sure you're properly outfitted.

How about that?"

Tonio's heart lifted. "Deal!"

John smiled. He sipped his coffee. "This is sort of nice," he said after a minute. "We don't talk enough."

"Well, that's because —"

Before he could get the whole sentence out, the alert went off. John grimaced as he pulled out his cell phone. "Ruiz. Yeah? Oh, hell! Not another one?! Yeah, I'll be right there. Twenty minutes." He hung up.

"I gotta go." He got up from the table and went to swing his coat off the rack and top his head with the cream-colored John B. Stetson hat he favored. "Don't stay up too late, okay?"

"Okay. You said 'not another one,' " Tonio ventured. "Another gang shooting?"

John nodded curtly. "You keep away from any boys with ties to Los Lobitos, you hear me? I'm not burying you!"

"I meant it. I don't do gangs," Tonio promised. "They know who got shot?"

"Not yet. We still haven't even identified the other victim, the Serpiente who was killed. Now this! Keep the doors locked."

"I will," Tonio said.

And with a wave, his father was off to the wars again. Tonio sat back in his chair. It was a shame. Just when they started to talk, to really talk, the job came barreling in to put another wall between them.

But now, Tonio had a new friend. That nurse, at the hospital. She was sweet and kind and she listened. He hoped he'd see her again. She made life seem hopeful.

Sunny had barely slept. She'd had nightmares the night before, probably a result of the conflict with Rado and the gang near the hospital. She'd relived her own tragedy, the one that Rado was part of. It had been a sad and terrifying dream. She woke sweating, crying. Not the best start to the day. Or what was left of it. She worked nights, so she slept late usually. Not today, though.

She made herself a sandwich and some black coffee and finished it before she dressed in her comfortable scrubs, picked up her purse and walked to work, a half hour early, again. She was going to work a double shift tonight, too, because she was covering for a woman with a sick baby. She didn't mind. It was just that she'd be asleep on her feet by the time she got off the next morning. At least she wouldn't have to get a cab home after work.

She always took a cab home when it was dark, despite the proximity of her apartment to her job. She had a real fear of being assaulted by one of Rado's goons. But in the daytime, there were a lot of people on the streets. She felt fairly safe.

She walked in the front door and there was her new young friend, sitting in the canteen with his eyes on the door.

He spotted Sunny and his whole face lit up. She smiled, too. There was the oddest bond between them. He was young enough to be the son she'd always wanted and never had. Perhaps she reminded him of his mother, who had been a nurse, too. Whatever the reason, he made her feel happier than she'd felt in a long time.

She walked into the canteen. "Got time for a snack?" she asked him.

He laughed. "Always." He studied her, frowning. "You don't look so good."

"Bad night." She laughed. "Bad day," she corrected. "I have nightmares, sometimes," she confessed. "How's the hot chocolate?"

"Great. I think they cleaned the machine," he teased.

She got her own, and an energy bar, and sat down to eat it. "How was school?" she asked.

"Great! I may get to go out for soccer in the spring!"

"You like soccer?" she asked. "It's my favorite sport! What's your team?"

"Madrid Real," he said at once.

She grinned. "Mine's Mexico. The World Cup comes up next year. I can hardly wait! We're going all the way this time, idiot referees notwithstanding. Last World Cup, we got penalties we never should have had, because one of the referees made bad calls."

"I saw that," Tonio confessed. He cocked his head. "You don't root for the American team?"

"Well, it's like this," she said. "My great-great grandmother was one of Pancho Villa's band during the Mexican War, back in the early part of the twentieth century."

"Really?!"

She laughed. "I know, I don't look it, do I?"

He shook his head. "No. You don't."

"Well, there are lots of blonde women in northern Spain. That's where my ancestor came from. She married an American and they lived in Mexico. She was a character. She flew planes, drove race cars, they even said she was a spy for a while."

"Gosh." He was impressed. "Our people came from Spain originally, too," he confessed. "But our family came to America from Argentina."

She caught her breath. "Argentina," she said with a sigh. "I've read about it for years.

82

The gauchos. The pampas. The dances!"

"Dances?"

"The tango. It was almost invented in Argentina," she said. "It's the most beautiful dance I've ever seen."

Tonio almost blurted out that his dad was a past master of that dance, and many others. But he didn't want to talk about his dad. Very often, when people knew his father was in law enforcement, they started backing away. He didn't want to lose Sunny when he'd only just found her.

"When I grow up, I'll learn it, just so I can dance with you," Tonio teased.

"Gee, by the time you're grown, I'll be walking with a cane," she teased back.

"Will not!"

"I'm twenty-three," she pointed out. "Old, compared to you."

"I think senior citizens are very cool," he replied with twinkling eyes. "So I'll keep your cane polished and repaired. How's that?"

She smiled from ear to ear.

"There was another gang shooting last night," he said after a minute.

"Another one?!" She didn't stop to question how he knew. She looked at him worriedly. "You don't have gang members where you go to school, do you?" she asked.

She was concerned, and it showed.

Tonio felt warm inside, seeing that. "No, of course not," he said at once, lying because she seemed really worried about him. "Just regular kids, like me."

She let out a breath. "Thank goodness!" She finished her coffee. Her eyes were sad. "That Rado," she said with quiet venom, "should be locked up and the key thrown away. He's gotten away with more murders than he's even been charged with."

His heart jumped. "He has?"

She looked down at her coffee cup. "It was his gang that killed my mother and my little brother," she said, and then regretted saying it out loud. She grimaced. "You don't tell anybody that, okay?" she added worriedly. "I shouldn't have said it."

"I never tell anything I know," he replied. "They killed your family?" he added, shock in his voice.

She nodded. "They were after the former tenant, who'd sold them out. They didn't know he'd moved." She swallowed down the memory. It was horrific. "That didn't bring my family back, of course. He and the boy who did the shooting were arrested. The boy did time. Rado had a convenient alibi. They couldn't break it."

Now he understood that sadness in her,

that showed even when she smiled. He could only imagine how it would feel, if his own family had been shot to death in front of his eyes.

"Do you have anybody else?" he asked.

She managed a smile. "I had an elderly aunt, but she died two years ago. I've got nobody, now."

"Yes, you do," he said, and he smiled at her. "You've got me. I'll be your family."

Tears welled in her eyes and spilled over. She grabbed a napkin and dashed them away, embarrassed.

"Sorry," he said quickly. "If I offended you . . ."

"No! I'm not offended." She swallowed, hard. "It was the nicest thing anybody's said to me, in a very long time."

He sighed, and smiled, relieved.

She stuffed the napkin into her pocket. "I've got to go or I'll be late for my shift." She paused as she started to leave. "Do you have family?"

"It's just me and my dad," he said reluctantly.

"At least you have somebody," she pointed out. She hesitated. "But you've got me, too. If I'm your family, you're my family, too. Right?"

He cocked his head. He grinned from ear

to ear. "Right!"

She laughed. "Okay. See you."

"See you."

One of the nurses on duty had seen the story about the gang shooting on the news, but it was only a flesh wound. Police had been at the hospital to take the boy into custody, but his companions rushed him out the door before the police could get near him. The name he'd given was an alias. They noticed tattoos on him. Wolves's heads. Retaliation, probably, for the dead Serpiente gang member. The nurse said they were still hunting for the victim.

Sunny worried about Tonio. He was just the right age for Rado to want to recruit him. She didn't know what she could do to protect him, but she'd do anything she could. She was already fond of him.

Two days later when she came on shift early, Tonio was in the canteen again, waiting for her. One of the nurses noticed this and teased Sunny about her young gentleman friend, only to be informed that he was her family. The nurse knew her background and understood. She just smiled.

After her shift, Sunny was thinking about Tonio as she went down the hall. She was almost due for her days off, so she wouldn't see him again right away. She was almost to the elevator when she noticed a San Antonio police detective who came onto the ward and paused at the desk. She knew that he was probably asking about yet another shooting victim who'd been brought in the night before.

Sunny knew he was going to want to talk to her, because she'd been the nurse on duty when he was placed on the ward following emergency surgery. She'd pulled another double shift, tonight, this time because two nurses were down sick and they were shorthanded. The gang shooting victim on her ward was only ten, a painful reminder that gangs didn't care about the age of anybody they targeted.

Odd child, to be so young and sound so mature when he talked in his sleep. He had tattoos. Wolf tattoos. It didn't bode well that this was the third gang shooting in recent days. And it was the second shooting of a member of Los Diablos Lobitos.

The detective spoke to the nurse in charge of the shift, who indicated Sunny and motioned to her. She went to the desk, her coat over her arm, her purse strap over her shoulder.

The man was tall and blond and drop-dead gorgeous. He'd have turned heads anywhere. There were all sorts of rumors about him. The most persistent one was that he'd been with a group of mercenaries in Africa some years ago. That was before he joined the San Antonio Police Department and worked his way up through the ranks to Captain, the position he held now.

Sunny knew him, because he'd been a lieutenant when her family was killed and he'd worked the case. Cal Hollister was a good man, with a kind heart. If Sunny had liked fair men, he'd have been at the top of her Christmas list. But she had a gnawing yen for an olive-skinned man with black dancing eyes.

"Hi, Captain Hollister," she greeted him, smiling.

"Hi, Sunny. How've you been?" he asked gently.

"Life is hard, then you die?" she teased.

He grinned. "So it is. Can I buy you a cup of coffee in the canteen so you can stay awake while we talk?" he asked. It was morning. She'd been up all night and she was tired. He knew it without being told.

"Sure you can," she said, stifling a yawn.

He led her into the canteen and purchased two cups of black coffee from the machine.

He placed one in front of Sunny as he dropped his tall frame into the chair. There were only a couple of people in the canteen so far, an elderly couple she recognized from the cancer ward; they had a grandchild there, in serious condition.

She forced her attention back to Hollister. "Are things so bad that the brass has to work cases now?" she teased.

He laughed shortly. "I ducked out of a meeting and said I'd promised to help Lt. Marquez interview a witness. I hate administration. I miss working cases."

"You were good at it," she said, smiling. "How can I help?" she asked.

"It will be hearsay, and not worth beans," he began. "But I wondered if your young patient said anything after he went on the ward?"

She hesitated. This was a slippery slope. Anything a patient told her wasn't supposed to be shared with anyone without permission from the administrator. It was to protect the hospital from lawsuits, that modern pastime that so many people seemed to love.

He chuckled. He produced a signed paper and handed it over. "I always go through channels when I have to. Recognize that signature?"

She did. She'd seen it on memos often enough. It was the hospital administrator's.

"Okay, then," she said, relaxing. "He hasn't said much. He hasn't had visitors, either. But he did say something, last night," she confessed. "Although, it was an odd sort of comment, and I'm not sure he was completely out from under the anesthesia at the time. You know that it can make you goofy for a few days after surgery?"

"I know it all too well," he said somberly. "I'm carrying about three ounces of lead in my carcass that they could never remove." His face hardened, as if he was remembering how he collected that lead.

She cocked her head.

"Give it up," he said with faint amusement. "I don't talk about my past, ever. Well, maybe to a local priest, but he's an old friend."

She pursed her lips. She knew a priest downtown who was a former merc. He did a lot of outreach work. "I wonder if we could possibly be thinking of the same priest?"

He glowered at her.

She held up both hands in mock surrender. "Okay, I'm done. Honest."

He shook his head with a heavy sigh. "Some people!" he scoffed.

She grinned at him. He'd been so kind when she was living through her own tragedy.

"Okay. What did he say?"

She sipped black coffee. It was at least strong enough to keep her awake, if badly brewed. She made a face.

"Listen, if you'd ever had coffee made over a campfire with the grounds still in it," he began.

She sighed. "Good point. At least it's not that bad." She lifted her eyes to his pale ones. "He said that he loved wolves, and that his boss was getting ready to poison a few snakes."

Hollister whistled softly. "Oh, boy."

"Like I said, it could have been the aftereffects of the anesthesia."

"Or it could be code for what's really happening." His eyes narrowed. "You know what's going on. Your hospital got the last two victims . . . the dead kid who was in Los Serpientes, and the wounded Lobitos member who skipped out before police could question him."

She nodded. She was thinking of Tonio and the treatment he'd had at the hands of Rado and his friends. She worried for him.

"There's a gang war starting," Cal told her. "I don't want a gang war in San Anto-

91

nio. I still remember the last one and it makes me sick at my stomach."

"I remember it, too." It was the one that had resulted in her family's death.

"I'm going to set up a task force," he said. "We have a Texas Ranger here with a good knowledge of gangs and gang activities. I'm going to ask him to join."

"Does he know about this latest shooting?"

He smiled secretively and glanced past her. "Why don't you ask him yourself?"

She half turned in her chair, and there was John Ruiz, staring at the two of them with narrow black eyes. And he wasn't smiling.

FOUR

"We were just talking about you," Hollister chuckled.

"Was it something printable?" John asked as he joined them at the table.

"Mostly." He held up a cup. "Want coffee?"

"I have too much respect for the beverage to ever drink it out of that counterfeit machine," John said haughtily.

"It makes very nice hot chocolate," Sunny said in its defense.

"It also steals dollar bills," John muttered. "Someone should give it an attitude adjustment."

"You wouldn't ever have gone down to Palo Verde with a baseball bat?" Hollister asked hesitantly, and with a grin.

John chuckled in spite of himself as he pulled up a chair and straddled it. "No, but I understand the officer who did is still paying off the damage on a monthly basis. The circuit judge put the fear of God into him."

"What am I missing?" Sunny asked, her eyes glancing off John's. A faint blush colored her high cheekbones and he seemed to relax, all of a sudden.

She didn't realize that he'd seen her with Hollister and that he was suddenly jealous. The other man drew women like flowers drew bees. Her flush delighted him, because it was proof that she was more attracted to him than the good-looking blond man sitting with her. He hadn't been able to get her out of his mind since he'd seen her in the cathedral. Crazy, to feel possessive about a woman he hardly knew!

"There was a soft drink machine in the police department in Palo Verde," John told her, bringing his attention back to the incident Hollister had alluded to. "It ate dollar bills and refused to give either change or soft drinks. One of the officers accidentally hit it with a baseball bat several times and it had to be replaced. So the story goes."

She burst out laughing. "How in the world can you accidentally hit a soft drink machine with a baseball bat several times?!"

"Funny, the judge asked the same question," John replied, his black eyes twinkling.

"And what was the officer's excuse?" she asked.

"Muscle spasms," he said with a grin.

She chuckled. John loved the way she laughed. It made her look very pretty, with her face animated and those dark eyes bright with humor.

"Needless to say, the muscle spasm defense failed," Hollister chuckled. "Actually, I had a similar mishap with an office shredder after it ate my credit card," he confessed. "I use it so often that I generally leave it on. It's automatic. So I accidentally dropped my card when I pulled it out of my wallet, and the damned thing shredded it."

"I hope the issuing institution was reasonable about replacing it," John asked amusedly.

"They were, after they stopped laughing," Hollister said, sighing. "But the captain at the time wasn't as understanding about the big dent in the shredder and the matching dent in the wall. I ended up buying a new shredder and paying to have the wall fixed. I'm still being ridden high about it, at the office."

"I shot a vacuum cleaner once," John confessed. He laughed. "I hate housekeeping. We have a woman who lives on the ranch and does it for us part-time. But she was down with the flu for a week, and I was left with the chore. Damned things! You have to drag them around furniture and they catch on every single thing they can find."

"You shot it?" Sunny asked, appalled. "Your poor neighbors!"

"I don't have neighbors," he returned. "I have a cattle ranch near Jacobsville, down in Jacobs County. Closest neighbor is about three miles away."

"Gosh, all that space," Sunny said with a wistful smile. "I live in a renovated broom closet."

They both stared at her.

"Kidding," she said. "It's an apartment, but if I had mice, I'd have to move. There wouldn't be enough room for all of us."

They both smiled.

"I was going to call you when I left here," Hollister told John. "We have a new shooting victim."

"I know. That's why I'm here," John said. "I've got a police psychologist out in the waiting room. I need permission to question the patient."

"He's asleep right now," Sunny volunteered. "He's had a lot of pain, so the doctor ordered medication that would put him to sleep about two hours ago."

"To sleep for how long, do you think?" John asked.

96

"A few hours, I should think," she said. "He didn't sleep last night at all. He was in and out of lucid speech. He just said that he loved wolves and his boss was going to feed some snakes to them."

John and Hollister exchanged worried looks.

"I'm going to put together a task force," Hollister said. "I'd like to have you on it."

"I'm game." John sighed. "Well, I'd better send my psychologist home. She gets paid by the hour." He shivered. "Keeps snakes."

Hollister's eyes widened. "Emma Cain."

"Well, yes." John was surprised. "How in the world . . . ?"

Hollister sighed and smiled secretively. "I have a checkered past. She was part of it." He glanced at his watch and got to his feet. "When do you go back on duty?" he asked Sunny.

"Not for three days," she said. "Sorry."

"It's okay. I'll ask Merrie York. She takes the shift when you're off, doesn't she?"

"Usually."

"I know her brother, Stuart," he said. "We have a mutual friend, Hayes Carson, who's sheriff down in Jacobs County."

"I know Hayes," John said, chuckling. "He's had to help me with a few issues out in the county. He's a great guy. Odd father-in-law," he added, tongue in cheek.

"Yes," Hollister chuckled. "His father-in-law is the biggest drug lord in the North American continent."

"What?" Sunny asked, aghast.

"It's okay," John assured her. "He doesn't practice his vocation in the United States. He has a brand-new granddaughter. No way he's risking his visiting privileges by breaking the law around Jacobs County."

Hollister sighed. "Still, half the undercover narcs in south Texas are employed by him."

"Does he know this?" Sunny wondered.

"We've never been sure," John said with a laugh.

"Didn't his enforcer work for one of those Middle East dictators who was killed?"

"Former enforcer," John replied. "He's the son of Dane Lassiter, who heads a well-known Houston detective agency. From what we hear, the son is actually a fed working several undercover cases with international perpetrators."

"Dangerous work," Hollister said.

"He graduated from MIT with a degree in theoretical physics," John mused. "Hell of a profession for an egghead."

"MIT." Hollister shook his head. "Now I've heard everything." He got up to shake hands with Ruiz and smile at Sunny.

"Thanks for the help," he added. "You take care of yourself."

"You do the same," she replied and laughed. "I'm just a nurse. You're right in the front lines in any gang warfare."

"Goes with the job. And I love the job. I'll call you," he added to John.

They both watched him leave.

There was an awkward silence.

"He likes blondes, and he's been around the world more than once," John said abruptly, and his eyes were faintly hostile.

"It's not like that," she said gently. "He was the detective on the case when I . . ." She hesitated. "It was a long time ago."

She picked up her purse and coat. "I have to go."

"Give me a minute, before you leave. Please," he added with a smile.

He walked out toward the waiting room. She wondered why he wanted her to wait. She wanted to go to bed.

But he wasn't long. He came back in not more than the minute he'd promised.

"I'll walk you home," he said.

Her heart jumped. She just stared at him. "But, it's broad daylight," she stammered.

He stuck his hands in the pockets of his jeans and smiled at her. "There are manholes," he pointed out.

She blinked. "Yes?"

He shrugged. "You could fall in one. I'd be there to pull you out again."

She laughed, flushed, delighted at his interest and without the experience to hide it. "Okay, then," she said in her soft voice.

He smiled and jerked his head toward the door.

The parking lot was full. During the holiday season, there were many visitors on the children's wards. Even Santa Claus made weekly visits to ask children what they wanted for Christmas.

"Still brooding about Bess, aren't you?" he asked after a minute.

She sighed. "It's hard, losing little patients," she confessed.

"It's hard losing people you care about."

"Yes."

She recalled her visit to the church to light candles and that he'd said he lit them, too, for lost members of his own family.

"What did you mean, that Hollister was the detective on your case?"

Her steps slowed. It was painful to talk about it.

He reached down and tucked her soft hand into his big one, lending her its warmth and strength. "Tell me," he said gently.

She drew in a breath. The parking lot was deserted. There was nobody close by. They might as well have been alone in the world.

"There was a gang war," she said, "six years ago. The Lobitos wanted to get even with a family that lived in the apartment my mother and brother and I had just moved into. They didn't know that the former tenants were gone." Her eyes closed on the pain. She could still hear the gunshots, hear the mocking cries outside as glass shattered and her mother screamed, and her little brother fell to the floor covered in blood.

He caught her to him, enveloped her in his arms, held her close and rocked her. "How old was your brother?"

"Four," she said brokenly, tears rolling down her cheeks. "He was just four years old!"

"Dear God," he whispered reverently, and held her closer.

The embrace gave her enough comfort to continue. "It was Rado," she said bitterly. "Rado and the four boys who still run with him. They gave up the boy who fired the shots to save themselves. He was tried as an adult, and he's on death row." She ground her teeth together. "I wish Rado was sitting in the cell beside him. He's killed so many people. They know, and they can't do a thing. He's always got an alibi!"

He drew the flower scent of her hair in through his nostrils. She smelled good. He liked the way she felt, close against him, too.

She liked it far too much. After a minute, she drew back and he loosened his hold. "Thanks," she whispered, without looking at him.

"You've gone without comfort, haven't you?" he asked, as if he knew.

She looked up, grimacing. "It's . . . hard for me, letting people get close."

"Yeah. I know all about that." His face was hard with memories. "When I lost my wife, I had nobody else. Well, maybe one person," he said, not mentioning that it was his son, Tonio. "But I drew into myself. I couldn't bear to talk about her. She was so young. I thought we'd have years and years. Nobody knew she had heart trouble. She got into an argument at work. She never argued," he added with evident sorrow. "She was the sweetest woman I ever knew. Her boss didn't like her. Maria was very conventional. She went to church, loved to knit . . ." He swallowed hard. The memories were painful. "Her boss was one of these new women, who look down on anyone conventional. She rode Maria, all the time. She pushed her too far one day and Maria talked back." His eyes closed. "She just . . . died. Right there."

"I'm sorry," she said huskily. She pressed close, holding him, as he'd held her. She laid her cheek on his broad chest. "I'm so sorry."

His hand tangled in her soft blond hair. "I thought her boss didn't give a damn," he said through his teeth. "I was going to see her the next day, after the funeral. I was going to give her hell."

"What happened?"

"She took a handful of pills, very strong pills. They found her body the next morning."

She lifted her head, shocked.

"Maria wouldn't have wanted that," he added quietly. "She'd have forgiven even the woman who helped kill her. It was the sort of person she was." His face hardened. "I'm not like that. I'm vindictive. I hit back."

She drew in a long breath. "I don't have the heart for revenge," she replied. "My mother always said that God uses people to teach us things. That sometimes a person who hurt your feelings did it for a reason, to make you see the world a different way, to make you understand an opposite position." She searched his black eyes. "She said that people came into your life because you needed them to. Some people make you happy. Some make you sad. But there's always a reason. There are no coincidences."

He lifted her ponytail and ran his fingers through her long silky hair. "So why are you in my life, now?" he teased.

"I was going to ask why you were in mine," she returned with a pert smile.

He shrugged. "Maybe we're going to solve some big crime together and make headlines, huh?"

She grinned. "I would love to solve a big crime."

"I'll keep my eye out for one," he promised. He looked around. People were coming into the parking lot. "We should probably get moving before we become a tourist attraction."

"For that, you have to carry a controversial sign," she assured him.

"Point taken."

He kept her hand in his while they walked. "This isn't the best neighborhood," he said as they approached her apartment. "And the memories must be pretty bad, if this is where you lived when it happened."

"It is," she replied. "But I know the

landlord. He's very protective and he hasn't raised the rent once, in all these years. He's filthy rich. He said he likes providing a safe haven for people like me, whose jobs are to help other people. I have neighbors who are rescue personnel, cops, public defenders . . . the list goes on and on."

"Nice guy," he commented.

She grinned. "You'd pass out if I told you his name."

"Try me."

She stopped walking and looked up at him. "It's Marcus. Marcus Carrera."

His thick eyebrows arched. "The mobster?"

"He isn't. Not anymore. I mean, he still owns casinos and things. But he's married to a Jacobs County girl, and they have a little boy. I know her through Merrie York."

"Small world," he mused.

"It's that star," she said, tapping it through the shepherd's coat. "You don't see much of the bright side of life. You see horrors."

He searched her brown eyes. "So do you."

"I never used to think I could bear to be a nurse. I was squeamish. But after my little brother died, and my mother, I went into nurse's training. I kept thinking, if I'd known any sort of first aid, I might have saved them."

He smoothed his big hands up the sleeves of her soft coat. "My best friend had a father who beat up his mother, and the kids. One night, he got stinking drunk and hit his wife. My friend intervened." His face hardened. "His father hit him over the head with a fire poker. Killed him instantly. The father went to prison. He was sorry, when he sobered up. But my friend was still dead. I wanted to help make sure that it didn't happen to some other innocent child." He sighed. "But I'm not doing so much good right now. One dead kid, another wounded one, and now one almost dead, and in my district."

"It takes time to solve criminal cases," she pointed out. "But you'll get the perpetrators. After all, you're a Texas Ranger." She smiled.

He traced her soft mouth with just the tip of his finger. He loved the way she flushed when he did that. She was so deliciously innocent. "What are you doing tomorrow?" he asked.

"You mean besides helping the president with his foreign policy and suggesting new legislation to the House?" she asked blithely.

He burst out laughing. "I was going to offer you a fast-food hamburger, but I can see that you're far too important for that," he teased.

She grinned. Her heart seemed to be flying overhead. "I love hamburgers."

"Do you?"

"When?"

"Eleven?"

She nodded.

"Wear your hair down, will you?" he added.

"Why?"

"I love long hair," he said softly. "And yours is sexy as hell."

Her lips parted. "My hair?"

He nodded. "Men have preferences," he mused. "Some like big . . ." He cleared his throat. "Suffice it to say, I like hair."

She laughed softly. He wasn't crude. She knew what he was going to say, just the same. "I'm challenged in that area," she pointed out.

His eyes fell to her chest. "Oh, no," he said with a tender smile. "Not challenged at all."

She could have flown. She'd never known such a connection to anyone before, least of all a man. She couldn't believe that he wanted to take her out. She shouldn't go. She couldn't offer him anything, especially not a casual affair. Wasn't that what men expected these days, when they took a woman somewhere? She had so little experience with men . . .

He tipped her chin up. He read her worried expression very well. "Just a hamburger," he said softly. He smiled sadly, thinking of Tonio, of how impossible it would be to let himself become involved with her romantically. Still, he was becoming fond of her, and it was just a hamburger, after all. "Friends."

Her eyes lit up. She could manage that, surely! "Friends," she replied huskily.

He winked. "See you tomorrow at eleven, *rubia,*" he teased. "Stay out of trouble."

"Why? Don't you like getting the opportunity to practice your profession?" she asked dryly.

"Not that way, and certainly not with you," he returned. "Keep your doors locked," he added.

"I always do." She smiled. "Don't get shot."

He pulled back his coat to reveal the gun on his belt. "Bullet deterrent," he replied. "Works wonders."

She laughed, waved and went inside. She felt happier than she had in years.

But, of course, once she was alone, she started brooding about the future. He was a gorgeous man. He could have had any woman he wanted. Sunny was just a new face, a new personality, to him right now. But if he wanted to take things further, there were too many risks. She didn't want him to ever find out why she never dated, why she never encouraged men.

She was twenty-three years old and she'd never had a love affair. She'd never even had a serious romance. She was green as grass and there were reasons, very good reasons, why she could never be intimate with a man.

Was it fair to John to let this continue? She was vulnerable when she was with him. What if she lost her heart, and then he found out? What would become of her, afterward?

She brooded about it all night. The next day, she decided, she was going to have to refuse the date. It would be for the best. She had nothing to give him. It might hurt now, in fact it was going to hurt very badly, but it would save a lot of heartache later on.

But she didn't call it off. She had a dozen excuses. She didn't have his cell phone number. She didn't want to have to call the Ranger office and ask for it, and they probably would want to know why or they wouldn't give it to her. And on and on. In the end, she just couldn't call it off. She wanted his company too much. She paced until it was time for him to come and pick her up. Eleven o'clock arrived. But he didn't.

He didn't seem like the sort of man who stood up dates. Not that you could tell —

Her cell phone rang. It took a minute for her to realize that it had. She picked it up. So few people had the number. Mostly, people at work . . .

"Hello?" she asked hesitantly.

"It's me," a deep, soft voice came over the line. "I got your number from your supervisor — I'm interviewing you about the shooting victim on your ward," he added with a chuckle.

"Abuse of power," she began, feeling elated.

"Guilty. Listen, I'm sorry, there's been a robbery. I have to stand you up."

She let out the breath she'd been holding. She was delighted and sad and uncertain. "That's okay," she said. It was for the best. Or maybe he was just letting her down easy.

"How about we try it again tomorrow, same time?" he asked abruptly, and her heart started beating again. "I have a wild life. I'm pretty much on call twenty-four hours a day if I'm needed, and you can't say no to a crime in progress. It's a hectic life."

"It's okay," she said at once.

"Tomorrow?" he persisted.

Say no, she told herself. *Say it! Say it right now!*

"Okay," she said softly.

He chuckled. "I'll try to make it all the way to your door next time. Honest. See you, *rubia.*"

He hung up. She turned off the phone and muttered at her own weakness. This, she told her stupid heart, was not going to end well.

There was something in the back of John's mind about the gang problem. He couldn't quite access it, but he knew he'd seen something, heard something, about Los Diablos Lobitos and a case several years ago. Talking to Sunny had stirred a memory.

They had a Ranger who worked cold cases. He had an assistant, but most of the legwork was up to Sgt. Colter Banks. He had an office in the basement of Rangers HQ in San Antonio. If anybody could connect something, it would be Banks.

So John drifted down to the basement between phone calls and working up reports to talk to him.

Banks was in his midthirties, tall and rangy with black eyes and dark brown hair. He was personable, but on the job, there weren't many law enforcement officers who were more relentless when on a case.

"No windows," John murmured as he tapped on the door and walked in. "I'd get claustrophobic in here."

Banks lifted a thick eyebrow and chuckled. "If I had a ranch the size of yours, I'd get claustrophobic in a building!"

John shrugged. "Dust and cattle and headaches twelve months a year."

"Fresh beef." Banks sighed. "What I wouldn't give for a nice twelve-ounce steak with mashed potatoes and green beans . . ."

"Haven't you had lunch?"

Banks glowered at him. "Lunch is for people who don't work cold cases. I'm knee-deep in an investigation that suddenly went hot. I may get a guy out of prison who's served five years for a crime he didn't actually commit."

"Nice work."

"I said I might, not that I would," Banks replied, leaning back in his chair with a sigh. "It's a lot of legwork, and there's just me and Clancey to do it."

"Clancey?"

"Oh, sure, but when they start handing

out the credit, it'll be, 'Oh, what a great job Banks did! Isn't he wonderful?' " came a mocking voice from behind another door.

"Oh, can it," Banks muttered. "You get plenty of credit."

A woman with short dark hair and pale gray eyes glared at him as she came into view in the doorway. She was slender and tall, wearing jeans and boots and a blue-checkered, long-sleeved shirt. "I never get credit," she retorted. "I spend my whole life in here, poring over dusty files, while the man of my dreams wanders around out there —" she indicated the general direction of the staircase "— being stalked by predatory females!"

"Yeah? Well, you shot the last predatory person who was seen around here," he reminded her.

"I never!"

"We had to take him to the emergency room," Banks told John.

"He shot himself," Clancey replied. "It was his own fault. He was trying to impress me with the size of his gun and it went off accidentally."

"Not to hear him tell it," Banks drawled.

"It wouldn't have gone off accidentally if he hadn't had his hand on my butt!" she said with towering indignation.

"Was he a Ranger?" John asked, appalled.

"No, he wasn't a Ranger," she said curtly, "he was a Reserve Deputy Sheriff serving papers in the building to one of our workers who's being divorced."

"Then what was he doing down here?" John asked, curious.

"I went up to get a soft drink and he followed me down here into the black pit of doom," Clancey muttered, glaring at Banks. "He —" she pointed to the other Ranger "— was offered an office in the building where the district attorney has his, where all the pertinent files for old cases are kept. But, oh, no, he likes it down here in the dungeon!"

"It's not a dungeon. And it's quiet. Usually," Banks added under his breath.

"Well, that's why the volunteer thought it would be a good place to chase women, obviously," she added.

"There aren't any women down here. There's just you, kid," Banks said with faint venom.

She drew herself up. "I'll have you know I just hit twenty-two!"

"I'll order a case of Ensure for you," he promised, alluding to a protein drink for older people.

"Order it for yourself, why don't you, you

old fossil?" she shot back, looking him up and down. "One job. There was one job going in the whole city, and I was desperate enough to take it." She looked up at the ceiling. "Why?" she asked. "Why didn't I just keep looking for that dishwashing job I've always dreamed of doing?"

"I've got dishes," John volunteered.

She rolled her eyes. "I'm going through the sixth box now," she told Banks. "And I still haven't found one single reference to that man you're looking for information about. I'll go blind!"

"You've got more lights in there than I've got in here," he pointed out. "I'm trying to save an innocent man."

"No, I'm trying to save an innocent man. You're talking to people!"

Banks's dark eyes narrowed. "I swear to God, I've killed chickens that didn't complain half as much as you do!"

"You heartless man!" she said. "Poor, fluffy little things . . . !"

"Floured. Fried. Crispy and delicious," Banks said with a wistful smile. "Nobody cooked fried chicken like my mother."

"Chicken," John scoffed. "I'll take a juicy steak any day."

"Poor, sweet little cows," she began, glaring at John.

"Steers," he corrected. "We don't eat heifers or bulls or cows. We eat steers."

She stared at him.

"It's useless to try and share knowledge with her," Banks said, waving his hand in her direction. "You can't fix stupid."

"No, you can't, that's why the captain busted you back to sergeant," she told Banks with a vicious smile.

"At least I don't shoot men in my own office," he retorted.

"Peasant," she said haughtily and went back into her office.

"Nasturtium," he called after her.

"And will you stop calling me that?!" she snapped.

Banks hid a smile. Her door slammed.

"Nasturtium?" John asked.

"It's a flower. If you call her one, she leaves you alone, at least, temporarily." He shook his head. "Never a dull moment down here since they stuck me with her," he added, his mouth turning down at one side. "I've thought of accusing myself of a crime so they'd lock me up and I'd be rid of her. But with my luck, they'd arrest her and with our unisex society being what it is these days, we'd be sharing a cell." He looked up. "What can I do for you?"

"I'm not sure."

Banks chuckled. "Well, you're honest."

John took off his hat and tossed it onto a chair, running his fingers through his thick hair. "I've got one dead kid and another missing wounded one, and one half-dead one, all three members of warring gangs. I keep trying to remember something similar, years ago, but I can't quite —"

"McCarthy," Banks said quietly. "Melinda McCarthy."

John drew in a quick breath. "Yes. Of course!"

FIVE

Melinda McCarthy had been the daughter of a state senator. Her death, two years earlier, had made national headlines. She'd been found in a back alley of San Antonio, dead of an apparent drug overdose. The thing was, she never used really hard narcotics and she wasn't suicidal. Her father was still trying to prove that it was murder.

There were only a couple of clues that might lead a jury to believe that it was. She was found with Propofol in her body and the body had been moved. It was a potent anesthetic usually given by infusion, which took time and indicated a need for privacy to give it. She was found in an alley right downtown. There was no tube in her arm for infusion, either, only a syringe. But it wasn't the right arm, at that.

It wasn't well-known, but she'd been estranged from her parents for a time, and she was known to the police. She made a living as a high-class call girl. The last person to see her alive was her landlady, who said that she was upbeat and happy because she'd found a way to go back to school and get off the midlevel drugs she was using. Her dad was going to help her. She also mentioned a murder that she knew about, and a drug dealer high up in law enforcement that she was going to blow the whistle on.

At the same time this was going on, there was a gang war over territory. But it wasn't the Serpientes. It was a lesser-known San Antonio gang, trying to infringe on Los Diablos Lobitos' territory. There had been four gang deaths. One of the dead was a low-level pusher whose sister worked as a call girl, just like Melinda, a boy named Harry Lopez. He, like Melinda, died of an apparent drug overdose, but under suspicious circumstances. Like Melinda, the boy had Propofol in his system. The blame had been placed on the leader of the gang opposing Los Diablos Lobitos, who was conveniently dead. The other three dead were high-level members of the opposing gang, and with their leaders in the morgue, the gang disappeared.

There were whispers at the time that the Lobitos were hand in glove with a high-level person in the DEA, and they'd had help disposing of the invading gang. It seemed that the opposing gang wouldn't make a deal to kick back part of its profits to the DEA mole.

Law enforcement officials thought Melinda's death was murder, but there was no evidence that pointed to it. No fingerprints, no clues, nothing to indicate that anybody had used the needle on her except herself. The only thing that pointed to murder was that she was left-handed and the needle was in her left elbow. Also, the drug that was used, Propofol, was usually used to anesthetize surgical patients and was most often inserted by drip. Odd drug for a street user, and only a syringe was found; no tubing to insert the heavy sedative. It had been used notoriously by some famous people as a drug of choice. Its most notable side effect was a complete loss of memory directly afterward. In other words, people who used it didn't remember using it, or anything that happened to them just before it was used. Oddly enough, the leader of the invading gang, now dead, had overdosed with the exact same drug.

Melinda's killer, despite the efforts of various law enforcement agencies to prove there had been one, had never been found. Nor was there any apparent motive for her death except the fact that she knew something about a high-level drug dealer. It was a motive, but with no suspects. Her death had saddened everyone connected to the case, because she was a kind and sweet woman who went out of her way to help the impoverished people in the apartment house where she lived.

"And how ironic," Banks added. "Because that's one of the cold cases I'm working on right now."

"Did something connect?"

"Yes. I had a tip a few days ago. A woman broke up with her live-in boyfriend after he beat her up for the tenth time. He was involved in drugs and prostitution. Well, so was his girlfriend. He ran because she called the police, and when they came, she fingered him for an accessory in a two-year-old murder. Melinda's murder."

"And?"

"She said that it was no suicide. She told police that her boyfriend had a part in the senator's daughter's death, but that it was somebody high up in law enforcement who'd ordered her killed and he didn't actually commit the murder. She didn't know why the senator's daughter was targeted. Her boyfriend never told her. But the boyfriend knew who the killer was."

"Who is he? The boyfriend? Have you tracked him down? It might be possible to offer him a plea deal. You could check with the DA."

"That's the thing. The name he used with her is an alias. He's more or less vanished."

"Great," John said heavily. "That's just great."

"That's why I've got Clancey going through paper files from three years ago, looking for any case that might have ties to mine."

"And she's not even getting overtime!" Clancey yelled through the door.

"At least she still has a job, for the time being!" Banks yelled back.

There was an insulting noise, and then, silence.

"I never thought it was suicide," Banks said, unperturbed. "She wasn't the type. She made her living as a call girl, but she was high ticket. She didn't take on clients who weren't loaded."

"Oppressive men, driving desperate women to acts of sinfulness!" Clancey interjected.

"I wish somebody would drive you to an act of desperation," Banks muttered. "There must be at least one sanitation worker in

Texas who needs an able assistant."

"Neat idea! Why don't you apply?" she called back.

Banks rolled his eyes and ground his teeth together.

John managed not to laugh. He leaned forward. "Do you think there's any possibility that the hit was gang related?" he asked.

Banks sighed. "I don't know. I'm pretty sure now that she was actually murdered and not a suicide. Her father calls me twice a month, hoping for any progress on the case. He lost his wife years ago. It was just him and Melinda, and he drew inside himself after his wife died. They hardly spoke. Then they had a major disagreement over her new boyfriend and she moved out. The boyfriend was the one who got her hooked on drugs and into prostitution. She'd just come out of a rehab clinic. She wasn't using anymore and she had plans to go back home. It's a sad story."

"Your informant said that someone high up in law enforcement ordered the hit." John was thinking, his black eyes narrow and thoughtful. "There was a case about two years ago, involving an assistant district attorney who was murdered in San Antonio."

"Yes!" Banks said, sitting up straight. "The

123

murderer was wearing a designer paisley shirt and a very expensive wristwatch that played music. The watch and the shirt tied him to the assistant DA's murder, and to the politician who ordered him killed. The politician was actually appointed to a vacant US Senate seat. It sent shock waves through the country when he went up for conspiracy to commit murder. State's evidence was turned by a former cop named Fred Baldwin, who was on the politician's payroll."

"I'd forgotten all about that. Sheriff Hayes Carson in Jacobsville was shot. An attempt was made on one of the Kirk boys in Wyoming, the one who'd been a Border Patrol agent. Both attempts were made by the same man, the one who'd pinched the shirt and watch from the murdered assistant DA, because he didn't want them to remember that he'd been wearing the DA's shirt!"

"He made an attempt on Carlie Blair in Jacobsville as well, didn't he?" Banks asked.

"Yes. She had a photographic memory and she'd seen him in the shirt. He wiped out everyone he could think of who had. He even wiped Sheriff Carson's computer in the sheriff's office and killed the computer programmer who'd been hired to recover the data on it. But when he put the hit on Carlie, he messed up. He was high as a kite and he got it confused, so the killer he'd contracted went after her father instead. Incidentally, the murderer in the stolen paisley shirt burned to death trying to kill two women up in Wyoming, one of whom was engaged to the Kirk who was a border agent."

"Complicated," Banks mused.

"Very. It came out that the DEA had a mole. They thought it was the guy who died in Wyoming, who actually posed as a DEA agent. But they found out later that the mole's still involved. They don't know who he is or where he is, or how to find out. If you mention it to Cobb, the senior DEA agent in Houston, he starts foaming at the mouth," John chuckled.

"A DEA mole who's still undetected. A dead girl who'd just gone through rehab to get off hard narcotics but was found self-injected with a high-ticket drug. A murdered assistant DA. What about the man who turned state's evidence?" Banks asked.

"Fred Baldwin. He was a cop in Chicago years ago, fired for being overly rough with a man who'd just killed his baby son. His name was cleared and he worked for Jacobsville Police Chief Cash Grier for a while."

Banks chuckled. "I know Grier. He was a Texas Ranger some years back."

John whistled. "I remember. He slugged our temporary captain and got fired."

"I learned some new words," Banks recalled wistfully. "I wish he'd hit the man twice as hard. Our temporary boss gave Rangers a bad name. He didn't last long after that. You know that Grier's related to the state attorney general, right?"

John nodded. "And a few people in DC as well."

"He and I are third cousins. His brother's SAC at the Jacobsville satellite FBI office," Banks remarked. "Good man, Garon."

"He is. I've worked with him from time to time."

"We all have." Banks leaned back again. "A two-year-old murder that nobody would admit was a murder. A mole in the DEA office, somebody high up and never fingered. A dead assistant DA. A murderer who can be identified by a disgruntled former girlfriend, but we can't find him because he used an alias with her."

"All true." John shrugged. "So I guess we dig and dig in our spare time."

"What spare time?" Banks asked, nodding toward a two-foot stack of file folders on his desk.

"Tell me about it." John got to his feet. "Hollister over at SAPD is putting together a task force to sort out the gang warfare we're currently embroiled in. I've been recruited for it. I've got a dead boy who was in Los Serpientes, a missing wounded boy in Los Diablos Lobitos and a hospitalized wounded boy who's covered in wolf tattoos. He said his boss was going snake hunting. So we're going to try to find the shooters before more blood flows."

"I'd offer to help, but my caseload is pretty formidable. I really want Melinda's killer," he added coldly.

"So does the senator. You might ask him to pull some strings for you at the political level," John suggested. "It never hurts to have a powerful politician in your corner."

"No, it doesn't."

John was conflicted after he left Banks. Like many law enforcement people in San Antonio, he wanted Melinda's case solved. Some lowlife had gotten away with murder. He needed to be caught, even if it was two years too late.

He remembered that he'd promised lunch to Sunny and he smiled. One bright spot in his day, at least, he thought as he got into his black SUV and headed toward her apartment building. A few minutes of pleasant company might clear his head.

■ ■ ■ ■

Sunny was sure that he wasn't going to show up, and part of her hoped he wouldn't. She was already a nervous wreck. She'd tried on four outfits before settling on jeans and a pretty green sweater with a turtleneck. She'd brushed her long blond hair so that it settled around her shoulders, and she'd used the lightest trace of lipstick. She wouldn't win a beauty contest, but she didn't look too bad, she considered.

Just as she was about to fix herself a sandwich, there was a tap on the front door. Heart racing, she ran to answer it. And there he was. Gorgeous. Six feet of virile, sensuous man.

He smiled to himself, because everything she felt was right there on her face. She didn't have the experience to hide it. He loved that about her. She was so sweetly naive. He wondered how a woman reached her age in the modern world without falling into an affair, or several affairs. It seemed to be the norm with people around him.

"Ready to go?" he asked softly, and with a smile.

"Oh, yes!" She grabbed her purse and

pulled out her door key. "I'll lock up," she said.

He followed her out and waited while she fumbled the key into the lock. "It's cold," she laughed, shouldering into the light jacket she wore with her jeans.

"It is. Unusually cold, for south Texas," he added.

She fell into step beside him. "Where are we going?" she asked.

"To a little place down near Floresville that has the best barbeque in Texas," he said.

She turned to him. "How did you know I liked barbeque?" she asked, surprised.

"I didn't. He has other meats, but it's the barbeque that keeps us coming back. It's an office favorite," he added with twinkling black eyes.

"I'm crazy about it," she confessed. "My mother used to make barbeque ribs in the slow cooker," she added. "She was a wonderful cook."

"Are you?" he asked.

"I do my best," she said. "I can make breads of all sorts, and I'm pretty good with vegetables. But I have problems with bouncing chicken."

He turned and stared down at her as they reached his black SUV.

She laughed. "I'm always afraid I won't

get it done enough, so I usually overcook it and it bounces."

He opened the door for her, admiring the long, beautiful sweep of her pale blond hair around her shoulders. "I know an easy fix for that," he said.

She waited, curious, while he went around and got in under the wheel and started the big vehicle. A police radio crackled softly with static between them. The back seat was full of paraphernalia.

He caught her glancing at the disorder and chuckled. "I'm messy," he confessed. "I think I was left behind when they taught how to put things in order. I was raised by my grandfather, and he was so disorganized that he made me look neat. But he loved me, and he raised me to be useful rather than a layabout."

"I know what you mean. My mother used to say that character was worth far more than wealth."

He nodded. "It is." He glanced at her. "When you cook chicken, put a fork in it. If it brings up blood, it's not cooked enough."

"Is it that easy?" she asked, laughing.

"I don't cook much, but when our house-keeper goes on vacation, I pretty much have to. I don't like takeout." He didn't add that his son loved it. He didn't want to mention

Tonio. She liked him, but her opinion might change if she knew that he had a ready-made family in tow. It was too soon, at any rate, to be that personal with her. After all, what he had in mind was simple friendship. Somebody to date occasionally. She was good company.

"Everything's so bleak in winter," she said with a sigh.

"It's not."

"Excuse me?" she asked, turning her head.

He chuckled. "It's not winter. Not until the twentieth."

"Oh!" She shook her head. "I always forget. When it gets cold, I always think it's winter beginning."

"I have more trouble with the time changing than the seasons changing." He sighed. "I wish they'd leave it alone. I always forget to change the clock and I'm either too early or too late for work."

She loved it, that he wasn't perfect. She looked at the purse she was rolling in her lap. The truck was nice. It seemed to have every device known to man, including power windows and a CD player. It even had a sunroof.

"What do you drive?" he asked.

"I don't." She sighed. "I know how to drive, I mean, but I can't really afford a car.

131

I can't make payments, for one thing. And for another, what I could afford would mean gas and repair bills and maintenance. Won't fit my budget," she added with twinkling eyes. "I like being able to walk to work. I can afford to replace shoes," she added.

He chuckled. He had no such issues. If he'd wanted to, he could afford to run a Jaguar sports car. In fact, he'd owned one when he was in his early twenties, before he married Maria. And before Tonio came along.

She glanced at his boots. They were big and hand-tooled. But they showed evidence of being working boots. Not for show.

"I like boots," he remarked when he noticed the attention his feet were getting. "I spend a lot of time with the cattle when I'm not on the job here. We have pasture on the bottoms, and when it floods, we're all out pulling cows and calves out of mud."

"Ranching must be interesting."

"It's magic," he said, trying to find a word that really expressed his love for it. "I love animals," he confessed. "I've nursed motherless calves and treated sick bulls and horses. I've never had one single day when I was bored."

"Do you have a lot of cowboys?"

"A good many," he said. "It's a big ranch.

I inherited it, along with the workers. Some of them are third-generation cowboys on the ranch," he added, to her surprise. "They know exactly what to do, so I just stand back and let them do it. I don't micromanage."

"I've seen nurses who did that," she said. "Supervisors who had to detail every single task and then stood over you to make sure you did things exactly the way they said." She grimaced. "It didn't make for a happy working environment."

"I can imagine. No problems where you are?"

"Oh, no," she said, and her face brightened. "I love my job. I have wonderful coworkers. I hate the bad times. But the good times more than make up for it. There's no greater joy than helping save the life of a child."

He smiled. "My job has echoes of that," he said. "If I can catch a killer and get him off the streets, that saves lives, too."

"You Rangers go all over the world on cases, don't you?"

"We do. I've been as far west as Japan and as far east as Egypt on cases. I've certainly seen the world."

"I've seen Texas," she laughed. "Well, actually, I've seen San Antonio. I've never been anywhere else."

"Never?" he exclaimed, glancing at her.

"Some of us are just homebodies," she pointed out. "Besides, I don't have a car," she reminded him.

"There are buses."

"There are tickets. They cost money."

"*Rubia,* you're hopeless," he teased.

"I guess I am," she said, but she smiled. "I like my life. I don't like change."

"Shame."

"What?"

"You don't have anything to jingle in your pockets. You don't like change," he reminded her.

She got it, belatedly, and laughed.

"You're a tonic," he mused as they drove down the long stretch of road that led past sprawling ranches with endless fencing, on the road to Floresville. "I haven't laughed so much in a long time."

"I haven't, either."

"Do you like movies?" he asked abruptly.

"Not many. I tend to enjoy cartoon movies and action ones more than comedies or horror. I do like science fiction, though."

"Me, too. I'm excited about next year's *Predator* movie —"

"That's my favorite series!" she exclaimed. "I love the *Predator*s. I have all the movies and all the books and a lot of comics and graphic novels."

"You're kidding me!" he exclaimed. "So do I!"

She laughed. "What a coincidence."

"How about the *Aliens*?"

"I like those, too." She glanced at him. "I'll bet you've never gone to a cartoon movie in your life."

"You'd be wrong." Tonio had loved those movies when he was little. He and Maria took Tonio to the theater almost every time a new one came out. It made him sad, remembering little Maria. They hadn't been a passionate couple, but he'd adored her for her gentle, kind heart.

She noticed his sudden withdrawal. There must be something sad in his past that was triggered by her comment. She was sorry she'd made it.

"What sort of music do you like?" she asked, changing the subject.

He came out of his memories and back into the light. "Almost every sort," he said. "But I'm partial to Latin music."

She laughed. "So am I. I'm crazy about it. My father taught me the tango when I was just nine years old —"

"The tango!"

"Yes. It's such a wonderful dance. So

complex. Nothing like most of the American movies that include it."

"Absolutely," he agreed. "It's as much an art form as a physical thing."

Her lips parted. "Can you do a tango?"

"Yes, I can." He almost added that he was from Argentina, and that he'd grown up with it. But he hesitated to mention his background. Not just yet. He smiled. "It's hard to find a partner who can do it."

"I know what you mean. I don't go out much. In fact, I don't go out at all. But there's a flamenco place downtown where I eat occasionally, when it doesn't get dark until late. They always have somebody who does a tango."

"It's something of a contest down in Jacobsville," he mused. "We have three couples who fight it out on the dance floor. The Griers, the Caldwells, and the Kantors. They're all accomplished, but the rumor is that Stanton Rourke Kantor and his wife are the true champions. Rourke was CIA, stationed in Argentina. His cover was as a dance instructor, so that gives him an edge on the others. A slight edge."

"Wow. We hear all sorts of rumors about people in Jacobsville," she added. "Is it true that your police chief used to be a government assassin?"

"It is," he said, eyes dancing. "We have a whole complement of ex-black ops and military people, as well as retired mercs. A drug lord found out the hard way a few years back that it wasn't just rumors."

"Cara Dominguez," she said abruptly.

His eyebrows arched. "How do you know about her?"

She laughed self-consciously. "My best friend on the ward is Merrie York. Her brother has a ranch in Jacobsville. She knows all the news."

"I know the Yorks. They're nice people."

"Very nice. Merrie's so good with children."

"You must be, too," he replied.

"It's why I work at a children's hospital. I love them all."

"Yet you haven't married and had some of your own," he said with a gentle smile.

The reaction he got was surprising, and it made him self-conscious. She nodded, but she averted her head and her face drew up. Why? A failed love affair? A romance gone wrong?

"Bad memories?" he wondered.

She sighed. "Very bad," she confessed, staring out the window. "I don't talk about them."

"You were alone after your mother and

137

brother died," he recalled. "It must have been very hard."

She drew in a breath. "It was. I've had my run-ins with Los Diablos Lobitos," she added, drawing his attention. "I'd love to see Rado go up for murder one," she said harshly. "He's like an eel. They can't hold him."

"Hard facts," he replied easily. "You have to have proof, not only of the crime, but of intent. It's not easy, when a gang leader surrounds himself with people who are more than happy to provide him with an unbreakable alibi."

"True," she said sadly. "I guess he'll go on until he gets too old to intimidate people."

"Does he intimidate you?"

She made a face. "I'm afraid of him. I don't let it show, ever," she added doggedly. "I won't give him the satisfaction."

"You have to walk home alone at night," he began, and the thought concerned him.

"Oh, I get cabs home," she said. "Even though it's close, I never take chances going home. I won't give Rado a free shot at me."

His black eyes narrowed as he pulled into the restaurant's parking lot and cut off the engine. He turned to her. "Why are you afraid of him?" he asked gently.

"Because he's made threats," she said

reluctantly. She forced a laugh. "It was probably just showing off, in front of his friends."

"What sort of threat?" he persisted, and his blood ran hot. She was a gentle, shy woman. He hated the thought that a thug would target her, for any reason.

"Just the 'I'll get you' one," she said, delighted at his concern. "I stopped him from bullying a child," she added. She didn't add anything else.

"I see."

"He was trying to get someone to take drugs into the hospital, to give to the children," she said, almost choking on her anger.

His face hardened. "He should be charged for that."

"How would you do it?" she replied sadly. "It would be my word against his, and his friends who were with him would swear that I lied. It's that simple."

"Still," he said, thinking. "It might be a good idea to have someone undercover at the hospital."

"From your office?" she asked.

"No. That would be SAPD's jurisdiction. I'll talk to Marquez about it."

"Marquez?"

"Rick Marquez. He's a lieutenant of

detectives. An old friend," he added with a smile.

"I was going to suggest Hollister."

He drew in a long breath. "We don't get along, as a rule," he said. "He's very fond of throwing out orders, and I don't respond well to prodding."

Her eyebrows lifted over mischievous brown eyes. "I thought you were that kind of man," she teased.

He grinned at her. "Actually, I'm worse. And we're here."

He went around to open her door for her. He lifted her down from the high seat, his hands tight around her small waist. He didn't put her down immediately. He held her at eye level, searching her big, brown eyes quietly while her heart tried to beat her ribs to death.

"You don't wear makeup," he said, his voice deeper, softer as he studied her.

She swallowed. "I don't really like it . . ."

"It wasn't a complaint, *rubia,*" he said softly. His black eyes fell to her mouth. It was the most perfect bow shape, lush and gently curved. He thought how it would feel under his lips. He hadn't wanted to kiss a woman in a long time. He wanted very much to kiss this one.

But it was too soon. And unwise.

He put her down and stepped back. "Barbeque," he said, ramming his hands into his pockets with a chuckle. "I like mine red-hot."

She fought to calm down as she fell into step beside him. Her heart was still racing like mad. She'd thought he was going to kiss her. But he'd pulled back and now he was as distant as he'd been at their first meeting. She forced a smile so her disappointment didn't show too much.

"I like mine edible," she retorted. "I have taste buds. They still work."

"I burned mine off years ago, eating raw jalapeño peppers," he laughed.

"To each his own," she replied, smiling.

They had a booth in the back of the sprawling restaurant. Their waiter was young, short, very friendly.

John knew him. They conversed in Spanish while Sunny listened, fascinated. The young man had a brother who was in trouble with the law. John had helped him, apparently, because he was asking if the brother was keeping himself straight. The waiter chuckled and said, yes, he was, because he didn't want to let John down.

Sunny smiled to herself. Her companion

had a big heart. She was already fascinated with him. She had to try to keep those feelings under control, though. She had nothing to give him, in any sort of intimate way.

He seemed as content for friendship as she was, and it made her relax even more. He was a widower. Perhaps he was still grieving. That would explain his reluctance to get involved with her. She hoped he never had to learn why she didn't want to get involved with a man. Friendship, though, that was fine.

They both ordered barbeque plates and cleaned them.

"I was starving," she laughed.

"I noticed."

"I forget to eat when I'm at home," she confided. "I get busy with household chores, or cooking, or crocheting, and I pass over mealtimes."

"I'm the same," he mused. "I rarely have time to sit down in a restaurant. Odd thing, that crime seems to balloon this time of year, during the holiday season."

"People are more open to other people. So they're more easily taken advantage of," she said simply. "It brings out the best and the worst in people, this time of year."

He nodded.

"Why were you named Suna?" he asked while he sipped coffee.

"For my mother's grandmother," she said. "It was her nickname. She was called Susanna. My mother couldn't pronounce that when she was small, so she called her Granny Suna," she laughed. "So Suna, she was."

"It's a pretty name." He searched her eyes. "Do you have another name besides?"

"Angelica," she said with a shy smile.

"Now that suits you," he teased. "But so does Sunny. I like it."

Her high cheekbones colored, just a little, as she met that even gaze and felt her heart skip.

He fingered his coffee cup, his eyes narrow on her face. "How about dessert?"

She shook her head. "I don't like sweets very much. Except when I'm pulling a double shift and I need an energy boost," she laughed.

"I don't like sweets much, either. But I carry granola bars around in my pocket when I'm on a case," he confessed.

The waiter came back with the check.

"La comida estuva muy buena," she said gently. *"¿Puedo pagar con tarjeta de crédito?"* she added, reaching for her purse.

Two sets of male eyebrows lifted, because

her accent was flawless.

"Yes, the meal was very good. No, you can't pay with a credit card," John said, with a soft laugh. "It was my invitation, so my treat. Next time, you can take me, and you can pick up the check. Deal?"

She grinned and laughed a little self-consciously. "Okay. Deal." At least, she thought brightly, he wanted to see her again. But she'd have to work up the nerve to ask him out. Maybe later.

Six

"You didn't tell me that you spoke Spanish," he said when they were in the truck.

"I have to. We have a lot of people here who only speak Spanish," she added, smiling. "Most of them have a child or grandchild with them who can translate. But it's not a bad idea to be bilingual. Besides," she added with soft laughter, "I love Spanish. My mother was bilingual. She taught me."

"I grew up speaking it," he said. "When I came to this country from Argentina, I had to learn English. Even at the age of ten, English is hard!" he said.

She smiled. "You grew up in Argentina?" she exclaimed.

"Yes. It's a beautiful country."

"I've seen videos of it on the internet," she said. "I love to watch the gauchos ride. Did you grow up in a city?" she wondered.

He laughed. "No, *rubia*. In the Pampas. My grandfather was a gaucho." That wasn't quite true. He was a wealthy landowner who rode like one, though.

"Wow," she said softly.

He grinned. "His wife, my grandmother, taught me the tango," he added. He glanced at her. "One day, we'll have to try out that flamenco club downtown."

Her heart skipped. She tried to hide her excitement. "I'd love that."

"You know, so would I," he said, smiling.

He drove her back to her apartment. Conversation was light and comfortable, nothing heavy. They found that they thought alike on politics, something of a surprise. It was a volatile subject, especially in modern times.

He pulled up in front of her apartment, but before he could cut off the engine, his phone rang with the FIFA World Cup theme, easily recognizable by a soccer fan, which Sunny was.

"Ruiz," he said at once.

He listened, sighed, glanced at Sunny with a rueful smile. "Okay. On my way. Text me the address, will you? Sure."

He cut off the phone with a wry smile. "Well, I would have walked you to your door, but I've got another robbery across town. SAPD requested our help. Sorry."

"No. You don't need to apologize. It's your job."

He reached over and touched her long, soft hair. "We'll do this again. Maybe a movie some weekend, you think?"

Her spirits lifted. It was unwise to let this continue. She should just say no and get out of the SUV. She knew that she should . . .

"I'd like that," she said instead.

"We'll talk about it later. You got a cell phone?"

"Well, yes . . ."

He held out his hand. She gave it to him. It was a generic phone, nothing fancy. "Can you get text messages on it?" he asked.

"Yes. That's mostly how I communicate with people at work," she replied.

He smiled. He pulled up a screen and input his name and cell phone number. He did the same on his own phone, with hers. He handed it back to her. "Now. You get hassled on the way home, any night, you text me. I'll bring handcuffs."

She laughed with pure delight. "Okay," she said softly.

He pursed his lips and studied her with warm eyes. "Or you could just text me for no reason. I'm easy."

Her heart skipped again. Stupid organ. It

147

was going to get her in hot water, eventually. "Okay," she added.

He winked. "I'll see you, *rubia.*"

She started to say okay, realized that she sounded like a parrot and laughed out loud. "I'll see you. John," she added huskily.

His eyes glittered at the sound of his name on her lips. She made it sound different. It made him warm inside, just to be with her.

She didn't notice his expression. She climbed down out of the big vehicle, closed the door and waved him off with a smile.

He threw up a hand as he drove off.

She unlocked her door and went inside, her heart swelling with new emotions. It had been a wonderful lunch. She hoped it wouldn't be the only one. Yes, it was risky. But life was risky. They could be just friends. It would work out.

She was early for work, shortly after her lunch date, and her young friend was sitting in the canteen, looking as if the world had fallen on him.

She draped her coat over a chair at his table. "Such a long face," she said gently. "Can I help?"

He looked up and the sun came out again. He smiled. "Not really. But thanks for asking. I haven't seen you lately."

"I was working a different shift," she said. "I traded with another nurse, who needed to be off."

"That was nice of you."

"She's a nice person," she replied. "How's school?" she asked when she'd filled a cup with hot chocolate and was sitting across from him.

"It's okay," he said. He was sliding his own cup of hot chocolate around on the table.

"Something's wrong," she said, noting his expression.

He looked up, surprised. "Sort of," he said after a minute.

"Would it help to talk about it?"

He let out a breath and sat up straighter. "It's Rado," he said heavily. "He beat up a friend of mine."

She frowned. "Why?"

He grimaced. "He thought David was telling tales about him to somebody," he said. He looked up at her with sad black eyes. "Broke his arm," he said worriedly. "David said he laughed while he did it."

Her face tautened. "He needs to be put away," she said coldly. "Someplace that he can't hurt other people."

"Everybody's scared of him," he replied. "Well, except you," he said, and smiled, remembering her fierce defense of him in the parking lot when they first met.

"Don't kid yourself. I'm scared of him, too," she confessed. "I just hide it well."

"David's sister had to take him to the emergency room and tell them he fell off a wall," he said.

"Did she bring him here?" she asked.

"No. Downtown. The old hospital."

She frowned. That sounded odd.

"She knows a doctor who works there, who'll treat him and not charge her," he said. He didn't add that the doctor was a client of hers. David's sister was a prostitute.

"I see."

"He's the only friend I've got, really," he told her.

"If you spend any time with him, make sure Rado isn't around," she advised gently.

"I do. I go when his sister's there. She and Rado get along. At least, they seem to. He doesn't do bad stuff in front of her. He caught David after school," he added quietly. "When nobody but Rado's gang was around. They held him while . . ." He stopped and sipped hot chocolate. It stuck in his throat.

"I don't suppose your friend would talk to the police?"

"No, he wouldn't," he said at once. He couldn't tell her that his father was in law enforcement. He couldn't take the chance that she might say something and it would get back to Rosa, who worked in the hospital here, and from Rosa to his dad. He didn't tell his father anything about Rado or David or David's sister. He was afraid.

She frowned slightly. "Are you in trouble of some kind?"

He grimaced. "Not really. Rado just wants me in the gang. He keeps pestering me about it."

He knew why. It was because his dad was a Texas Ranger. It would be a strike against law enforcement if he could recruit a Ranger's son. It would beef up Rado's rep in the community, too.

"Don't you do it," she said.

"I wouldn't," he promised. "It's just . . ." He sipped hot chocolate. "David just told somebody that Rado knew a guy in the DEA. He didn't say who or anything. He was just talking, you know. Rado went crazy."

Her heart jumped. "Don't you say anything to anybody," she cautioned.

"I know. I wouldn't." He finished the hot chocolate. "I don't want him to hurt my friend. He told David he'd do worse if he ever opened his mouth again."

"Can you talk to your father about this?"

151

"No!" he said at once. He averted his eyes. "He's never home. It's always work, work, work. We never talk. If he's not eating, he's on the phone, and then he's off to some . . ." He started to say crime scene, and caught himself. "Off to some meeting," he amended. "He only notices me if I do something wrong."

She pursed her lips and smiled. "So you do something wrong, to get his attention," she guessed.

He laughed. He looked sheepish. "Yeah. I guess so."

"You need to tell someone who can do something about Rado," she said.

"He'd kill me if I talked to anybody about his business," he began.

"Not if he never knew it was you," she replied. "I have a friend. He's a policeman, but he was a mercenary, a professional soldier, before he started working in San Antonio. He's a great investigator and he's also a clam. He doesn't gossip. Suppose I asked him to talk to you?"

His heart jumped. It might save David's life, if he could tell somebody what Rado was doing. But he was afraid. "If I go to see him," he began.

"No," she replied at once. "He can come here, to talk to you."

That might work. He wouldn't be seen with the policeman. But Rado might find out. He looked up at her. "You're sure, that he won't sell me out?"

"I'm very sure. When my family was killed, he was the investigating officer," she said quietly. "I've known him a long time. He's a good man."

"Do you like him?" he asked curiously.

She laughed. "Not that way," she said. "He's just a friend." She looked down at her hot chocolate. "I don't . . . get involved with men. I like being on my own."

"You don't want to get married and have kids?" he asked, wondering why he felt so empty when she said that. His father wasn't married. Sunny was sweet and kind, not like that stern, unsmiling woman his father had brought home two years ago.

She drew in a long breath. "It's complicated," she said finally. "It's just complicated. Would you talk to my friend?"

"Yes," he said after a minute.

"Then I'll call him tonight."

"Okay."

Her phone beeped. She pulled it out. There was a text.

New movie. Saturday matinee. 2 p.m. What do you think, rubia?

She brightened. Her face lit up like a Christmas tree. Okay, she texted back.

See you then, he texted back.

He hung up. She put the phone back in her purse.

"A guy, huh?" Antonio asked, faintly disappointed.

"A guy who's a friend," she corrected. "I don't have boyfriends." She glanced at her watch. "I have to run. I'll see you tomorrow, okay?"

"I'll be here."

"You be careful," she added as she picked up her empty cup to put it in the trash container. "I'd do anything I could to help you, you know."

He felt warm inside. "I'd do the same, for you, if I could."

She smiled. "See you."

He nodded. He watched her walk away and he felt scared. She said the policeman would keep his name confidential. He hoped so. He couldn't tell his dad what was going on, or he'd know that David was in the gang with Rado. He'd forbid Tonio to see his friend again, and that would leave him alone with nobody to talk to. Well, that wasn't quite true. He had Sunny.

He smiled as he watched her walk away. She was one of the nicest people he'd ever met. So he had two friends now in San Antonio. He just hoped he could keep the youngest friend alive.

Sunny called Cal Hollister that night when she got home. She knew from experience that he hardly slept at night. He had nightmares from his adventures overseas. He'd let that slip, just once. She had her own night terrors about the loss of her family. It gave them something in common.

"I have a young friend," she told Hollister. "He has a friend who's in Los Diablos Lobitos. Rado broke the friend's arm because he thought the boy was talking about him. I think my young friend would talk to you, if you wouldn't mind coming over to the hospital one afternoon. He's afraid of Rado. But I think he may know something about what's going on with the gang problems."

"That would be a help, if we can manage not to get your young friend killed in the process. Rado has eyes everywhere."

Her heart jumped. She was less confident now. "I don't want him hurt. He doesn't have much family, just a father who seems to be a very occupied businessman with no time for his son. He says he can't talk to his father."

"He can talk to you, though, apparently,"

came the amused reply.

"He's a sweet kid," she said softly. "I'd like to help him, if I could. Rado's dangerous."

"Yes, he is. Would the boy with the broken arm be willing to testify against Rado, if we provided protection?"

"I don't know, Cal," she said honestly. "You know what Rado is. He wouldn't mind killing a child."

"Not him," he agreed. "Okay. How about if I show up at the hospital one afternoon? You can tell me what time. I'll be meeting you there, in case anybody asks."

She hesitated. It was unlikely that John would be around then. She was uneasy about being seen with another man, and it getting back to him. She wouldn't be able to tell him the truth, and she didn't want to lie. She hadn't realized until then how much John Ruiz meant to her. If he thought she was getting involved with Cal, he might go away and not come back.

"I'll be asking you about a case," he continued, having read the hesitation correctly. "You've got a case on Ruiz, is that it?" he teased.

She flushed. "He's just a friend."

"Sunny," he said gently, "you're letting life go by without even trying to join in. You can't live in the past. It won't matter," he added firmly. "You think it will, but it won't. Not to a man who cares for you."

She drew in a breath. "I'm too much a coward to want to find out," she said, trying to make a joke of it. "John is really just a friend. I like him a lot, but it's not a man-woman thing."

"If you say so. Okay. When do you want me to show up?"

"Tomorrow's Friday. How about in the canteen, about three thirty?"

"Will your young friend be there then?"

"He's there most afternoons. I'm sure he will."

"Okay. I'll come talk to you about some nonexistent case," he said on a laugh.

"That works." She paused. "You won't mention it to John? The boy's really scared, and John might let something slip . . ."

"He's a clam," Hollister returned. "But if you're that concerned, I won't mention it. Not unless we hit pay dirt," he added.

"It would be nice if we could find a way to put Rado behind bars," she said on a sigh.

"I'll second that. So, I'll see you tomorrow."

"I'll be there."

When she hung up, she wondered if she should have told Cal that the boy had told someone that Rado knew somebody in the DEA. But it was probably nothing.

She was at the canteen on time. But Tonio wasn't. She and Hollister waited for twenty minutes, but she had to go to work and the boy still hadn't arrived.

"I guess we'll try again next week," Hollister said as he got up to go.

"I'll make sure he's going to be here, next time. I hope he's all right," she added worriedly. "He was really nervous."

"Do you know who his father is?"

She shook her head. "I don't even know the boy's last name," she said with a rueful smile. "We've had snacks together a few afternoons. I saved him from Rado," she added. "I was scared to death, but Rado was being really mean to him. I hate bullies."

"So do I," he returned.

"Rado wanted him to bring drugs into the hospital and pass them to the little patients," she said through her teeth. "He refused. He was angry about it."

"Nice kid," Hollister said.

"Very nice. It's a shame he doesn't get more attention at home. His mother's been dead for some time. I guess his father buried himself in work and just sort of forgot that his son might need him."

"Don't be judgmental," Hollister chided. "You've only had one side of the story. There are always two."

"I guess there are. He's such a sweet kid. I feel sorry for him. He has a relative who works in the hospital, but I have no idea who it is. It's a very big hospital. I only know my own ward."

"He's secretive about his family, is he?"

"Very."

"He may have a reason for it. One he doesn't want to tell you."

"I got that impression," she confided.

"Well, we'll try again next week. And if you hear any gossip, about the patient who was shot, how about getting back to me? John tried to get the psychologist back over there to talk to him, but the boy's guardian spirited him out of the hospital before he had the chance. We have no idea where to find him. That makes two gang members who've given us the slip."

"I know. The name he gave us wasn't his real one, apparently," she said. "Gangs. Why do we have gangs?"

"Why do we have criminals?" he mused. "If you figure it out, please tell me. I'd love to solve the problem."

"Wouldn't we all? Thanks, Cal."

"No problem. See you around."

She went on her shift. It was a hectic night. All through it, with two emergency surgeries and one crash cart episode, she worried about Tonio. Surely Rado hadn't done something to him? She hoped and prayed that he was going to be all right. She wouldn't see him on the weekend, because he wouldn't need a ride home after school. She'd have to bide her time until Monday, when she'd hopefully find out where he'd been.

Tonio was at home. He'd come down with a stomach virus and couldn't go to school Friday. Adele sat with him, feeding him ice chips while his poor stomach finally began to settle down again. His father had looked in on him, but the phone had gone off almost at once, and John was out the door and gone.

"I wish I had a dad," Tonio said sadly as Adele placed a tray with soup and crackers in front of him in bed.

"You have a dad," she chided. "But he's a lawman. A lot of people depend on him. He saves lives."

"Yeah. I know." He sipped soup. "It's just, he's never here." He looked up at her with sad brown eyes. "When Mom was alive, it was different."

"Your father might marry again . . ."

"No! I don't want another woman here," Tonio said harshly. "He brought that awful woman from work. I hated her! She was cold, all business, she didn't even smile . . . !"

"He was just dating her, my darling," Adele interrupted gently. "He wasn't going to marry her on the spot, you know."

"I ran away," he muttered. "I'd do it again, if he brought someone else home. He can't talk to me about anything, ever. He's too busy. But he had time to bring her here, didn't he?"

She frowned. She didn't know what to say to him. He'd loved his mother. So had Adele. Maria had been unique.

"You can't expect your father to spend the rest of his life alone, Tonio," she said, trying to reason with him. "There are nice women in the world. Really nice ones."

He thought of Sunny. She was nice. If his father had brought someone like Sunny home, it might have been different. But his dad seemed to like brash, blunt, law enforcement-type women, if that one he'd brought home was any indication of his taste.

He didn't answer Adele. He felt terrible. He was worried about David. He hoped Sunny wasn't worried about him. Under different circumstances, he could have asked his cousin Rosa to speak to Sunny and tell her that he was okay. But he didn't want Rosa to know about Sunny, because she knew who David was and he couldn't afford the risk that she might tell Rosa about Rado and the gang. It would get back to his father, who might send him off to military school. That had been discussed, just before John enrolled him at the alternative school. Tonio tried very hard to stay out of trouble. He was certain that he wouldn't be able to fit in at a military school. He didn't want to find out for sure.

"You eat that," Adele instructed, indicating the soup that was just sitting on the tray. "It will settle your stomach. If you need me, you call, okay?"

He managed a smile for her. "Okay. Thanks."

She went out, leaving the door open. He finished the soup and lay back down. Maybe he could sleep, and he'd stop thinking about poor David. Rado was a bad man. Really bad. One day he might kill David, and then Tonio would have nobody his own age to talk to.

■ ■ ■ ■

John picked Sunny up at her apartment a few minutes before the matinee. He'd told Tonio he had to work on a case. Well, it wasn't a complete lie. Sunny knew about Rado, so she was technically part of the cold case he was working on. He didn't want to spook Tonio with fears of another woman. Having him run away and join a gang once was more than enough.

The boy was worried a lot lately. John had tried just once to talk to him, but the phone rang. The phone was always ringing. John was in a better situation than some of the other Rangers when it came to late-night crime. He had someone to watch Tonio, and he had no wife or small children to be concerned with. So when a Ranger was needed, he was usually called. And he'd always go, without complaining.

Now he wondered if he hadn't been hiding behind his job. He'd grieved for his late wife. He'd drawn into himself. Tonio had needed his father badly, and John had buried himself in work. It was something he regretted. Perhaps he could find a way to get back on the old footing with his son, if he worked at it. If they were closer, perhaps

Tonio wouldn't get so bent out of shape about John bringing a woman home.

He was growing ever more fond of the blonde woman sitting beside him in the big SUV. She was sweet and gentle and she made him feel protective. He liked being with her. He didn't want to like being with her. Always, in the back of his mind, was the fear of losing Tonio. He'd made a lot of mistakes with the boy.

"You're very quiet," Sunny remarked.

He chuckled. "I'm working." He glanced at her from dancing black eyes. "I gnaw on a case like a dog on a bone while I drive. I don't usually have anybody riding with me," he added. Not quite true. Tonio rode with him. But he wasn't sharing that.

"I didn't even ask, what movie are we going to see?"

"It's a honey," he replied. "It's a foreign language film —"

"Oh, dear, not one of those very racy ones . . . ?" she interrupted.

His eyebrows arched and he chuckled. "No, Miss Prim and Proper, it's not one of those racy ones. It's part of a film revival they're showing at the Diamond Cinema downtown." He glanced at her. "It stars Jean Reno, and it's set in France and —"

"— and Japan!" she exclaimed, all eyes.

"He's a policeman with a really bad temper and he has a daughter he didn't know about who's Japanese!"

"Her mother dies and he has to assume guardianship and she hates cops." He grinned from ear to ear. "It's called *Wasabi.* You've seen it!"

"I own it," she corrected. "I fell in love with it the first time I ever saw it. I bought the DVD. I discovered Jean Reno years ago, when he was in that *Godzilla* movie. I thought he was a terrific actor, so I looked for other films he'd been in, and I found *Wasabi*! It's great!"

"Subtitles and all?" he teased.

"Subtitles and all. I'm crazy about foreign films. I love Toshiro Mifune, too."

"The Samurai Trilogy," he said. *"The Hidden Fortress* Dozens more."

"Oh, yes. He was one of my favorite actors."

"Mine, as well."

"It's a small world," she said, shaking her head.

He smiled. "So it is, *rubia.*" And that was a very odd coincidence, that they enjoyed the same sort of movies. He felt as if he'd always known her.

She was feeling something similar, and fighting it tooth and nail. Despite Cal

Hollister's reassurances, she was worried about John's reaction if he knew the whole truth of what had happened to her when the bullets started flying through the apartment she shared with her mother and little brother. He was in law enforcement. He'd seen terrible things, just as nurses and doctors and rescue personnel, cops and firemen saw terrible things. But it was different, when the terrible things were part of strangers. It didn't mean that John would react any differently than the boy she'd dated so long ago.

She stared down at her purse. She should never have agreed to go out with him. It was going to end badly, she knew it was.

A big, warm hand came down on both of hers, where they gripped her purse.

"You worry all the time," he said quietly. "It shows. What's bothering you so much?"

She wanted to tell him, but she couldn't betray Tonio's confidence. She'd promised she wouldn't say anything to anyone about his friend David.

"It's been a long week," she said instead, forcing a smile. "One of our patients is very sick. They have her in ICU. They called a priest in last night, before I went off duty."

His hand lifted back to the steering wheel. She felt empty and cold, although she shouldn't encourage his touch.

"I imagine illness is harder, when the patient's a child," he agreed. He was remembering Tonio, in bed with a virus. And here John was, about to enjoy a movie when he'd told his son he was going to be working. It was just, he was so alone. Sunny filled the empty spaces in him. She made him feel warm, comforted. He didn't want to give her up, and that might cause some very big problems down the line.

"It is," she agreed.

He turned into the parking lot of the theater and cut off the engine. "We'll bury ourselves in the movie and forget our troubles for a couple of hours. How about that?" he teased.

She smiled. "That sounds very pleasant."

"To me, too."

They sat near the back of the theater with soft drinks and a huge barrel of buttered popcorn that they shared. Every time Sunny's fingers encountered John's in the popcorn, she felt thrills of pleasure go through her. He was the most attractive man she'd ever known. Which raised the question, why did he keep seeing her, because she wasn't really that pretty.

He could have picked any woman in San

Antonio to be with. She felt self-conscious about her injury, and she never spoke of it. But it made her uncomfortable. She worried about what a man would think if there was ever intimate contact . . .

She had to stop thinking like that. John was a friend. Just a friend.

While she thought it, he moved the popcorn barrel to the floor and slid his fingers into Sunny's, holding them tight while the movie ran.

It was an action movie, but parts of it were hilarious. Sunny didn't feel like laughing. Her heart was in her throat. She hoped John wouldn't notice. Her heart was going like an old-fashioned watch ticking.

He knew. Of course he knew. He was older than Sunny, and he'd been married. The signs were so obvious that she found him attractive. But she didn't want more than friendship, any more than he did. His reason was Tonio. He wondered what hers was.

Surely she wasn't married? No. That innocence he saw in her wouldn't be there if there had ever been a man in her life. She kept apart, alone. Why?

His fingers played with hers while Jean Reno and his French sidekick battled it out with Japanese gangsters on the screen. She was watching the movie, but her heart was jumping madly. He could see it bouncing under her coat.

She was wearing a high-necked sweater. He frowned. He'd never seen her in anything that wasn't high-necked. She even wore high-necked things under her work scrubs. It was as if she didn't want to call attention to her breasts.

His eyes narrowed as he looked at them, surreptitiously. Odd, the way the sweater fit on one side, the left side. It looked as if it had some sort of makeshift padding under it. The other side was normal.

He averted his gaze before she caught him looking. Her family had been killed by gunfire. If she'd been with them, he knew her well enough now to be fairly certain that she'd have thrown herself over them to protect them, perhaps even jumped in front of them to do it.

Had she been shot, and she was self-conscious about her body? She wasn't a poverty case, but her finances seemed to be about even with the poverty line. That meant there would have been no money for plastic surgery.

He'd almost worked it out by the time the movie finished. He kept her hand in his while they walked back to the SUV.

"You're very quiet," he remarked softly.

She swallowed. "Am I? It was a great movie. Thanks."

He shrugged. "You can take me to the next one," he said, and smiled tenderly.

She laughed. "Okay."

He stopped at the SUV and opened the door. But before she could turn to climb into it, he backed her gently up against the door that opened to the back seat. His big, warm hands framed her face.

She caught her breath at the look in his black eyes. "There are . . . people," she began in a rush, because he was looking as if he meant to kiss her, right there.

"When your family was shot, what did you do?" he asked quietly. "Did you jump in front of them, Sunny, to shield them?"

SEVEN

Sunny's heart stopped in her chest at the question. It went through her like fire. She ground her teeth together.

He nodded slowly, certain of what had happened. "It would be like you, to shield people you love by sacrificing yourself. You were injured, too, weren't you?"

She lowered her eyes to his shirt. There was thick, dark, curling hair peering out of the opening at his throat. It was very sexy. Like him.

She drew in a breath. "Yes. I spent several days in the hospital. A bullet collapsed my lung."

"And damaged you, in a way that makes you self-conscious and uneasy about relationships with men."

She shivered. She looked up, the surprise in her dark eyes. "How . . . ?"

"I work crime scenes, *rubia,*" he said gently. He brushed back her long, silky hair

171

and speared his fingers through its softness. "If you were involved in a shooting and two people died, it's pretty inevitable that you had to be a victim as well. I've seen gang shootings more than I care to remember. They're thorough."

She swallowed. She hadn't wanted him to know. But it was just as well that it was out in the open, she supposed. Now he'd understand why she didn't get involved with men.

"It's not pretty," she confessed. She still couldn't look at him. "I didn't have the means to fix it with plastic surgery. My dad had taken out insurance on all of us, so there was enough to bury them. There was nothing left over."

"Six years. How old were you?"

"I was seventeen," she said heavily.

Which made her twenty-three. That stung a little, because he was thirty-four. Probably too old for her, but he wouldn't think about that right now. "And you didn't date anybody until now?"

How had he known that? A lucky guess? Probably. She sighed. "I dated one boy." She hated the memory. It showed on her face.

He tilted her chin up. "Look at me. No, don't do that. Tell me."

Those black eyes were compelling. She

imagined the look worked very well on people he interrogated. It was hard to resist. "It was just after I lost my family. The rent on the apartment was paid up. Mr. Carrera did repairs very quickly and told me I could stay there rent-free while I was in nurse's training. He was so kind."

"A former mobster," he mused. "With a kind heart."

"Very kind. I'd graduated high school just before the gang shooting. I decided on nurse's training just afterward and enrolled at the Marshall Medical Center. Mr. Carrera offered to put me through school, but I told him he'd done enough, that I had to support myself. I worked part-time at a department store on the night shift, to help pay for my training. There was a boy there who was a stocking clerk in the same area I worked. He invited me out. I'd had a crush on him ever since I got the job. I was so thrilled. I bought a dress . . ."

She broke off. It was a bad memory. "So we went to a dance and he parked the car after, on a side street. He was a nice boy. I really liked him. So he kissed me, a lot, and then his hand slid under my blouse." Her eyes mirrored the pain. "To say he was shocked was an understatement. He drew back as if he was scalded. He took me right home, put me out and drove off like a madman." She smiled sadly. "I knew then that it would be the same, every time. So I never accepted another date."

"What a stupid boy," he muttered. "*Rubia,* you're a woman with a scar, not a scar with a woman attached. Do you understand what I'm telling you?" he asked.

She looked up into soft, kind eyes. She drew in a breath. "Yes, well, it's sort of hard to think that way after someone's treated you like someone with a contagious fatal disease."

"I can imagine. It must have hurt very badly, especially if you liked the boy."

"He didn't even speak to me at work, afterward. And it wasn't much longer before he quit the job."

"Maybe he just got a better one," he pointed out.

"Maybe. Nevertheless, I never saw him again."

"That wasn't a bad thing," he said, bristling. "Idiot."

Her eyebrows arched.

"Not you. Him!"

"Oh." She laughed self-consciously. "Well, anyway, now you know why I keep to myself. I have a job that makes me feel needed. I'm happy, in my way."

"And you don't have to worry about being rejected ever again."

She stared at him blankly.

"Idiot." He smiled, tracing her lips with one forefinger. "And this time, I mean you. Get in the truck."

She let him lift her up into it. She felt confused. "It's not a truck."

"It's sort of a truck," he conceded. "Fasten your seat belt."

He closed the door and went around to get in under the steering wheel. He fastened his own seat belt and cranked the engine.

But he didn't drive her back to her apartment. He went down the road that led to Jacobsville, in Jacobs County.

"Where are we going?" she asked.

He grinned. "I have to interview a woman who's a witness to a crime. I thought I'd take backup along. Unless you want to go home . . . ?" he added.

"No!"

He chuckled at the way she said it.

"I don't have a badge or a gun," she pointed out, flushing with delight that he still wanted her company after what she'd confessed.

"You don't need, either. I think the witness might feel more confident if there's a woman with me. So I'm deputizing you. For

175

the next few minutes," he teased.

"Oh, boy, I'm a Texas Ranger," she chuckled. "I feel more confident already."

"A few martial arts classes might not hurt. Not," he added, "to teach you to actually attack someone who's attacking you. That never works out unless you're a trained professional. You run if you get into a situation where you're threatened, or you scream. Most perps are bigger and stronger than you, and many are on drugs. Even a .45 won't stop a man who's high and angry unless you empty a clip into him." He glanced at her horrified look. "No, I haven't," he added. "But I know at least one man in law enforcement who had to. He drinks. A lot."

That surprised her. "But I thought shooting people when you had to went with the job," she said.

"It does. That doesn't make it easy to take a life. I've had to do that a time or two in the past . . . First in the military, then on the job." He grimaced. "I don't talk about it. It's like you and your injury," he said, glancing at her with a sad smile. "Both of us put the horrors out of mind and hope they'll stay there."

"What branch of the military?" she asked, changing the subject because she could see how much it bothered him.

"Army," he said. "Green Berets."

She smiled. "I should have known. Spec ops. It's why you sort of get along with Cal Hollister."

"He wasn't military," he pointed out. "We have a touchy relationship with mercs. They're often used as additional troops in combat zones, but some of them are rougher than they need to be overseas. It's led to problems."

"I don't doubt it. But Cal's one of the nicer ones."

His face hardened. "Is he, really?" His black eyes pinned hers as he drove. "I suppose he's all right, as long as he stays away from you."

Her expression betrayed her surprise.

"Think I'm joking?" His free hand felt for hers and tangled with it. "I don't want to get involved with you," he added shortly.

"Then why are you holding my hand?" she asked with exasperated humor.

"My hand's cold."

She burst out laughing. His hand was warmer than hers.

He glanced at her and grinned. "That's better. We were getting morose."

"I see."

"You don't." He drew in a long breath. "I've got complications. Lots of them. I haven't been serious about a woman since my wife died, and I can't get serious." He glanced at her again. "I'd like to. But it's not possible. Not yet."

"I have complications, too," she said.

"Yours aren't a problem," he said, and meant it. "You really do need to enroll in a martial arts class. It will give you self-confidence. You're the least assertive person I've known, since Maria," he added softly. "It's a trait I love. But it's not good for you."

"You can't change people."

"I don't want to change you. I just want you to be confident enough to say no to people."

"Like you?"

He chuckled. "Now, when have I done anything that you need to say no to, *rubia*?" he teased.

"Nothing, I guess."

"Exactly." His fingers toyed with hers. "So we'll be friends. For the time being, at least."

She looked out the window, but she was troubled.

"Now what's going through that quick mind?" he asked.

"I'm not modern," she began hesitantly.

"I'm not modern, either," he replied. "I don't talk about personal things much. But my wife was like you, very innocent. I waited until we were married. I wouldn't have disgraced her for anything in the world. She came from a very religious family. In fact," he added quietly, "so did I. I lost my parents when I was just ten. I came here to live with my grandfather, in Jacobsville. He was a great old gentleman. Crusty, but with a soft center. He raised me to believe that good character was far more important than wealth. And he took me to Mass every Sunday. Even when I didn't want to go," he added with a chuckle.

"My mother took me to the Methodist church one Sunday, my father took me to Mass the next. They alternated. I became acquainted with both faiths and I'm richer for it. But they were very strict. It wasn't until my mother died that I had my first real date."

"The idiot at work," he recalled.

She laughed. It didn't sting so much now, that memory. "Yes. Him."

"What a hell of a first date," he said harshly.

"It wasn't one of my better memories," she had to admit.

His fingers tightened. "We'll make better ones."

Her heart jumped. She felt the pressure of his strong fingers with real pleasure. He'd become so important to her, in so little time. It was a little frightening.

"Have you seen Rado lately?" he asked suddenly.

"No. But I've heard about him. He broke a child's arm for talking about him."

He frowned, glancing at her. "I heard nothing about that on the radio."

"He didn't tell anyone. His sister took him to the emergency room, to a friend of hers who's a doctor." She sighed. "Poor kid. They said that Rado laughed when he did it. He's a pig!"

"He is. Would the boy talk to us? Do you know who he is?"

"No. I spoke to a friend of his." She couldn't tell him about Tonio without getting the boy in more trouble. It was dangerous enough that she was getting him to talk to Hollister. She had reservations about that, more than she liked.

"Would the friend testify?"

"No," she said. "He's afraid of Rado. Most sane people are."

"What did he tell that made Rado attack him, do you know?"

"Something about a DEA agent who had ties to Los Diablos Lobitos —" She felt her seat belt catch sharply as he stopped the truck suddenly, right in the middle of the road.

"A DEA agent?" he asked, seeing ties that he couldn't explain. Ties to a cold case murder.

"That's what the boy told me. He won't talk to anybody in law enforcement. He says Rado has people everywhere. He'd find out and the boy who's his friend would be killed. Rado doesn't mind killing people. He told the child that he'd done it before to people who talked about him."

John let out a soft whistle. "Damn!"

He started the SUV moving again.

"What is it? Why are you curious about Rado?"

"I can't tell you," he said gently. "It's connected to a cold case that a colleague of mine is working on."

"And Rado's involved?"

"He might be. We're not sure. That's why I'm going to Jacobsville to talk to this witness." He glanced at her. "Anything you hear is privileged information. You're not to discuss it with anyone. Especially not with anyone who has ties to Rado. You understand?"

"Yes, I do. I won't say a word."

He smiled gently. "I knew that. I just wanted you to promise." He looked forward at the road ahead. "I know already that you don't give your word lightly. You have too many principles."

"Thanks."

"It was a great movie, wasn't it?" he asked, changing the subject.

She laughed. "Absolutely great. I loved it!"

"There's the new Star Wars movie coming out soon. Want to go with me?"

"Yes!"

"It will have to be a matinee," he added, grimacing. "Sorry. It sort of goes with the job. I'm less likely to be called in broad daylight on a Saturday, however odd that sounds."

"You get called out at night?"

"All the time. I'm more available after hours than the married colleagues with small children." He didn't add that he had a child, not small. Someday he'd have to tell her about Tonio. But not yet. That was a bridge he wasn't eager to cross.

"I see. I don't mind matinees. I almost never go out after dark."

His fingers contracted. "If you ever have to, you text me. I mean it. I don't care what time it is, either. I'll come. I sleep light, and the phone's always on."

That protectiveness made her feel warm

all over. "I wouldn't, unless I really felt threatened," she said.

"Still. I'll always be around if you need me," he said softly.

She smiled. "I'd do anything I could for you, too," she said. "Although if it involved fighting off big tough guys, I might have to enlist aid."

He chuckled. "Know some really big tough guys you could call on for aid, do you?"

"Just Hollister."

His fingers went still in hers.

"He's a friend," she emphasized.

"Does he know, about the injury?" he asked, remembering that Hollister had been the detective on her case.

"Yes." She sighed. "He said that it wouldn't matter to someone who cared about me. He's been very kind. But I don't really like blond men," she confessed sheepishly.

"You just saved his life," he mused.

She laughed. She felt years younger, green and happy and full of life. It was a feeling so new that it was precious.

"I like to hear you laugh," he commented.

She started to answer him when he pulled off the road and into the driveway of an isolated house that looked very new, with landscaping that was unfinished.

"We're here."

He got out and helped her out. He didn't hold her hand on the way to the front porch, and he looked suddenly concerned as they approached it. He stopped, noting that there wasn't a light on in the house and that the door was ajar.

He pulled out his 1912 .45 Colt ACP automatic and took off the safety. "You stay right here," he said firmly. "And if I yell for you to run, you get in the truck and lock the doors."

"I will," she promised. "You be careful."

The words went on the wind, because he was already moving to the porch, the sidearm raised in both hands beside his ear. He went inside cautiously.

Sunny waited, her arms folded over her chest, praying softly that she wouldn't hear a gunshot. Or more than one.

But only a couple of minutes later, he came back out, tight-lipped. He shoved the sidearm into the holster at his belt and pulled out his cell phone. He called 911 and gave the code for a body and another for an ambulance and local law enforcement to respond.

She knew the codes, because law enforcement people were in and out of the hospital emergency room when she was on duty. She was responsible for getting little patients to their rooms when they'd been treated. She'd picked up a lot of things from law enforcement people over the years.

He hung up.

"She's dead?" she asked gently.

"Very dead." He looked down at her. "You know the codes."

She nodded. "We have cops in the hospital emergency room pretty frequently with our little patients. Victims of domestic violence, accidents, other things."

He drew in a breath. "This is going to be bad," he told her. "*Sensational,* is probably the best word. I just hope we don't have any eager beaver reporters around hoping to make a name for themselves."

"Not likely in a small community."

"We had one such, here in Jacobsville, working for the local paper. Its publisher is Sheriff Carson's wife, though, and she fired the reporter last year. She doesn't do sensational stories."

"That's good."

It wasn't another minute before flashing red and blue lights came down the road. No sirens. She knew, as John did, that sirens were almost never used unless the ambulance or squad car was boxed in by traffic or behind cars that wouldn't get out of the way. It alarmed people, sometimes even caused accidents.

The Jacobs County EMTs exited the ambulance, exchanged a word or two with John and staged while the uniformed deputy in the sheriff's car went inside with John.

While they were in the house, a Jacobsville police car rolled up and stopped, obviously having heard the call over the police band. A man with a long, black ponytail and a dark attitude got out of it. He spotted Sunny and his eyebrows lifted, but he didn't speak to her. He went on into the house as well.

Minutes later, the EMTs were allowed in. John and the officers came back out. The deputy went to his car and got on the radio.

John came back to Sunny, with the tall, intimidating officer beside him.

"This is Jacobsville Police Chief Grier," he introduced. "This is Sunny. She's a nurse at a children's hospital in San Antonio."

Grier nodded.

She nodded back. He was very dignified, and Sunny remembered suddenly what John had told her about his past.

"We'll get the TBI out here with their crime tech and have the body transported up to San Antonio after the coroner examines the victim. In fact, one of the TBI investigators lives here — Alice Mayfield Jones Fowler. She's married to Cy Parks's foreman."

"Alice." John rolled his eyes. "She's a legend."

"She is that." Grier's black eyes, almost as black as John's, went back to Sunny. "Did he bring you down to examine the witness?" he asked curiously.

She flushed, uncertain of what to say.

John chuckled. "I had a call to interrogate a witness and I brought her along, because I thought she might put the witness at ease. It's okay. She's a clam," he added, smiling down at her. His smile faded as his eyes went back to Grier. "The victim was a witness in a cold case that Colter Banks is working on. This is going to set the investigation on its ear. She had vital information."

"I know about the case," Grier said. "Banks and I keep in touch. Good man."

"Good investigator," John agreed.

"We have some ideas about her contacts," Grier said. "If you'll stop by my office Monday morning before you go to work, I'll put you onto somebody who might be able to tell you who the mysterious missing boyfriend is."

"That would be a great help," John said.

187

"We all remember Melinda," Grier said curtly. "She got a rough deal, all around. Her dad's still trying to cope with the guilt."

"Some kids become headaches at an early age," John said.

"And that's something . . ." Grier began, and John knew he was going to mention Tonio.

"I have to get Sunny back to San Antonio," John said. "I'll talk to you Monday."

Grier wasn't slow. It was obvious that John liked the nurse and that he hadn't told her about his son.

He smiled. "Sure. That's fine. Nice to meet you," he told Sunny, shook hands with John and went back to the crime scene.

On the way to San Antonio, Sunny was curious.

"He's city law enforcement, but that was a county crime scene," she pointed out. "Wouldn't the sheriff's department have jurisdiction?"

"It would, normally. But in Jacobs County, a murder is a rare event. The call went out on the police band and Grier heard it. So did a lot of other local law." He chuckled. "Before long, you'd have seen cars from every single department in the county out there. It's a small-town thing."

"Your police chief is intimidating."

"He is. He has something of a reputation for that. I hear that speeders he stops rush to town to pay fines. He never has to say a word. His eyes say it for him."

"I noticed that. I'd never want to break the law down here."

He smiled. "He's married to one of the most beautiful women in the country. Tippy Moore, she used to be known as when she modeled."

"The Georgia Firefly," she exclaimed. "I used to see her on covers of fashion magazines. And those movies she starred in were hilarious."

"She gave up her career for him," he said. "He didn't ask her to. She's devoted herself to raising their little daughter and son, and her brother, who's in middle school now."

"She must be quite a lady."

"She can also do the tango," he told her with some amusement. "Grier taught her."

"Hard to imagine a man like that dancing."

"It's not, if you see him at it," he said. He thought of the annual Christmas dance and wanted very badly to invite her to it. But he didn't want Tonio to find out yet that he had a female interest. It was too soon.

"I'll take your word for it," she said,

smiling.

He let her out at her apartment. But he got out with her. The damned phone went off just as he got to her door.

He sighed as he answered it. "Ruiz."

"I know, you don't want to hear it," his captain said with resignation. "But this is a federal case and they've asked for help. I can't get in touch with anybody else —"

"It's okay," John said, chuckling. "I'm used to it. After all, it's Saturday," he added, looking down at Sunny. "Anybody who has a home life is at home, living it."

"You have one of those, too, you know," the captain replied, tongue in cheek.

"It goes on fine without me, mostly. What do you need?"

"We've got a body," he said. "SAPD found it stuffed into an outdoor trash can, badly beaten, almost unrecognizable."

"Gang stuff?" John asked.

"Not this. The guy was in his forties," he added. "Dressed nicely. He had the keys to a Mercedes in his pocket. We're still looking for it. The feds are on scene with the crime investigation unit. I've just texted you the address."

"Okay," John said. "You know about the cold case Banks is working on, don't you?"

He paused, frowning. "No, he didn't call me about the body. I was going to call him. I went down to Jacobsville to interview the female witness who gave him the tip and found her dead."

"Dead?"

"Yes, sir," John replied. "It was pretty bad. Somebody was sending a message, I think. Jacobs County SO is investigating, but Cash Grier was on scene as well."

"I remember Grier," the captain laughed. "Never liked him more than when he knocked that excuse for a temporary Ranger captain through the door onto the street. I'd have cheered, but it would have cost me my badge."

"The temporary captain didn't last long," John chuckled.

There was a rough sigh. "Old times. They were somehow less pressured than today. Banks is going to meet you where the feds are staging," he added.

"Why?"

"There may be a link to that cold case. The feds found something on the body . . . Well, I'll let Banks tell you. Get moving."

"Yes, sir," John said. "On my way."

He hung up and put the phone back in its holster on his belt. He sighed. "Life is never easy," he said.

"It's going to be a hard day for you," she said sadly. "I'm sorry. Two bodies in one day."

"That makes three within ten days," he added. He herded her toward the door. "Unlock that," he said.

She did, curious about why he was rushing her. Did he sense some danger?

He let her go ahead, then he went in behind her and closed the door.

"They can wait five more minutes," he murmured, taking off his hat and tossing it in the general direction of her sofa.

He lifted her off the ground in his arms and held her, his mouth hovering just over hers. In the silence of the apartment, she could hear her own heartbeat.

"I can't get involved with you," he whispered as his mouth brushed lazily against hers. "So this is a very bad idea."

She nodded, her eyes on his sensuous mouth. "Very bad," she whispered.

He nibbled her upper lip, loving the way her arms curled around his neck, as if they belonged there. He smiled against her mouth. "And since we can't get involved, you have to pretend not to like this."

She nodded again. "Not to like this."

"Are you listening to me, *rubia*?" he whispered.

She nodded. "Listening . . ."

While she spoke, she lifted toward the tormenting hard mouth that was daring her, provoking her, tempting her into indiscretion.

He drew in an audible breath. "What the hell. It's the holidays . . ."

His mouth opened tenderly on hers, every slow motion coaxing, not demanding, as he made her hungry for him.

She'd been kissed. Not often, but kissed. This was . . . different. He tasted of coffee. His breath was clean. His lips were firm, but slow and gentle, and the experience behind them was noticeable even to a novice. Well, he'd been married, of course he was experienced, she thought absently.

"This is very nice," he whispered. "And I don't have time for it."

"I know."

But he carried her to the sofa and sat down on it with Sunny in his lap while he made a virtual banquet out of her soft mouth.

"You taste like honey," he whispered huskily, bringing her closer. "I could get used to this."

"Me, too," she said shakily.

His mouth opened and pushed her lips apart, bearing down on them, insistent as the kiss caught fire and ignited them both.

She moaned helplessly. She felt swollen and shaky all over. She didn't feel like a woman with a bad scar. She felt like, just a woman. It was so new, so exciting, that she lost herself in the sweetness of it.

He held her tight for just another minute and then, with a groan, he put her away and stood up.

"I do not want to leave," he announced heavily. "But if I don't, they'll send Banks after me."

"It's okay," she said, still reeling from the pleasure.

He swept his Stetson off the other end of the sofa and looked down at her with soft, black eyes. They swept over her flushed face, down to the rapid heartbeat that he could see under her jacket.

"We can't get involved," she reminded him.

"No." He searched her eyes. "But we can practice kissing together," he added outrageously, and grinned.

She laughed. "That sounds innocent enough."

"Five more minutes, and it wouldn't have been innocent at all," he murmured. "I have to go. I'll text you. Maybe next weekend, we can take in another movie or eat out, when

I have some time off."

"You never have time off," she pointed out.

"I'll make some. Just for you, pretty girl," he added and laughed when she flushed again.

He moved to the door, glanced back at her with hungry, possessive eyes. "Don't practice that with anybody else. Especially Hollister," he chided.

"There isn't anybody else," she replied, and meant it. Her heart was in her eyes.

He smiled, very slowly. "Same here. See you later."

She watched him close the door. Five minutes after he'd gone, her heartbeat still hadn't calmed down one bit.

John pulled up at the curb near the rodeo arena where a still form lay on the sidewalk. Crime scene technicians were working the area around the body while local police made and enforced a barrier around it, keeping the press out. It wasn't easy. Overhead, a news helicopter was trying to home in with a telephoto lens.

"If I were a really good shot," Colter Banks mused as John joined him, "I'd take out that lens."

"You'd get us sued," John laughed.

"We have really good attorneys. They could say we were duck hunting. Helicopter looks a little like a duck if you squint."

"You couldn't sell that to even a crooked judge. Why are we here?" he added.

"Well, it's like this," Banks drawled as he shoved his hands into his pockets. "Know that ex-boyfriend the dead witness told us about?" He indicated the body. "He was carrying a note from her. Apparently he's the missing boyfriend."

"Oh, boy," John said. He never touched hard liquor. But he'd never felt more like getting drunk.

EIGHT

Hayes Carson was also in his office, on the phone and exasperated when John knocked and walked in. Hayes motioned him into a chair.

"I don't care who he knows in Washington," Hayes was growling at someone on the phone. "Yes, I'm aware that the traffic light is out. I've called the power company. They've promised to get on it just as soon as they finish restoring the other twenty very important outages, one of them at our hospital! In fact, Copper Coltrain raised the devil and insisted that the hospital had to have priority. Which it should." He paused and started smiling. "Say, why don't you tell him that Dr. Copper Coltrain insisted on having power restored there first and that's why the traffic light is still out? He might like to air his grievances to the doctor. Yes, I'm sure it would make an impression." He laughed. "I'd like to be a bug on

197

the wall, too. Tell him. You bet."

He hung up. He glanced at John, who was leaning against the door facing him with his arms folded over his chest.

"Somebody had a wreck," John guessed.

"Our newest ranch owner, in fact," Hayes said. "He slid through the traffic light and wants to blame us because he doesn't know how to use his brakes in several inches of snow. He's been yelling at my deputy."

"So you referred him to Dr. Coltrain." He shook his head. "Cruel and unusual punishment. Copper will have him for lunch."

"On a toasted bun," Hayes agreed, nodding enthusiastically, "which is why I suggested it."

"Wicked."

Hayes laughed. "The guy is from New York City. He bought the ranch through a local Realtor, stocked it with Holsteins and plans to sell his beef to selected overseas markets."

John stared at him. "Holsteins are dairy cattle," he pointed out.

"Apparently the rancher learned his craft by watching old B movies about ranching on YouTube. He'll go bankrupt and leave, and somebody who knows how to raise cattle will snap up the property."

John laughed. He and Hayes both owned

cattle ranches. They knew cattle. No cow-calf producers around Jacobsville would stock Holsteins for beef. Milk, maybe.

"What can I do for you?"

"It's what I can do for you, actually," John said. "I'm here to give you an affidavit since I found the body outside town."

"Nasty crime scene," Hayes replied quietly. "The murderer was making it personal. Stabbed ten times, beaten in the face until she was almost unrecognizable. Hell of a thing. Do you have any idea why someone would do that to her?"

"A good one. Colter Banks is working a cold case . . . You remember Melinda McCarthy?"

"That case." Hayes grimaced. "I never bought the suicide theory."

"It's not a theory anymore," John told him. "Our witness, the dead woman, called in a tip on the McCarthy case. She said that her boyfriend was involved, and that it was murder. The senator's daughter had something on a high-level person in law enforcement. They shut her up because she threatened to tell."

Hayes whistled. "Any luck tracking down the boyfriend?"

"Sure. We found him late yesterday in an alley in San Antonio. Dead."

"Some cold case," Hayes pointed out. "Is there a stupidity epidemic going around? Because there's two murders tied to one case, and it's going to encourage people to start asking questions."

"We're already asking them. Cash's cousin is the state attorney general. If we get any threats to shut down the investigation, he'll call Simon Hart and we won't have any more roadblocks. It seems Cash is also related to a US senator."

"Calhoun Ballenger." Hayes nodded. "He was targeted by a dirty politician with ties to the drug lords over the border. That is, until some of the drug lords were mysteriously blown up with a hand grenade. The survivors ran afoul of El Jefe." Hayes smiled sheepishly. "My father-in-law. So when the dirty politician was arrested, Calhoun was appointed as interim senator until the general election — which he won."

"You guys have some pretty intimidating relatives," John pointed out.

"It helps when we get stonewalled. The other US senator from Texas, Fowler, is the father of Cy Parks's foreman, Harley. He's married to Alice," he reminded John.

"Alice Mayfield Jones Fowler." John sighed. "How would we manage crime investigation without her?"

"I'm not sure we would. I called her in after my deputy worked the crime scene and ascertained that the EMTs weren't really needed. Alice came down from the San Antonio crime lab about the same time the coroner did. She found a few things, too," Hayes added. "Let me show you."

Hayes led John back to the locked evidence room. "San Antonio crime lab's got most of it. I kept this back for my own investigation." He pulled out a small piece of paper with writing on it.

"I saw one similar to that at the scene of the male witness's body," John said at once. "Same sort of paper."

"I can't decipher the writing," Hayes began.

"If you'll trust me with it, I'll take it up to Longfellow at the crime lab," John said. "She deciphered the other note. It was the same handwriting. I'd bet money on it."

"In that case, if you'll sign for it, it's yours. But I want it back when it's processed."

"You have my word," John promised. "Now, if it just has something useful written on it!"

"Alice got some trace evidence, including what looks like animal fur. Just a couple of hairs, but it might help if it can link to somebody's pet."

"Imagine a murderer keeping a pet," John muttered.

"You never know. It's a long shot, but it might pan out. She also got a partial shoe tread pattern in blood from the dining room. The murderer or murderers apparently knocked over a chair while they were beating the woman. The print was under the chair. I guess they missed it."

"Lucky for us."

Hayes nodded.

"I'd bet money we'll trace it eventually to one of two gangs in San Antonio. We've got a gang war going. Just like the one that happened about the time Melinda was killed. The Department of Public Safety was tasked with helping law enforcement in the city handle the gang problem last month. A lot of arrests were made, but that effort's concluded. SAPD Captain Hollister has set up a new task force to help deal with the teenage gangs and I'm on it. It's bad up there."

Hayes frowned. "Speaking of Melinda's murder, there was a young man who died about the same time. Don't you remember? He was found in an apartment near hers. Drug overdose. But his family said he'd never used drugs."

"Great memory, Hayes. Son of a gun!"

John pulled out his cell phone and checked his notes. "The victim's name was Harry Lopez," he said. "He had wolf tattoos on his arms." He hesitated. "Funny, how familiar that name sounds."

"There must be a hundred Lopezes in San Antonio," Hayes chuckled.

"Yeah. I guess so. Anyway, Lopez left behind a sister and a brother. They might know something. I'll tell Banks."

"Let me know what you find out. And don't you lose that," he chided, indicating the clue he'd given John.

"I never lose evidence," John chuckled.

He gave Hayes the pertinent facts of the case and watched the sheriff's fingers fly over the keyboard on the computer while he inputted the data.

"You're faster than me," John noted.

Hayes chuckled. "That's why I'm doing this instead of asking you to."

When they finished, Hayes turned the computer screen around and let John read what he'd typed. John made one correction. Hayes made it, printed out the information on a form for John to sign and date.

"Hey, Fred, come notarize this!" he called to a deputy nearby.

"I'm going to start charging. I am, after all, a notary public," Fred said with mock haughtiness. But he chuckled and brought his seal. He watched John sign and date the statement and pressed his seal into the paper, making the affidavit admissible in court.

"Thanks for coming by so promptly," Hayes said. He shook his head. "Brutal murder. Really brutal."

"Brutal means personal," John said. "I'll keep in touch. If I find anything, you'll be the first to know. I'd appreciate knowing anything you did find out."

"I'll keep you in the loop," Hayes promised. "The crime lab should have something shortly. You'll go to the autopsy?"

"I will."

"Get all the evidence you can. I've seen hairs solve crimes."

"Me, too."

"I could send one of my deputies up to observe," Hayes said deliberately with a wicked glance in Fred's direction.

"Not me," Fred called from his desk. "I have an urgent appointment whenever the autopsy is scheduled!"

"He's squeamish," Hayes told John.

"I am not squeamish. I just faint when they start cutting up dead people," Fred replied. "I also break out in hives. Honest."

"I could send Marlowe, our newest investigator. He served in the Marines overseas. Nothing fazes him," Hayes chided.

"I'll drink to that." Fred nodded. "Thanks, sheriff." He grinned. "See? That's why we work for him. He has a marshmallow for a heart."

"Not when you point a gun at him," John said with a wicked grin.

"I'll concede that," Fred agreed at once.

Hayes Carson had been in two gun battles during his time as sheriff. He'd been shot three times. The third was an attempted assassination that failed. Hayes still had limited use of the arm that had been injured, but it didn't stop him from doing the job. He had nerves of cold steel.

"You won't need to send anyone," John told Hayes as he was leaving. "I'll make sure we have whatever we need. SAPD will send a detective from their homicide squad as well. Between us, we'll get something. Even if it's just a hair," he added with a smile.

"Good luck."

"We could use some. Well, I'll go to work and see what I can find out about the victims," John said. "See you, Hayes."

"You take care of my clue," Hayes said firmly.

"I will."

■ ■ ■ ■

John puzzled all the way back to San Antonio about the violence of the murder. Profilers in the FBI often said that the more personal a murder was, the more brutal it was. The first person on his suspect list was Rado, but he had no probable cause to even interrogate him. There were no connections to the gang leader. At least, not now.

He left the note with a technician at the crime lab, who signed for it. Longfellow wasn't in, but she was expected back the next day, he was informed. Then he went back to the office and knocked on the lieutenant's door. He was invited in.

"Something?" Lieutenant Gadsden Avery asked, dark eyebrows arched.

"Something. The note on the latest victim's body came from the murdered woman outside Jacobsville," he said, dropping into the chair Avery motioned to. "It was a confession that she'd spoken to law enforcement and a request for the victim to go and see her in a hurry. I've got another note, in the same handwriting. I dropped it off at the crime lab on the way here. I asked them to have Longfellow look at it — she can read the writing — but she's off today sick."

"This whole thing is one big tangle," Avery said with a rough sigh. He leaned back in his chair and propped his boots on his desk, hands behind his head as he stared at John through narrowed, piercing gray eyes in a tanned lean face. "If Melinda McCarthy was murdered, and I think she was, whoever's involved at the federal level is going to make pursuing an indictment very, very difficult."

"It may be political suicide to push it," John said.

Avery grinned. "Let them try. We have enough high-level connections to put even a senior DEA agent against the wall. If all that fails, and we get threatened, I'll ask Cash Grier to go speak to them."

"Grier has a way with words," John said on a laugh.

"That's not all he has a way with. One of my friends got caught for speeding in Jacobsville a couple of years ago." He let out a whistle. "My friend said Grier didn't say a single bad word or even raise his voice. It was the way he looked at him. It sent my friend rushing to the police station to pay the fine. Now, if he goes through Jacobsville, he watches that speedometer like a hawk."

"They tell tales about Grier," John mused.

"And most of them are true," the lieutenant replied. "So. Where do we go from here?"

"I'm going over to talk to Marquez at SAPD. His detective on scene was going to backtrack and see if he could find any friends or acquaintances who were willing to go on record about the two victims. I want to see what he found, if anything."

"Want a hint?"

John nodded. "Anything would help."

"Go talk to Cal Hollister instead."

He frowned. "He's heading up the joint gang task force. Is that why?"

"No. Hollister has ties to a minister who used to be a merc. The minister works in the center of Los Diablos Lobitos gang territory. But the boys leave him alone. They know what trade he used to practice, and they don't provoke him. They say he can walk into the darkest alleys at night and nobody touches him. That's mainly because of his connections. He's friends with the leader of Los Serpientes in the city. If anybody harmed the priest, he'd have not only the Serpientes to deal with, but many of the priest's old friends as well. They won't take the chance."

"I've heard about the priest. Never met him."

"Get Hollister to introduce you," Avery advised. "The priest is bound by oath not to disclose anything he hears in confession. That's probably why he's still alive. Well, that, and his contacts. But he might be able to tell us something about any connections the victim had, if there are any. He knows most of the Lobitos gang, and the latest victim here was a member."

"It might be the break we need," John said, encouraged. "Thanks, lieutenant."

The phone rang as the older man was about to speak. He answered it, put his hand over the mouthpiece and said, "This is going to take a while. I'll talk to you later."

John nodded and left the room.

He hated the idea of Hollister, because the man knew Sunny far better than he did. She wasn't attracted to the police captain, however, which made the visit at least tolerable.

"What can I do for you?" Hollister asked with a smile.

"I need an introduction," John began.

Hollister's blond eyebrows arched. "Does Sunny know that you're trying to meet other women?" he teased.

John glared at him. "I need an introduction to a priest," he clarified.

"That sounds ominous," Hollister replied, tongue in cheek.

"I don't need one for myself." John took an exasperated breath. "There are two new related murders . . ."

Hollister sat forward. "One in Jacobsville, badly mutilated, and one, a member of Los Diablos Lobitos, in an alley here in the city," he said, quickly serious. "I know. We've got men on the street trying to find any friends or family or acquaintances of either victim. We've also got as many officers as we can spare going door to door around the crime scene looking for witnesses."

"Thanks," John said.

Hollister nodded. "We all have to work together to get these gangs stopped. We've had our share of murders recently."

"Yes, we have."

"The priest. Which one?" Hollister asked.

"The one who used to be a merc," John replied.

Hollister's face closed up. His eyes narrowed, glittered.

John knew the man didn't like to talk about his past. He respected that. "He works in the area where Los Diablos Lobitos operate. He has a friend who leads the local Serpientes gang. We need the contact. You don't have to go with me. If you could just write a note of introduction . . ."

Hollister's lips made a thin line. He drew in a harsh breath and pulled a sheet of letterhead out of the drawer.

He wrote something, signed it and placed it in a sealed envelope. On the envelope, he wrote *Father Eduardo Perez, Catedral de Santa María.*

He handed the envelope to John and gave him the address, which John put in the notes app on his cell phone.

"Listen," John said softly as he put his phone in its holster, "I know you don't talk about the past. But there's a dead kid, two wounded kids, two murdered adults, and I think they all tie in to this one gang and a cold case involving the death of the daughter of a state senator. This . . ." he indicated the note ". . . may help me catch the perps, before they can do it again. Whatever I find out, I'll share with you."

Hollister relaxed, just a little. "I don't like remembering," he said.

"We all have things in the past that hurt us. Things that sting from time to time."

Hollister smiled sadly. "I lost everything," he said tightly. "Including a woman I would have died for."

John didn't speak. His black eyes were curious.

"Not Sunny. In case you wondered," he added suddenly.

John laughed. "Am I that transparent?"

"She's a sweet woman. And I'm partial to blondes. But there was never any sort of spark there. She . . . reminds me of someone I lost."

That made sense. John recalled that Hollister was a widower and concluded that he was speaking of his late wife. He smiled back. "Okay."

"I've never seen Sunny as happy as she is lately," Hollister added. "She smiles. She laughs. She was the saddest person I've ever known, before you came along."

John beamed. "Yeah. It's that way with me, too. I love just being with her."

Hollister sat back in his chair. "You'll let me know, if you dig up anything?"

"Certainly." John got up. "My lieutenant thinks Father Eduardo may know something about the cases. I hope I won't get him in any trouble with the gang by going over there."

"You won't catch any Lobitos gang members within a city block of the church," Hollister said with pursed lips. "When Father Eduardo first settled into the parish and started watching out for victims of the gang, Lobitos decided that he was an interloper and they were going to get him out. They walked into the church with weapons drawn." Hollister let out a whistle. "The emergency room was full. And I mean full! Eduardo stayed with the victims while they were treated and advised them to leave his parishioners alone in the future. They listened. One man against seven armed gang members. They still talk about it, even today."

John laughed. "Okay. Now I really want to meet this guy!"

"He's unique, I'll say that for him."

"Thanks again," John said. "And I'm sorry I had to ask for this." He held up the envelope.

Hollister's face was hard. "I made a lot of mistakes in my past, did a lot of things I wish I could undo. Eduardo and I have a history. He's been a good friend. He'll help you. He has no fear of Los Diablos Lobitos. In fact, it's sort of the other way around," he added whimsically. "Tell him I'm free most Friday nights if he wants to go watch them do the tango at Fernando's."

"I'll tell him."

Father Eduardo was tall, powerfully built, with jet-black hair and dark eyes. He had scars on his face, and he looked like a man that no sane criminal would tangle with. John recalled what Hollister had said, that seven gang members hadn't been able to take him down.

"Yes? What can I do for you?" Father Eduardo asked congenially.

John handed him the envelope.

The priest raised his eyebrows curiously before he opened the envelope and read the note. "Ah, yes," he said. "Cal."

"He said he's free most Friday nights if you want to have supper at Fernando's and watch the guests do the tango."

"Amateurs," the priest chuckled. "The tango is not for the weak of heart."

"I know," John said. "My people come from Argentina."

"¡Compadre! So do mine!" Father Eduardo laughed. "Who are you?"

"John Ruiz." He shook hands. "I work for the Texas Rangers. I'm investigating a string of gang hits in the city."

"Oh, yes, we know about those," he said sadly. "I have counseled survivors. I would love to see the gangs go the way of the dodo bird. Sadly, that is a pipe dream."

"I'm afraid it is."

"Come into my office. We can talk."

He led the way through the cathedral, past a small group of people milling around the candles, lighting them for loved ones.

"I did that not long ago, at San Fernando," John said, indicating the guests.

"You lost family?"

"My wife, three years ago. A heart attack."

"I am most sorry," the priest said quietly. He closed the door, and turned to John. His face was hard with memories. "I lost my wife and two sons to a man whose brother I killed while I was practicing my former profession. He murdered them in front of me while I was tied up and helpless. I took the collar soon after," he said. He hesitated. His eyes asked a question.

"I'm sorry for your loss. I do know what your former profession was," John confessed. "My lieutenant told me about you." He cocked his head. "So did Hollister. Seven armed gang members it was, I believe . . . ?"

The priest's face lightened. "Yes, they thought it would be a simple matter to get rid of an annoying priest. They had no idea what I used to do for a living. It seemed to be a great surprise to them." He smiled. "Two of them joined the church afterward."

"I can see why. You seem to have a powerful ally." He glanced up at the ceiling.

"Divine connections," the priest agreed, smiling. "I do what I can for a congregation that defines the word *poor*," he added. He shook his head. "It never ceases to amaze me, that in a country of such plenty, there are so many in need. We spend millions, billions of dollars, developing weapons that can never be used, biological and otherwise. What I could do here with just a fraction of that," he said sadly. "I contacted a group of wealthy patrons and got them to provide clothing for a family of eight whose father lost his job. They found him another one." He smiled. "I believe in angels. Some don't have wings."

"We have good people here in the city," John agreed.

The priest sat down at his desk and invited John into a chair across from it. "What do you need?"

"I won't ask if you're squeamish," John said, because he knew the man wasn't. He pulled out his cell phone and went to the photo app. "I need you to look at these photographs and tell me if you've ever seen any of them before."

He handed over the phone. It contained pictures of the Jacobsville woman, the well-dressed dead man who was in Los Diablos Lobitos and the Serpientes gang member who'd been killed. The photo of the woman was painful to see.

The priest crossed himself. "To do that, to a woman," he said, wincing.

John was sorry that he'd had to include that photograph. Eduardo's wife had been murdered. It must bring back painful memories. But he had to do what he could to catch the killers.

Eduardo turned his attention to the man in the photo. "Yes, this one is familiar," he said, and John's pulse jumped.

"How so?" John asked.

"His mother is my parishioner. I went to see her this morning. She could not stop crying. He was a good son, although he was certainly involved in the selling of drugs, and he belonged to the Lobitos. His name was Alberto. Alberto Fuentes." He frowned as he looked at the photo. John was taking notes on his cell phone. "This chalk drawing beside his head," the priest commented as he thumbed through the photos, "it's the mark Lobitos leave at a crime scene." He looked up. "They killed one of their own?" he exclaimed.

John nodded. "I have a suspect. I just can't prove a connection."

"Rado," the priest said with venom in the pronunciation. "I would give much to see him off the streets. Even with the old gang leader, the one now on death row, there was not so much blood spilled. Rado uses. It makes him more dangerous than a rational man."

"I have noticed that. He broke a child's arm —"

"Yes, David Lopez's," he interrupted. "He was . . . What is it?"

John's caught breath stopped him before he could finish the sentence. "That name. Lopez. There was a Harry Lopez. Died of a drug overdose at the time Senator McCarthy's daughter Melinda also died of one. Neither of them was known to use hard drugs. In fact, Melinda had just come out of rehab and was looking forward to getting her life back together. Everyone we talked to said that Harry Lopez had never been known to use drugs of any kind."

"Harry Lopez." The priest winced. "He was a good boy. One of the better gang members, if there is such a thing. He took excellent care of his sister and little brother, although he did it with money that was not legally earned. When he was killed, Rado took over the family. He put Tina out on the street and made her prostitute herself for him. She comes to confession." His face hardened. "I cannot tell you what she told me. You do not know what I would give to tell you."

"I can guess." John studied his boot, where one long leg was crossed at the ankle over the other one. "Lopez. No, the case, that's not why I remember the name. It's something else. Tina Lopez. That name sounds familiar, but I had no contact with her when her brother was killed. Banks was working that case." He frowned. "She's a prostitute?"

"Yes. It is a sad life. She has great fear of Rado. He threatens her brother when she defies him."

"The brother, what's his name again?"

"David. David Lopez. He's a troubled boy. They put him in an alternative school, hoping to straighten him out. Now Rado does this to him." He sighed. "Lawmen and priests. The things we know and have to live with," he added with a sad smile. "Not much different than being a merc. You see only the bad things."

"You also see some good ones," John countered. He smiled. "A man with a gun trading it for a collar, and changing lives for the better. That's not one of the bad things."

"Thanks, *amigo*," the priest replied sincerely.

"Do you think Tina would talk to me?"

"Do you think crocodiles might speak English or learn to fly?" came the whimsical reply. "Just being seen with you might condemn her brother to death. She risks enough coming to confession. They stay away from me, and they know I never reveal anything I learn at confession. That's the only reason she's still breathing."

"What a way to have to live," John said.

"Agreed. But perhaps we may find a way to get Rado off the streets. If you want to talk to Mama Lupita, I can have her come here for confession and have you waiting in the office afterward. You might have to come in something a little less noticeable than your present attire."

John chuckled. "I own a ranch in Jacobsville. I'll come up in my work clothes on a Sunday. Any Sunday you like. I'll even go to Mass first."

"*¿Es catolico?*"

John laughed. *"Toda mi vida,"* he replied. "What is Mama Lupita's last name?"

"Fuentes, like her poor son. He was Alberto, but they called him Al."

"Criminals have parents just like everyone else," John said. "A child commits a crime, and they say, that's a kid with bad parents. But it isn't always. You can do the right things, make the right choices and still have your kid end up in an alternative school," he added bitterly.

220

"I do understand," Father Eduardo said, and he saw a lot more than John realized.

"Would you like to get her here this Sunday?" John asked.

"I would. But would Saturday be better for you . . . ?"

"Sorry, no," John chuckled. "There's a party at my boss's house this Saturday. I'm taking my best girl. She doesn't know it yet."

"What's she like?"

"She's a nurse," John said. "With the kindest, sweetest heart I've known since my late wife. I've never known anybody like her."

"A nurse. Well, it's not a profession one chooses for the money. Like yours, and mine," he added with a chuckle.

"That's true, and she works at a children's hospital," he replied.

"Even better. She must have a very soft heart."

John nodded. "Soft and very innocent." He ground his teeth together. "I took a woman home with me a year ago. My son ran away from home. He said if I got involved with someone else, he'd run away and join a gang and I'd never . . . Oh, my God!"

"What is it?"

John stood up. "He ran away. He got

221

mixed up with Los Diablos Lobitos. The woman he was staying with when I tracked him down was a prostitute with gang ties. Her name was Lopez. Tina Lopez!"

NINE

"Your son?" Eduardo asked.

"Yes. My son. I just made the connection." He shook his head. "No wonder the name sounded familiar. The woman was protective of my son until she had proof that I was his father." He recalled her. Tall, dark, beautiful. "She was a knockout," he added. "And Rado's making her prostitute herself?"

"He pairs her with rich men who can afford all sorts of luxury gifts, which he then confiscates, along with whatever cash she gets," the priest told him. "She hates it. She was a good girl. Innocent and sweet until one of her brothers mixed her up with Lobitos." He shook his head. "I will never understand greed."

"Nor will I," John replied. "Well, now I have some answers and many more questions, and I can't go near the Lopez woman without getting her or her brother killed, or both. And if I try to have you bring her here, after the Fuentes woman comes, Rado may find out and it could cause even more tragedies."

"Hollister."

"Excuse me?"

"Have Hollister send one of his officers to pull her in for prostitution, put the word out that one of her johns wants to press charges, hold her overnight. While she's there, you'll have a free hand to question her. If you're worried, send a lawyer to do it instead and have him tape the session."

"I like the way you think," John said.

Eduardo smiled. "I do my best. Meanwhile, I'll do what I can, without divulging anything I know." He stood up. "I may not be in the profession anymore. But I know plenty of people who are, including a high-level security guy for Ritter Oil Corporation. He was a merc longer than I was. We're still friends. He's pretty good at interrogation."

"Colby Lane?" John asked with an amused smile.

"Yes. You know him?"

"He was down in Jacobsville on the Dominguez case, when she was arrested and charged with drug dealing," John recalled. "In the process, Colby Lane's little girl was kidnapped, as insurance to keep the authorities away. Lane had them find him one of the drug runners and he questioned him about his daughter's whereabouts. They say that afterward, he ran to the nearest officer and confessed to things he hadn't even done to get him away from Lane."

Father Eduardo grinned. "Yes. Colby has a unique method of asking questions. He worked for Eb Scott for a while, but he was forbidden to teach any sort of interrogation tactics to Eb's recruits. Sad thing. Colby and his family were going to live in Jacobsville, but his wife couldn't give up her DEA job. So they went back to Houston, where another of our friends is the top security guy for Ritter, Phillip Hunter. Sarina had a little boy and went right back into the field. Colby's resigned to it now. He says he'd rather have her with her little quirks than go back to being a bachelor. Besides, he loves the family life." He shook his head. "If you'd seen him in Africa . . ."

"If you mention Africa around Cal Hollister, he gets this look," John said. "I can't even describe it. That must have been one bad campaign."

"One of the worst any of us ever lived through. After that, Eb and Cy came to live in Jacobsville, Colby worked as a security guy for the L. Pierce Hutton Corporation. Hutton builds oil rigs, among other things. When the company relocated overseas, Colby went to work for Ritter in Houston, doing security."

"You know some interesting people," John said.

"You have no idea how many. If I can be of further help, please feel free to call on me." He pulled out a business card and gave it to John. "That's my cell phone number." He indicated it. "I keep it with me night and day. I don't sleep much, so it won't bother me if you call at night."

"I'll remember. Thanks again, for your help."

"It was my pleasure. If you can put Rado away," he added with a flash of cold eyes, "it would be the best blessing of my recent life."

"I promise you that I'll do my best. I'll be in touch, about Sunday."

"Okay."

John wanted very badly to talk to Tina Lopez. He stopped by the San Antonio police department and went to see Hollister again.

The blond man was unloading the clip from his pistol. He had a cleaning kit on

226

the desk. He looked up, grimacing. "She did it again."

"Excuse me?"

"Gwen Marquez — Rick's wife. Outshot me. A hundred bullseyes out of a hundred shots." He sighed. "I think I'll go live in Fiji."

"You can go with Colter Banks and me," John said. "We're already looking at ticket prices."

Hollister chuckled. "Come on in."

John closed the door behind him. "The priest and I made a connection, and I need a favor."

"Shoot."

"There's a call girl. Tina Lopez. I need you to have an officer arrest her, and I need access to her while she's here."

"Tina?" he asked, surprised. "She doesn't belong to a gang."

"You know her?"

"Yes. She dances at Fernando's on Friday nights. That's how Rado gets her rich patrons. It attracts some of the wealthiest patrons of any restaurant in town."

"Small world," John said. "Getting smaller all the time. No, Tina hasn't done anything. But I've heard that her brother had his arm broken by Rado, and she had a connection to Melinda McCarthy . . . They were friends."

Hollister ground his teeth together. "Ruiz, I can appreciate the effort to get Rado, but if he knows you've talked to Tina —"

"I know an attorney who works down in Jacobsville at the district attorney's office," John interrupted. "I'll ask her to wear a wire and record anything Tina tells her. Rado will never know."

"If the attorney can keep her mouth shut."

"You don't know this one," he chuckled. "She's Jason Pendleton's stepsister and she's married to DEA agent Rodrigo Ramirez."

"Glory Ramirez," Hollister replied, smiling. "She was a crackerjack assistant DA here. I hated to see her relocate to Jacobsville."

"Me, too, but she does a good job for our DA in Jacobs County. And she can keep secrets. Tina won't be in any danger. Even if Rado knows she's been talking to a female lawyer, he won't know anything else. I'll make sure Glory uses a fake name and says she's with the public defender's office here."

"The public defender's office will barbeque you. Over a flame."

"Not likely," John said, with a chuckle. "I'll clear it with the chief over there. He thrives on defending poor criminals, but he wants Rado behind bars, too, even if his office has to give up someone to defend him. We all want Rado off the streets. We've had enough murders."

"I can't argue with that." Hollister picked up the phone. "Marquez, can you step into my office for a minute? Thanks."

Rick Marquez opened the door and was motioned to the desk. John closed the door again.

"What's up?" Rick asked.

"The Texas Rangers need a favor," Hollister said, grinning. "And if you could persuade your wife to let me outshoot her just once . . . I am the captain here, after all, you know. I outrank her."

Rick was laughing heartily. "I could try, but you know these hotshot former FBI agents," he replied. "Even two daughters haven't slowed her down with that pistol or this job."

"I noticed." He glanced at John. "He has two of the prettiest little girls you've ever seen. One looks like him. But the other . . ."

Rick, encouraged, pulled out his cell phone and brought up the photo app. There was his wife, Gwen, and his daughters, Jackie and Bella. One was dark haired and had pretty brown eyes. The other was blonde and light eyed, like Gwen.

"They really are pretty," John agreed, handing back the phone. "Nice family."

"My whole world," Rick replied, smiling.

"What's this about your mother and Fred Baldwin?" Hollister asked suddenly.

Rick cleared his throat. "I know nothing."

"Marquez?" the captain persisted.

Rick grinned. "I know next to nothing. It's just the ballet. She's taking him. I've been asked to provide handcuffs."

"What for?" John asked.

"To keep him in his seat while they watch *The Nutcracker*," Rick explained. "He's not a fan of the arts, but mom thinks she can convert him." He laughed. "It's so cool, to see them together. They're not alike at all, but they are, if that makes sense."

"It does," Hollister said.

"So, what can I do for the Rangers?" Rick asked John.

"I need a woman arrested for prostitution."

"Ruiz, what have you been doing?" Rick teased.

"I am an upstanding member of law enforcement," John said haughtily. "I would never engage in any sort of clandestine activity that involved prostitutes."

"Think McKuen Kilraven," Hollister said in a stage whisper.

Rick's eyebrows raised.

"Okay. What's that look about?" John wanted to know.

"Kilraven was married and had a little girl. His wife and child were both murdered."

"I didn't work the case, but I know people who did," John replied somberly. "It was a nightmare of a crime scene."

"So Kilraven finally married again, to Winnie Sinclair. Her brother —"

"Owns one of the biggest ranches in Jacobs County," John interrupted. "I know him. We both belong to the local cattlemen's association."

"Yes, Boone Sinclair," Rick agreed. "He and his wife, Keely, eat at Mom's restaurant."

"Everybody eats at your mother's restaurant," John chuckled.

"True. Anyway, Kilraven had been a widower for seven years when he remarried and the gossip was that he'd gone high and dry all those years in between wives." He gave John a steady, amused look.

John's high cheekbones flushed, just a little. He glared at the other man.

Rick held up both hands. "No wonder you and Cash Grier get along," he said, grimacing. "Honest to God, Ruiz, you could set fires with that look!"

"Are you wearing asbestos?" John drawled.

Rick chuckled. "No, so I take back any inconvenient comparisons I may or may not have made. Who do you want arrested?"

"Tina Lopez," Hollister interjected.

Rick grimaced. "She's such a sweet woman."

"It's not a real arrest," John said. "She has a connection to Melinda McCarthy's murder. I'm going to get Gloryanne Ramirez up here to question her, pretending to be from the public defender's office. She'll wear a wire and Rado won't find out that she's talking to anyone about what she knows. If she'll talk at all."

Rick was somber. "You know that Rado broke her little brother's arm?"

"I do know. That's why I'm taking elaborate precautions. If we had to, we could get Eb Scott to hide her and her brother at his place in Jacobsville. Even Rado wouldn't dare go there after her."

"No, he wouldn't," Hollister said. "That's not a bad idea, if it comes down to that. But if she can give us some leads, it might be enough to bag Rado without involving her. At least, until the trial."

John nodded. "I wouldn't want to endanger the boy, either. What sort of lowlife bum breaks a child's arm?"

"Rado's kind," Rick said. "Okay, when do you want me to do it?"

"I'll talk to Glory and the public defender's office here and let you know," John said. "And none of us is going to mention this. Right?"

The other two agreed. John left and went straight over to the public defender's office to explain what he was going to do.

He drove by the Jacobsville District Attorney's office on his way home, just as the staff was heading for the doors at quitting time.

Blake Kemp, the district attorney, gave John a curious look. "Do you need to talk to me?"

"No, I need to talk to Glory," John replied with a smile. "I need a little help with a confidential witness."

"Nobody better than our Glory for that," Blake chuckled. "She's always the last one out." He indicated a blonde woman backing out the door to lock it behind her.

"Glory, you have company," he told her.

She looked up. "Ruiz," she said, smiling. "How are you? How's Tonio?"

She knew about Tonio because she'd been at the hearing when he was expelled from school, representing him against the school's

attorney. She didn't often do private practice, since she worked for Kemp, but she
took the case because John had asked her
to.

"Tonio's fine. I've got a problem in San
Antonio. Can I buy you a cup of decaffein-
ated coffee and we can talk for a minute?
Barbara's Cafe doesn't close until late."

"Okay. Let me text Rodrigo and tell him
he'll have to watch Jack until I get home."
Their son's full name was John Antonio
Frederick Ramirez, but they called him
Jack. He was the spitting image of his father.

She did that and walked with John to the
cafe. Everybody knew that Glory had a bad
heart, so decaffeinated coffee was a neces-
sity. Her job was stressful, but not nearly as
bad as being an assistant district attorney in
San Antonio, where she and John had
worked together on a couple of federal cases
being tried in the city. They got along very
well.

John sat sipping hot black coffee. It was the
dinner hour, so diners were filing in and
out of the restaurant. John and Glory had a
private booth in a corner, where they
weren't likely to be overheard.

"I have a woman who's in danger of being
killed if she's seen with anybody in a uni-

form," he said. "I don't even know if she'd talk to us voluntarily. But another woman might make an impression. She knows something about Melinda McCarthy's death. A gang leader killed her brother for talking about it. She's terrified of Rado, so she's kept her mouth shut. He pimps for her."

"Rado. Even down here, I know that name," she replied. "I knew it when I worked in San Antonio. We tried for years to find anything that would put him away. He's too slick."

"This time, we might get lucky. I need you to talk to Tina Lopez and wear a wire while you're doing it, so that nobody can connect me with it."

"Why particularly you?"

"I'm working Melinda's cold case with Colter Banks."

She whistled. "They tell stories about Banks."

"They're mostly true," he chuckled. "He's a character."

"Putting it mildly," she agreed. "I was an assistant DA in San Antonio," she pointed out. "If she knows —"

"You're going to be a relief public defender. I cleared it with Tom Simmons."

"Oh. Okay. That might work. When?"

"When you have time."

"I could give up an hour's sleep," she laughed.

He sighed. "I know how that goes. The captain has me on speed dial. How about tomorrow evening, about seven? I'll have Marquez pull her in earlier and you can talk to her in an interrogation room."

"I can do that. I hope . . ." Her eyes widened.

Her handsome husband was walking in the door with a small boy by the hand. The child broke into a huge smile and came running.

"Mommy!" he exclaimed. "We came to have supper with you!"

"Yes, so Mommy doesn't have to cook after a long day," DEA senior agent Rodrigo Ramirez chuckled. He bent to kiss his wife. "I came right over when I knew he was going to be with you," he added with a wicked smile at John. "I don't trust this maverick around my wife."

John sighed. "It would never work. She's too crazy about you to look at anybody else. Pity I wasn't around when you married her," he added.

"You were around," Glory laughed. "But you were married." She grimaced. "Sorry, John."

He shrugged. "It's been three years. Th. memories are sweet, even though I miss her like hell. You two are lucky," he added, smiling at the child. "Hi, Jack!"

"Hi!" the boy replied. He cocked his head. "You got on a star," he said, pointing.

"Yes. I'm a Texas Ranger."

"My daddy works for the feberal goberment," he replied seriously, while mangling the name of his father's employment, to the amusement of his small audience. "My daddy got a badge!"

"Your dad is a great agent," John told the child, smiling. "What are you going to be, when you grow up?"

"I'm gonna fly jet planes," he said, making a swishing motion with his hand. "I'm gonna be a pilot!"

"Too many war movies, my darling," Glory chided her husband.

"I'm a pilot," he replied. "I love planes. He's my son. Of course he wants to be a pilot!" he added, laughing.

"No argument here," John replied.

"You've got a pilot's license, and a plane," Rodrigo said. "Why don't you ever use it?"

"No time," John said. "I'm a working stiff."

"You could live in Monaco and sail yachts," Rodrigo said, lowering his voice.

"Or live on the property in Argentina. This is small potatoes, for someone with your background."

John raised his eyebrows over twinkling eyes. "I could say the same of you," he pointed out. "You could buy a small country with what you inherited. But you work for the 'feberal goberment,'" he added, using the child's pronunciation with a grin.

Rodrigo sighed and smiled at his family. "I like my life as it is. Besides that, I want to do with my son what you've done with yours."

"Put him in reform school?" John said, sighing.

"He'll be a fine boy. He's going through a rough patch. It won't last. No, I meant I want Jack to grow up the same as his friends. I don't want him to stand out in designer clothes and think it puts him above other people."

"Tonio doesn't even know about the ranch in Argentina. My cousin runs the operation." He laughed. "He loves the lifestyle. Yachts, beautiful women, the best hotels. He sends me a check every month. It goes in the savings account and stays there. This ranch provides me and Tonio with everything we need."

"Too bad our kids aren't closer in age,"

Glory said, cuddling her little boy.

"It is."

"He's friends with Jake Barnes, though, isn't he?" Rodrigo asked. "Jake's father runs Hereford cattle and likes to play poker with Cash Grier."

"Chess is more my style," John said.

"Mine, too," Rodrigo replied. He grinned. "We'll have to get together one evening and wage war across the board."

"I'd like that. Except that my captain has me on speed dial."

"There's a mute button," Rodrigo said in a stage whisper.

"You and Banks," he sighed.

"Common brain patterns," Rodrigo agreed.

"Stay for dinner with us," Glory invited.

John looked at his watch. "Adele will have supper on the table. I might get a few bites before I'm called back out," he said wistfully.

Rodrigo gave him a steady look. "Tonio needs you more than the job does right now, John," he said quietly. "He really needs you."

The way Rodrigo said it was odd. He started to question the statement when his phone rang.

He answered it. "Ruiz."

"Autopsy starts in two hours," Longfellow

said. "Are you coming up for it?"

"Yes. I'll go home and eat and then I'll be along."

"I couldn't eat first," Longfellow said. "I never eat before or after. I just drink milk and cry on my husband's shoulder."

"Any luck on that note?" John asked.

"Yes. I'll tell you when you get here."

"Okay. Thanks, Longfellow." He hung up. "We've got an autopsy. I have to go."

"Which victim?" Rodrigo asked.

"Not sure. Probably the woman from here. The man was found later in the day, unless Longfellow's going to leapfrog it."

"Longfellow." Rodrigo sighed. "She's very by the book."

"But good at details. I'll call you tomorrow, Glory."

"That will be fine."

"Thanks again. See you," he said and smiled as he went out the door.

Tonio was sitting at the table, quiet and morose. He looked up as his father came in the door.

"You home for the night?"

John shook his head. "Sorry. I have to go to an autopsy on a case I'm working."

"One of the murder victims?"

John nodded. "It looks great, Adele," he

said as she loaded the table with food.

"Thanks. Dig in." She went back to the kitchen.

She'd made a nice beef dish with mashed potatoes and sliced apples. John ate hurriedly, because he didn't have much time.

"How's school?" he asked his son.

"It's good."

John finished his meal and sipped coffee. He glanced at Tonio and frowned. The boy was very pale.

"What's wrong?" he asked.

Tonio couldn't tell him the truth. He wanted to, so badly. But he was afraid for David and Tina. Rado had killed three people, just recently. He didn't want to cause more deaths.

He had to come up with a good excuse or his father might drag the truth out of him. He picked at his food. "There's this older boy. He picks on me."

"Stand up to him," his father advised quietly. "Bullies are full of hot air. Confrontation deflates them."

"He'd fight me."

John raised a black eyebrow. "Tonio, if he hits you, he's expelled. That's the rule. Just make sure you don't hit him first."

"I won't." He looked up. His father was so strong. He was like a sturdy oak tree, always tall and straight and unafraid. "How do you learn not to be scared of things?" Tonio asked him.

"You never learn that," John said. "There are always going to be things, people, situations that frighten you. Courage is doing what you must, in spite of the fear. People who tell you they've never felt fear are lying, Tonio," he added with a smile. "I feel it any time I'm face-to-face with criminals. But I do my job."

Tonio just nodded. It was easy to say it. Hard to do it. He wished he could help his friend.

"I have to go."

"You said something about a movie?" Tonio asked.

John grimaced. "I've got to work Saturday and Sunday, on this case," he said apologetically. "So we'll have to take in the matinee on Saturday," he added gently. He'd gotten to his feet, but he sat back down and looked at the boy. "Tonio, I'm not being a good father to you. I'm sorry that I've let my job separate us so badly. That's going to change, when I wrap up this case. What I'm doing right now is more important than I can tell you. It may save many lives."

"It's okay, Dad," Tonio interrupted. "I know you do the best you can. You miss

Mom, too, don't you?" he added.

John's eyes were sad. "I miss her every day. We knew even in grammar school that we'd marry one day. Even if I hadn't loved her, she was my best friend. She was the best of both of us, Tonio."

Tonio bit his lip. "Yeah."

John got up and turned away. It hurt to talk about Maria, which was why he rarely did it. He shrugged into his coat and put on his hat. "Hey, did you make a snowman?"

Tonio laughed. "I made a snow cat. He's out back."

"I'll have a look in the morning. Is he a good snow cat?" he teased.

"He looks more like a big mound with sticks coming out of him," the boy confessed.

"Art is good if you think it's good," John scoffed. "What do art critics know?"

Tonio laughed. It had been a long time since his dad had joked with him. He thought about Sunny and wished she could meet his dad. They'd be perfect for each other. But that wasn't likely to happen.

"I'll be late. Do your homework and don't stay up all hours playing that game," he added.

"Got nobody to play it with right now. The military guys went on maneuvers and

my friend's hurt his hand so he can't play."
He grimaced. "I'm just soloing stuff."

"Bummer," his dad said.

Tonio chuckled. "It's a great game. Even if I have to play it alone."

"Okay. I'll see you later."

"Sure, Dad."

He paused. "What was your friend's name? David, wasn't it?" he added with a smile, trying to show that he did take at least some interest in the boy's life. "He can cuss like a sailor, but if you like him, he must be a good kid."

"He is a good kid," Tonio said.

"Nothing like friends to help get you over the rough spots," John said. "See you later, son."

"Okay. Be careful. The snow's deep."

"Snow in Jacobsville," John mused, shaking his head. "Miracles never cease. I'm gone, Adele!" he called loudly.

"Okay. Be careful out there!"

"You, too," John muttered, but he grinned as he opened the door and went out to the SUV.

TEN

Sunny trod through the snow, laughing at the rare treat, exchanging smiles and greetings with neighbors and strangers as she made her way to the hospital, stomping her feet before she entered to get the snow off.

Her face was flushed and pretty with happiness when she spotted Tonio in the canteen.

"Hi," she greeted. "Isn't the snow beautiful?!"

"Yes, it is."

"You weren't here Friday," she said. "I was worried."

"I got a stomach bug. I'm much better," he added, glowing because she was concerned.

"I was off for two days," she said. "I never take sick days or vacation days, so I had to start taking some of them or lose them. I've missed talking to you," she added.

He beamed. "I've missed seeing you, too."

She got hot chocolate and a nut bar and sat back down. "That friend of mine that I wanted you to talk to . . ." she began.

He hesitated. "I talked to David," he said. His face was pale under its light olive tan. "He's so scared," he said. "His sister's scared, too."

"Why?" she asked gently. "Has something else happened?"

He bit his lip. He wanted to tell her, so badly. "I can't say," he said. "That guy, the detective. If he'll promise to be careful, I'll tell him. I won't tell you," he added, his face grim, his big brown eyes eloquent. "I don't want anything to happen to you, Sunny."

Her high cheekbones flushed. Her eyes brightened. "That's very sweet of you. But I want to help. I don't want you hurt, either."

He felt warm inside. He felt as if he'd known her all his life. "But he has to make sure nobody knows," he said. "David's got throwaway phones. It's the only way he can even talk to me, and not for more than a couple of minutes."

This sounded serious. She drew in a breath. "I've trusted him with my life," she said after a minute. "I told on Rado, when it happened," she added. "I told him, because I knew that Rado did it. He kept my confidence, even though he could never prove that Rado was directly involved. If Rado had known that I told Cal, he'd have killed me, too."

He relaxed a little. "Okay, then."

"Cal comes here on cases. Not very often, but if there's something like that boy who was shot, it's not unusual for him to be in the hospital." She grimaced. "He's easily recognized, because he's in the news so much." She smiled. "Female TV newscasters love him. They won't even talk to Rick Marquez, they go straight to Cal," she added, laughing. "He's a widower."

"Oh, like . . ." He almost said, *like my dad,* but he caught himself just in time. "I see."

"Do you want to try tomorrow after school?" she asked.

He hesitated. He was still uneasy about it. But if it would save David, maybe it was worth the risk. If he did nothing, his friend could die. "Okay," he said.

"Good. I'll phone him when I get off duty."

"You get off real late, don't you?" he wondered. "Will he be awake?"

"Cal doesn't sleep much," she said.

He recalled what she'd said, that the guy had been a merc. "He fought, didn't he?" he asked.

"Yes. He was in a war in Africa, a big one.

The group he was with was decimated. Only a few of them came home."

He frowned. "Why was he there?"

"The legitimate government was overthrown by a particularly vicious rebel leader. He thought nothing of butchering women and children. Cal and his friends put the elected ruler back in power. They saved hundreds of lives."

He smiled. "He sounds nice."

"He is. Try not to worry so much," she added softly. She frowned. "Can't you talk to your father about this?"

He shook his head. "He wouldn't understand. He'd go storming to the police and David would die."

"I see." She had a very poor impression of Tonio's dad. It was such a shame he wasn't more supportive. "Well, I'll help you all I can. So will Cal. You don't tell anybody, okay? Especially not your friend David."

He started to protest. Then he realized that she was right. David had let it slip about Rado's connection to the DEA. The boy couldn't keep secrets. "I won't tell him," he promised.

She cocked her head. "He knows something about Rado, doesn't he?"

Tonio's face was like still water. He just smiled.

"When you get older, I'm never playing poker with you," she said abruptly.

He grinned.

"Okay, then, I'll go to work. You be careful. Very careful. Do you live someplace safe?" she added worriedly.

He wanted to tell her that he lived on a big ranch, that it had lots of burly cowboys, that his dad was a lawman. But she was safer if she didn't know much. Even about him. Especially about his dad. All she had to do was let something slip around her detective friend, who might mention it to someone who knew his father. He didn't dare.

"I live someplace safe," he promised. "You be careful going home in the dark," he added and was concerned.

"I get cabs," she said softly. "I'll be fine. It will work out," she added solemnly. "You can get through anything if you just think past it, think ahead. Christmas is coming," she added, laughing. "Santa might bring you something awesome!"

"Dad's getting me computer software, instead of Xbox One games," he said sadly. "The only console game I have is *Destiny* 2. He thinks I game too much already."

"What sort of software?" she wondered.

"Educational stuff," he said with absolute disgust.

She burst out laughing. "I used to get perfume." She made a face. "I'm allergic."

"Gosh, that's bad," he said.

"At least I'm not allergic to flowers, and that's a good thing, because the ward's covered up in them this time of year," she added with a grin. She grabbed her coat and purse. "I wish I could play in the snow," she said ruefully. "Maybe it will last for a little while."

"Maybe it will. I'll see you tomorrow, Sunny."

"See you, Tonio."

He watched her walk away and wondered for the tenth time if he was doing the right thing. If he got David killed by talking about Rado, he was never going to get over it.

Sunny called Hollister on her way through the lobby.

"Tomorrow," she said when he answered. "Same time as last."

"Good news at last. Be careful in the snow," he added. "It's refreezing. Slippery as hell."

"I'll be careful," she said. "Good night."

" 'Night."

She went out the door and looked around.

There were usually cabs everywhere. But not tonight. Not one. She shivered faintly in the cold. It was only a couple of blocks. If it hadn't been for the ice, she might have risked it. What if she fell? Snow wouldn't stop Rado's gang from looking for victims. She gnawed her lower lip, worrying.

Just as she was thinking about sitting in the lobby until a cab drove up, a big black SUV pulled up at the curb.

"Hurry," John called. "I'll get ticketed. My lieutenant would never let me live it down," he laughed, throwing open the passenger door.

She ran to him, almost sliding down in the process. She jumped up into the cab and slammed the door. "How in the world . . . ?!" she exclaimed.

"I was working on a case with ties to a bank robbery last week," he said, looking both ways before he pulled into traffic. "Crime doesn't keep business hours," he chuckled. "I thought it was about time for you to go off duty."

"There were no cabs," she said. "I was debating whether to try and call one. Every time, I get put on hold or cut off, or I get somebody who doesn't speak English well enough over the phone. I really need to brush up on my Spanish."

"I'll read love poems to you," he teased. "You'll refresh it very quickly."

She laughed with pure delight. "You don't look like a man who's ever read a poem," she retorted.

"I have the heart and soul of a troubadour," he promised. "I'll prove it to you one day. Not tonight, sadly, I've got to write up the report while it's fresh in my mind. Then I'm going home for a couple of hours' sleep."

"You work long hours."

"So do you, *rubia*," he said gently. "We love our jobs."

"Yes. We do."

"My lieutenant is having a Christmas party at his horse ranch. We're all invited. Go with me?"

"Oh, I'd love to," she said. "But I'm working four more days this week."

"It's a week from Saturday," he said.

"Next Saturday. I'll see if Merrie York will cover for me. If she will, and my supervisor okays it, I'd really like to go."

He beamed. "Then it's a date." He made a face. "Hopefully nobody will commit a major crime that I'll be asked to assist in solving. At least, we might get to dance," he added.

"I love dancing."

"Me, too." He glanced at her with wicked black eyes. "I still remember our first dance."

She flushed. "I felt so bad . . . !"

He laughed. "You'll never know how flattered I was when my cousin mentioned what you said." He didn't mention that he was feeling really down when she rejected him. One of the nurses he knew had told him what Sunny said, and it had lightened his heart incredibly. Strange, to feel so deeply about the opinion of a woman he'd just met.

"You must know that you're gorgeous," she said shyly.

He raised an eyebrow. "I'm not. But I'm very glad that you see me that way," he added. "You fill my heart."

Her breath caught, because his voice was low and soft and full of feeling.

"I wish things were different," he said grimly.

Meaning, that he couldn't get involved with her. She knew, and understood. He had some sort of complication in his life. She wondered if it was another woman, someone he'd made promises to. She knew so little about him, really.

"You're worrying again," he chided.

"I guess I am. Sorry. I've had something

on my mind today."

"Anything I can do to help?"

She shook her head, smiling. "I'd love to ask you. But it involves a young friend of mine who's having problems. He won't talk to anybody in law enforcement." That wasn't quite true. But John didn't like Hollister and she didn't want to set him off, when things were going so well with them.

"A patient?" he wondered.

She hesitated, just briefly. "Yes. A patient," she lied convincingly. "He has a friend who's being threatened."

He pulled up in front of her apartment building and cut off the engine. He was very serious. "You don't need to mix yourself up in anything dangerous. I can help. Tell me what's going on."

Her face drew up. Her dark eyes were eloquent. "I wish I could. But I made a promise not to talk to anyone about it. I put him in touch with someone I thought could help."

"Someone in law enforcement?"

"Sort of."

"Sunny . . ." he began, exasperated.

She put her soft fingers over his mouth. She loved the feel of it. He had the most sensuous lips. "I can't," she whispered.

He felt her fingers with a sense of wonder

at the passion she aroused in him. He turned them and put his mouth hungrily against the palm.

She melted. The hunger she felt was open to him, almost painfully evident.

He ground his teeth together. "This will not end well," he said gruffly. He let her hand go and got out of the SUV. He came around and opened her door, lifting her down. He held her there for just a few seconds, hoping to subdue the passion he felt. He couldn't.

"What the hell," he said roughly. He caught her hand and tugged her along with him to her door. "Open it."

She fumbled her key into the lock. It was always like this with him. She wanted him. All he had to do was touch her, and she had no will of her own. It had to be a rare thing, this attraction. Probably every woman in the world who felt it thought that she was the only human to ever know such instant joy.

He slid off her coat, and then his. He drew her to him. "I have to go home," he whispered as his head bent. "I can't stay." His mouth brushed tenderly over hers. "I want to. More than anything in the world."

Her arms linked around his neck, pulling. "Me, too."

He felt her shiver as his mouth crushed down on hers, gentle for all its frustrated passion. His arms contracted slowly and he lifted her so that she was on her tiptoes, so hungry for his mouth that she had no thought of resisting.

He groaned. "I don't have anything to use," he said huskily. "I haven't had a woman since my wife died. Three years . . ." His mouth was invasive then, passionate and demanding. "Stop me!"

She was trying to. Her mind said no. Her body was pushing up against his, pleading with him. She was a virgin. She'd never slept with anyone. She went to church. This was wrong. She should say something, do something!

While she was thinking of ways and means to subdue her hunger, his mouth suddenly slid down onto her breast and pressed into it — the damaged one, the one she had to pad so that the wound didn't show. It didn't seem to bother him at all.

She felt a jolt of pleasure that went all the way down into her toes. Her caught breath was audible.

He lifted his head. His black eyes were glittering with feeling. "I have scars, too, little one," he whispered.

He bent and lifted her and carried her to

the couch, still kissing her. He dropped down onto it, with Sunny in his lap.

The kiss was so drugging that she couldn't protest even when he pushed up her long blouse and his hand trespassed onto the breast under the padding.

"Ah," he whispered, and smiled at her. "Is that all?" he teased, and his fingers drew over the scar, so tenderly. "I have far worse ones."

"You do?" she managed in a husky tone.

He unsnapped his shirt and pulled it to one side. His chest was broad and muscular, covered with thick, black, curling hair. He drew her hand to a long scar that ran from his left shoulder down his chest almost to his navel. "Feel it?" he asked. "I had to subdue a subject about four years ago. He pulled a knife on me before I could get him cuffed. It took a lot of stitches," he added with a smile. He cocked his head as her fingers traced it. "Does it make me less attractive to you?"

"Oh, of course not," she said at once.

He nuzzled her nose with his. "Then why would you think a scar would cause me to find you less attractive? It's what you are, Sunny, not how you look, that attracts me. You make me . . ." He paused and searched for a word. He frowned. "You make me whole."

Her heart jumped into her throat. "That's how I feel, too," she confessed.

His mouth settled tenderly over hers. He kissed her with pure reverence. "How strange," he whispered, "to find someone so unexpectedly who fits you like a glove."

She smiled under his warm mouth. "I was thinking that, too."

One big hand went under her and felt for the clasp of the bra. He freed it and pushed the whole works up, staring down at creamy breasts with hard dusky peaks. His face was rigid with self-control as he traced the scar that covered half of her left breast. "This must have hurt like hell," he said softly.

She swallowed hard. "Yes. But it was what the boy said on that date . . ."

He smiled. "The idiot?" he teased. He looked down at her soft body. "There's nothing wrong with you. Nothing, honey. Nothing at all."

While he spoke, his head bent to her breast. He took it into his mouth and worked the hard nipple with his tongue. She gasped and caught his head, her hands unconsciously tangling in the thick, cool wavy black hair.

"I won't hurt you," he whispered against

her breast. "Trust me."

She did. But what he was doing shocked her. It shocked her more that it robbed her of any resistance at all. She arched toward his mouth, her hands tugging at his head now instead of protesting.

He worked his way down to her waist and back up again, slow and gentle and passionate, all at once. It had been so long since he'd had a woman in his arms. It seemed a lifetime. And here was this angel, untouched, unwanted, and she wanted him back. It was like a miracle.

"Mi corazón," he whispered hungrily. "We have to stop."

She was on fire for him. She'd never really felt desire before. It was saturating her senses to the point that she didn't care what happened next. "Are you sure?" she asked dreamily.

He drew back reluctantly. He couldn't believe he was doing this. She was willing, he was starving. But it wasn't right. In the morning, she'd hate him. If she was untouched, it was as much because she had principles as much as she lacked self-esteem. He couldn't take advantage of her.

He smoothed back her long hair, holding her close. The thick hair on his chest tickled her breasts, but it felt like heaven. And not only to him.

"I never knew it would feel like this," she said, searching his black eyes.

"Two people can start fires together with such an attraction as we share," he replied. He looked down at her body and clenched his teeth. "I'm going to hit myself over the head with a fire poker later, when I remember that I walked away from you."

"You could stay," she offered hesitantly.

"Yes, I could." He traced her soft mouth. "And in the morning, Sunny, when you come awake and realize what you've done?"

She flushed.

"You see?" he asked, his voice deep and slow. "It isn't only because the stupid boy hurt your feelings. You go to church. You have a fragile conscience."

"It wouldn't bother you, though," she began.

"It would," he interrupted. "You're untouched. I can't offer you a future. Not right now, at least. That being the case, I won't risk putting a baby in here." He pressed down hard on her flat stomach and wanted suddenly, desperately, to do just that.

Her breath went out like the tide at just the thought of it. A baby. She'd wanted children all her life. With this man, she wanted them with all her heart. And that was in the face she turned up to him.

For just a few blinding seconds, he thought about it. He could make her pregnant. They could get married, have a life together. And with those thoughts came the memory of Tonio, running away to join a gang.

He groaned and put her to one side. He stood up, fighting a passion stronger than any he'd felt in his entire life. He took slow breaths, trying to calm the anguish desire had kindled in him.

Sunny tidied herself up, grimacing. Had she offended him somehow?

She got to her feet. "I'm sorry," she began.

He turned and drew her gently into his arms; not too closely, because he was still aroused. "For what?" he asked, smiling. "We wanted each other. It's not a crime. I'd know, too," he teased.

She managed a laugh.

"It's bad, when you start thinking about babies and how much you want one," he said with a long sigh. "And you know it's impossible."

"Babies are easy," she argued. "You just forget all your principles and beg a man not to stop." Her eyes twinkled at him.

He chuckled, deep in his throat. "Some-day," he said quietly, and the smile faded. "I promise you. Someday, we'll have a future."

"Those complications you keep talking about," she said, and started to ask what they were.

And his phone went off. He grimaced as he pulled it out. There was a text message, from Tonio.

Adele's going home, do you want her to leave you something in the fridge?

He typed, yes, omw, and sent it. He put up the phone. "I have to go."

"Another shooting?" she asked worriedly.

"No." He bent and kissed the tip of her nose. "Just a meeting I can't miss."

"At this hour?" She was worried. "You be careful. There are dangerous people in the city."

"I know." He grinned. "I'm one of them. I'll call you, *rubia.* The movies, this Saturday?"

"Oh, yes," she said breathlessly.

"I'll text you. Then Saturday week, we'll go dancing at my lieutenant's party."

"Something to look forward to."

"For me, as well." He bent and kissed her hungrily for a few seconds. He stood up. "Good night."

"Good night."

He swept up his hat and coat from the chair where he'd tossed them and put them back on. "Be careful outside in the morning if you have to go out," he cautioned. "It's going to be worse than tonight when the temperature falls."

"I will." She smiled dreamily. "Drive safely."

"Sleep well."

"I will. Good night."

"Buenas noches, mi alma," he whispered. He smiled once more before he left.

She locked the door after him, almost floating with joy. It had been so long since she'd felt anything even remotely like what she felt now, for John. He wanted children with her. He'd said as much. That meant he wasn't looking for a one-night stand.

She was grateful, because she had, apparently, no self-control or willpower where he was concerned. She wished she knew why he couldn't commit to a relationship. He'd said his wife had died. Was there some other woman to whom he'd made promises, and he was bound by honor to her? Was that why? She wished she knew. He seemed like an honest man, but what did she know about men? She'd avoided them since she was seventeen.

That was probably why John had become

so attractive to her. He was the first really adult male who'd ever paid her any attention. Was he just handing her a line, leading her on until he could take her to bed?

She thought about that, about what she knew of him. No, she decided. No, that was definitely not the sort of man John Ruiz was. She knew it. She turned out the lights, put on her gown and went to bed. Her dreams were sweet.

Tonio was still up when John started heating up the plate of food Adele had left him in the refrigerator. It had been a frustrating day, in some respects. Marquez had sent an officer to get Tina Lopez, but she hadn't been home and neighbors didn't know where she went. The officer tried again before he went off shift. Still no Tina.

"You should be asleep," John commented when the boy joined him in the kitchen.

"I can't sleep," Tonio said.

John glanced at him while his food heated. "Problems at school?"

"Sort of."

"Want to talk about it?"

He did. He couldn't. "Just normal stuff," he prevaricated. "How's work?"

"Tedious."

"You never talk about what you do," Tonio commented.

John turned to him. His face was hard and there were deep lines in it. "You don't know what I have to see at work, Tonio," he said quietly. "It isn't anything I can talk about with people who aren't in law enforcement."

"You mean like bodies and stuff?"

John nodded. "There are some terrible ways for people to die. I see them." He turned back to the microwave. "It never ceases to amaze me, what people can do to each other in a temper."

Tonio had some idea of that. David's broken arm was a prime example. He sighed.

"You should go to bed, son."

"I guess. We still going to the movies Saturday?" he added hopefully.

"You bet." He felt warm inside. Here was his son, who was finally willing to come closer after such a long period of alienation. He smiled. "What do you want to see?"

"That new movie based on the comic book," he said at once.

John chuckled. "Okay. It will have to be a matinee."

"No problem."

"Now go to bed. School tomorrow."

"I know. But if I get up early enough, I can build a snowman first!"

John just shook his head, smiling. He phoned Marquez later. There was still no luck contacting Tina Lopez. He phoned Banks. Nothing new on the murder victims yet. Longfellow's note had produced nothing except a grocery list, of all things. Another dead end. He was getting a lot of those lately.

Later, he texted Sunny, when he was in bed. My life is getting more complicated by the day, he texted. We still on for the movie Saturday?

Sunny answered the phone and saw the first line with pure misery. Then she read the second one. He wasn't backing away. He really wanted to go out with her. She was so elated that it took her two tries just to type an enthusiastic Yes! in the space and hit Send.

John read it with pleasure. She wasn't coy. She was up front, honest. She was the sort of woman he'd be proud to be seen with. He wanted her almost desperately. All he had to do was convince his son that the world wouldn't end if John brought another woman home.

Sunny wasn't like the very attractive fellow Ranger he'd brought home last year. She was a very feminine, caring, nurturing person. Surely Tonio would respond to her.

He just had to bring it up the right way, and go slow. He remembered with terror Tonio running away. He couldn't risk provoking another such episode.

He'd find a way, he promised himself. He thought about Sunny, remembering her warm, soft body, the way she responded to him. She was innocent, but she wanted him very much. It made him proud. He had to take excellent care of her. He couldn't risk making her pregnant, but he wanted to. The idea of Sunny carrying his child made his heart run wild.

Sure, he'd find a way to convince Tonio that he wasn't marrying the Wicked Witch of the West. It would just take time.

The next afternoon, Sunny was sitting with Tonio in the canteen when a tall, blond man came toward them.

"Is that him?" Tonio asked.

Sunny turned. She smiled. "That's him."

ELEVEN

Cal Hollister shook hands with Tonio. "I appreciate your courage," he said as they sat down. "This can't be easy for you, I know."

Tonio was impressed. "Thanks," he said, and flushed a little. "You won't tell anybody that I told you? You won't let David get killed?"

"I won't."

Tonio looked at Sunny. He grimaced. "You can't listen," he said gently.

She smiled warmly at him. "I have to go on duty anyway," she agreed. She ruffled his hair. "I'll see you tomorrow, okay?"

"Okay, Sunny," he promised. He smiled back.

"You like her, don't you?" Cal teased when she was gone.

"She's so much like my mother," Tonio said. "Mom died three years ago. It's just me and my dad, and he's never home."

"That's a shame," Cal said quietly. "What can you tell me?"

"Rado killed those people."

"Who?"

"The man and woman, the ones that were in the paper," he added, having remembered just in time not to say that his father had told him about them. "Rado did it. They were going to say that he killed that senator's daughter, the one who died of a drug overdose. It wasn't an overdose, David said. Rado did it. Now he and his sister are in real trouble, because Rado's watching them like a hawk to make sure they don't rat him out."

Cal let out a breath. "Tonio, this is big. Really big. Will David talk to me?"

"No," he said. "I can't ask him to. His brother died about the time the senator's daughter did. He's only got his sister. Rado makes her sell herself to keep him in money," he added sadly.

"This is where it gets hard," Cal said quietly. "Names. I need their names. I swear to you, nobody will ever know who told me."

Tonio drew in a long breath. It was now or never. "David Lopez," he said. "His sister's Tina." He gave Cal the address, unaware that Cal recognized them instantly and felt his heart lift. "Please," Tonio said.

"Don't trust anybody else with what I told you. I can't stand it if David dies on account of me. He's my best friend."

"I can promise you that he'll be safe," Cal said, with a solution already in mind. He smiled at the boy. "You've been very brave. I'm proud of you."

Tonio's heart jumped. It had been a long time since anyone had been proud of him. He grinned. "Thanks."

"Now forget who I am, and that you ever saw me," Cal said. He glanced around to make sure they weren't observed. "If anyone asks, you did something bad and I saw it and gave you a lecture. So don't smile."

Tonio made a face. "What did I do?"

"Tried to get something out of the vending machine using a washer," he replied with twinkling gray eyes.

"Can you do that?" Tonio asked.

"Never mind if you can do that," Cal said. He got up and shook his finger at the boy. "Don't you ever do what you didn't do again. Got that?"

"Oh, yes, sir," Tonio said, nodding enthusiastically.

"Good. I'll see you." He left the canteen just as Rosa came up.

"Who's that you were sitting with?" she asked curiously.

"Just a guy who was sitting at the table when I came in. It was crowded, so I sat with him. Nice guy," he added.

"Well, he was a dish," she said, with a soft whistle. "Why can't I ever meet guys who look like that?" she teased. "Maybe you could introduce me."

He managed not to blow his cover. "How?" he asked, laughing. "I don't know who he is."

"Darn. He looked almost familiar, isn't that strange?" she added, laughing, while Tonio prayed that she wouldn't remember Cal. Rosa had been a policewoman. Certainly she'd have recognized him if he'd been closer when she arrived. "Well, let's go. I hope we can get home without sliding into a ditch," she groaned.

"You're a great driver," Tonio told her. "We'll be fine."

She ruffled his hair. "Okay, buster, thanks for the compliment. Let's go."

The movie theater was crowded for the Saturday matinee. Fortunately the ticket taker wasn't the one John had seen when he'd brought Sunny here before. He didn't want Tonio to know about her until he could find a way to introduce them that wouldn't produce a traumatic result.

"Here, get us some popcorn," he told his son, handing him a twenty dollar bill.

"Want a Coke?" Tonio asked.

"Sure."

"Okay. Be right back."

John sat on the bench, studying the messages on his phone. One of them that he hadn't noticed was from Colter Banks, who was working overtime today. He'd found out something about Tina Lopez.

He read that and his heart jumped. He was tempted to leave the theater, but he couldn't do that to Tonio. The boy had been excited about the movie all week. He'd get through it and then he'd go see Banks. He typed him a text message and sent it. Then he sent another, to Sunny: see you later, pretty girl. He smiled when she typed back ok, and added a heart.

Tonio gave him a suspicious look. "Who're you talking to?"

"Someone I know."

"A woman," Tonio said, because his father's face had been radiant for those few seconds. His own face grew cold with mingled fear and concern.

"I'm only texting her, for God's sake, not trying to marry her!" John almost bit his tongue. He'd snapped at the boy, because of his reaction to his father texting a woman.

It stung.

"Sorry," Tonio said, averting his eyes.

John didn't speak. He took the Coke Tonio had brought him and waved away the change.

Tonio felt bad. He'd made a lot of trouble for his father. It must be lonely for John without Maria. Tonio missed her. He knew that his dad did, too. But he didn't want another woman around.

Except maybe Sunny. He adored her. He was sure that his father would, too, if he could just find a way to get them together. But he had no idea how to proceed. The woman in the text must mean something to his dad, because he'd looked . . . different suddenly. Happy. Tonio felt guiltier than ever. He loved his dad. But he just didn't want any other woman in his house. Well, that wasn't completely true. Sunny would do nicely. If only he could find some way to get them to meet.

Something was tingling at the back of John's mind all through the movie. Tonio had a friend with a smart mouth who played video games with him. The boy's name was David. Tonio said that he wasn't playing lately because he'd hurt his hand.

As he processed those thoughts, he recalled the name Lopez. Tina Lopez had been the woman who let Tonio stay with her when he ran away from home. Tina had a brother. What was the brother's name, the one who hadn't died about the same time the senator's daughter did? Harry Lopez was the victim of a drug overdose. Or so they said. The younger brother, what was his name? Wasn't it David?

Lights flashed in his mind. David Lopez. Tonio's friend. He pulled out his cell phone while Tonio's attention was on the action scene playing on the big screen. Tina Lopez had a rap sheet. She also had gang associations. Los Diablos Lobitos. Her brother was David. He went to San Felipe. Tonio's school.

He put up the phone. He was furious. The connection was right in front of his face and he hadn't seen it. David Lopez was a member of Los Diablos Lobitos. He hadn't realized it before and Tonio hadn't told him. Tonio also had to know that David's arm had been broken by Rado, but he hadn't told his own father. Why?

John was silent all the way to the ranch. Tonio watched him covertly, frightened. His dad looked furious.

"Did I do something?" Tonio asked when

they were walking in the front door.

John put up his coat and hat. He turned to his son. "Your friend is David Lopez."

"Well, yes," Tonio said hesitantly.

"He has a sister named Tina, a prostitute."

"She's not bad," Tonio said. "She was forced to go on the streets — !"

"Yes. By Rado," he replied coldly.

Tonio swallowed, hard. He looked tormented.

"Rado broke a kid's arm for talking about him. He laughed while he was doing it. Your friend David doesn't play with you, but not because he hurt his hand. It's because Rado broke his arm. Isn't it?"

Tonio almost panicked. "Dad —"

"What do you know about Tina and David, and their connection to Rado?" he persisted.

"I can't tell you," he began.

"You can. You will!"

"I told a cop," he replied quickly. "Someone I know got him to come see me at the hospital. I told him all about Rado and David and Tina. He promised to make sure David and Tina don't get hurt. If Rado finds out I told, he'll kill David! You can't go over there and make trouble for them. Please, Dad," he pleaded. "David's the only friend I've got, and he's scared to death of Rado.

He says Rado's over there all the time now, because David and Tina know enough to put him away for life. David called me on a throwaway phone. He's so scared!"

John cursed under his breath. "You told a cop," he said icily. "But you wouldn't tell me? I'm your father, Tonio!"

Tonio felt terrible. "Dad, you're like an avalanche when you're on a case," he said defensively. "I was scared that you'd go over there to talk to David. Rado would find out and David would die."

"I can be discreet," John argued. His face was hard as stone. "Who's the cop?"

Tonio ground his teeth together in anguish. "I promised I wouldn't tell. He's got friends in Los Serpientes," he added. "Well, not friends, maybe, but people he trusts."

"A cop with gang friends. A boy who's in danger of dying because he knows too much. A known killer standing in the shadows. Did it ever occur to you that you're putting people in the line of fire by saying anything at all? And worse, if Rado finds out that you talked to someone in law enforcement, he'll be after you!"

"The cop was sitting with someone I know, a woman," he replied. "It would look like they were getting together and I was just sitting at their table. Even Rado

276

couldn't believe I was telling the cop anything."

John ran a hand through his hair. "Damn it, Tonio," he bit off. "I put you in school in San Antonio to keep you out of trouble. Your friend David is up to his neck with the wolves, and you're his friend. Do you think Rado doesn't know? Do you think he believes you won't say anything?"

Tonio felt nervous. And not only for himself. Now he was worried about Sunny as well. What if he put her in harm's way? What if Rado was watching the canteen or had people watching it for him? What if he'd seen Cal Hollister with Rado and Sunny and thought Tonio was telling both of them things about Rado that he'd heard from David?

"I didn't mean to get anybody in trouble," he said miserably. He looked up at John with dark, solemn eyes. "I only wanted to help David. I didn't want him to die, or Tina, either. Tina isn't on the streets because she wants to be. Rado made her. Dad, he's so dangerous," he added quietly, going closer. "I was afraid to tell anybody, but this woman I know at the hospital said she knew somebody I could trust, because she trusted him. She's been hurt by Rado's gang, too."

"Some woman, a stranger, says you can

trust her," John scoffed.

"She's not a stranger," Tonio protested. "She's kind and sweet." He turned his eyes away. "She reminds me of Mom."

John bit his lower lip. The boy was alone too much. No wonder he was making friends at his school who were out of the mainstream. John had put him there to protect him and to straighten him out. Now it seemed, he'd put him in danger as well.

"I don't want you talking to David again," he said firmly. "I'm going to have one of my men shadow you, even at school from now on. Rado's not getting to you. No matter what I have to do."

"David's my friend," Tonio protested.

"If he knows something on Rado, I have to find out what it is," John said quietly. "This is bigger than us, Tonio. The man's killed people. Two, just recently. I can't let him walk."

"But he won't, that's what I'm trying to tell you! The cop's going after him. He said he can do it in a way that won't involve me or the woman who helped me. He can protect David and his sister."

"If Rado wants them dead, there's no such thing as protection, least at all from a police officer. He may have the best of intentions, but you can't go about something like this

278

in a covert way, Tonio. You have to go through the front door."

"Please don't get David killed," Tonio said miserably.

John didn't reply. He put his hat and coat back on. "I'll be late."

"Dad, please . . . ?!"

"I'm not going after them tonight," he said curtly, his black eyes cutting into his son's face. "I have to meet an informant." That was a lie. He was meeting Sunny. "But you keep your nose out of this, understand me? I don't want you near David until we can get Rado sorted out. Afterward, well, we'll see."

"I wish I'd never punched that teacher," Tonio said gruffly. "This woman I know asked me if I just did it to get your attention." He lowered his eyes, blind to his father's sudden flush. "I don't know. Maybe I did." He shrugged. "The movie was nice. Thanks. I'm going to bed."

"Tonio."

The boy turned on his way down the hall. John moved closer, his face troubled. "I know we don't spend enough time together. I'm trying to do something about it. It's just . . ." He hesitated and drew in a breath. "You don't understand how it is with me. I can't crawl into the grave with your mother.

I loved her. But life goes on. It has to. Do you really expect me to live the rest of my life alone?"

Tonio's face closed up. "There really is a woman, isn't there?"

John lifted his chin. "Yes. There's a woman. I take her out for a sandwich now and then. That's all."

Tonio's face hardened. "As long as I don't have to be around her," he said sullenly. He turned and walked away.

John looked after him, ready to fight. But Sunny was waiting, and he was tired of trying to change the boy's mind.

"Dad?"

He looked back from the open door.

"Please don't get David killed," the boy repeated sadly.

"I'll do what I can," he said curtly, and left. On the way off the ranch, he had a talk with his foreman about providing additional security for Tonio. As an afterthought, he phoned Eb Scott to see who he had who might be willing to shadow Tonio in San Antonio while he was in school and he put the man on the ranch payroll at once. That settled, he drove back to the city.

He sent Sunny a text and said he'd be a little late for the evening film. She sent him one back that said it didn't matter what time. She added that she had a new movie on DVD and maybe they could watch it at her apartment. He sent back an lol and a message that he'd like that even better.

Before he went to her apartment, despite Tonio's warning, he made a beeline to the Lopez apartment. Earlier in the week, Cal Hollister had promised to have Tina brought in for questioning on prostitution so that they could interrogate her, but the officer Hollister sent hadn't been able to locate her. It was Saturday night. If she had a "date," she might be at home. He was going to see.

He knocked on the door, but there was no answer. He couldn't see any lights on in the apartment from under the door. Odd, the boy at least should be there.

Troubled, he went by Father Eduardo's church. The priest welcomed him and took him into his office. He closed the door.

"How can I help?" he asked.

"I'm looking for Tina Lopez and her brother David," John said. "They aren't at her apartment, and it's dark. No lights."

The priest nodded. "They've gone into hiding, is all I can tell you. But things are in motion that will bring a good result."

"What things?" John asked.

The priest only smiled. "Good things. Be patient."

"They're witnesses in a murder investigation," came the reply. "I know that Rado's making threats. They're in danger."

"Not now," Father Eduardo replied. "They're safe, and in good hands. Rado's future is looking darker by the second. But that's all I can tell you. I gave my word."

John bit back a curse. Here was the worst dead end he'd had in ages. An active murder investigation, and the two people who might finger the shooter were out of reach. "Can you tell me if they're still in the city, at least?"

Father Eduardo laid a gentle hand on the other man's shoulder. "Rado will pay for his crimes, sooner than he thinks. And that is all I can tell you."

John just shook his head. "Okay. I'll get with my task force and hope they've got another solution."

"They will have. You worry so much," the priest said gently. "It is good, that you want to preserve the peace and protect others. It is bad that you give so little of that time to yourself. God guides us, you know," he added. "He sends us down the river of life with the illusion that we are in charge. But the reality is that we have no control over what happens to us, unless you discount prayer. You must relax and just live life."

"Sound advice, but I have a stressful occupation," John said with a faint smile.

"I came from an even more stressful one, to my present job. I can tell you for a fact that once I sat down and let God lead, the stress lessened drastically."

John chuckled. "It seems I have no choice, for the moment. Thanks anyway."

"*Buena suerte,*" Father Eduardo said. "*Y que Dios te bendiga.*"

"You, too, father. Merry Christmas."

The priest smiled. "It is good, that we can say this once again. *Feliz Navidad* to you, too, my son. *Y prospero año y felicidad.*"

"There's a song about that," John said with a twinkle in his black eyes.

"José Feliciano. One of my favorites."

"Mine as well. See you around."

"Yes. You will."

John worried the problem of the Lopezes and his son all the way to Sunny's apartment. He couldn't believe he'd been so preoccupied that he hadn't realized the David Lopez with the broken arm was the same David who was his son's best friend. He was working too hard, putting in too much overtime. He was neglecting his son.

He hated even the thought of Tonio in danger from Rado. It seemed that the boy was keeping many secrets from him. He'd said that a San Antonio cop was helping him. He wished he knew which one. He was also curious about the mysterious woman Tonio referred to. The way he spoke of the woman indicated great affection. It was amazing how much John didn't know about his son.

Perhaps they were right. He needed to be less obsessed with his job and more attentive to his only child. If only he and Tonio could work out their problems. John wanted him to know Sunny. If he could just meet her, it might change his whole attitude. But how to bring that about, without invoking tragedy — that was the thing.

Sunny met him at the door, in her sock feet, wearing jeans and a long red sweater with a reindeer on it.

He laughed wholeheartedly. "I could use a little Christmas cheer," he teased as he put up his hat and coat and joined her in the kitchen. "You're not cooking?" he wondered.

"I've had supper. Have you?" she asked.

"Yes . . ."

"So I made dessert." She indicated a

cookie sheet on the stove. There were several kinds of cookies. All of them looked delicious, even to a man who didn't normally like sweets.

"Forget the popcorn," he said at once. "I love cookies. Just enough sweetness without overdoing it." He made a face. "I don't like cakes much. And pies, only occasionally. But cookies! My favorite treat! And how did you know I liked chocolate?" he teased, taking her by the waist.

"I didn't. I took a chance." She looked up at him, laughing. She looked very pretty with her face scrubbed clean and her long, silky hair around her shoulders. She smelled of wildflowers and soap all at once.

He bent down and nuzzled her nose with his. "We could have gone out, if you'd wanted to."

"I'd rather be here," she returned. She smiled. "You can relax on the sofa. In the theater, not so much."

"True." He let her go and grabbed two cookies.

"Here." She handed him a red dish, which he filled to the brim. "Coffee?"

"Do you really need to ask?" he asked with a laugh.

"Silly question. I already made a pot. It's strong," she added and poured it out into two mugs.

"I love black coffee strong," he said when she joined him on the sofa. "I live on it."

"Me, too. Night shift gets long."

He stretched his long legs out in front of him. "It does, indeed."

"Why don't you take off your boots?" she asked. "I almost never wear shoes inside. Too confining."

He grinned at her. He tugged off his expensive boots and tossed them to one side, wriggling his toes in his thick white socks. "You're right. Much better."

He drew her up beside him after she'd started the DVD player. "What are we going to watch?"

"The new cartoon movie. Well, it's not new, but I haven't seen it."

"Moana!" he exclaimed. "I haven't seen it, either. I've heard great things about it from the people at work. Most of them have kids."

She smiled. "I love cartoon movies."

"So do I."

The music was lovely, the acting perfect. But about halfway through the movie, John drew her across his lap and kissed her softly.

She wreathed her arms around his neck and kissed him back. In between segments of the movie, his hands slid under her sweater and up her bare back to the fastening of her bra. This was familiar now, comfortable. She felt his hands on her firm breasts with a sense of wonder at how right it felt, how good. She never protested once.

He eased her down on the sofa and kissed her hungrily, his body moving slowly against hers in a sensuous, exciting way. His hands eased up the sweater. She was so far gone already that she never tried to stop him when he pulled it over her head and tossed it to one side, along with the shirt he quickly removed.

The feel of his bare, warm, hair-roughened chest against her bare skin was so exciting that she gasped out loud.

He held her close. *"Rubia,"* he whispered at her ear, his voice strained, "you are every dream I ever had of the perfect woman!"

"Not so perfect," she replied sadly.

He lifted his head and looked down at her. His fingers lightly traced over the breast with the scar. "This makes no difference," he whispered. "Except that I wouldn't have had you hurt for all the world."

"It's unsightly —"

Before she could finish the sentence, his mouth was on the nipple, moving down, coaxing, invading, consuming her with a faint suction that lifted her right off the couch in a helpless, anguished arch. Her nails dug into his thick hair as she shivered with unexpected pleasure that seemed to feed on itself.

"You like that?" he chuckled, deep in his throat. "I like it, too. So much!"

His mouth shifted to the other breast and he repeated the arousing caress, joy shafting through him as he heard her soft cries of pleasure, felt her body go rigid with desire, with delight.

While his mouth was busy, so were his hands. At first, she protested, a little, but another feverish caress and she let him unzip the loose jeans and push them down her legs. She was vaguely aware of his own jeans following, along with his gunbelt and pistol, but she was so intoxicated with pleasure that she had no will of her own left.

"This is going to end badly," he bit off at her mouth as his body covered hers. "Very badly . . ."

"I know," she whimpered. But she was pulling, not pushing. It was the most exquisite physical pleasure she'd ever known.

"You're a virgin," he ground out. "It will hurt!"

"Not much," she managed.

"Baby," he breathed into her mouth, "we

shouldn't do this!"

But while he was talking, he was removing the last barriers. He settled onto her and began to move her long legs apart while his mouth invaded her own, teasing, hungry, sweeter than honey.

She lifted up to him as his body slid up, so that he could find her where she was open and moist and hungry. She shivered as he moved down, one hand firm on her thigh as he lifted his head and looked into her misty eyes.

He pushed, very gently, and she bit her lower lip.

"Yes," he whispered, his voice slightly unsteady, because this was a rite of passage for her. "Let me make it easier," he added.

He moved away, just a little, and his hand moved against her, wise and slow and tender, bringing up her blood, making her shiver and shift, reaching up to tempt him closer. Her breasts had hard, dusky nipples. She was moaning with need, her eyes glazed with it. He probed softly and she began to jerk with the growing pleasure.

"Yes, that's it," he whispered, making a rhythmic motion that swiftly brought her to the very edge of ecstasy. "That's it. Here. Yes. Here, like this, hard, hard hard, *rubia,* hard . . . !"

His hand was on her thigh, his body invading hers, stretching it, in a mania of passion that blurred pain and discomfort, that defied reality. She moved with him, crying out softly as he went into her, all the way into her, so deep that she sobbed with every quick, passionate movement of his hips.

She was going to burst, like a balloon, like a dam. Her body throbbed. Her eyes opened to look straight into his. He ground his teeth together. He'd never watched. Now it seemed that he needed to.

"Yes," he bit off, just as her body stiffened and she began to sob, her hips jerking upward, pleading.

"John," she cried out.

"Yes!" He pushed down with all his might, thrusting into her as hard as he could. She convulsed, the pleasure was so overwhelming. It was unbearable. For him, as well. He cried out as his own body shuddered and shuddered, completion washing over him like hot water. They pulsed together in each other's arms, held tightly, tightly, while they endured the sweet agony of fulfillment.

It was a long time before he could get his breath. He lifted his head. His hair was sweaty. So was his body. Sunny looked up at him with the face of an angel. She was shy with him now, in the aftermath.

"No," he whispered shakily. "None of that." He turned her face gently back to his. "Nothing so beautiful should ever be a source of embarrassment. We loved."

Her face flushed. She searched his eyes, seeing not indifference or apathy, but the sharing of something intensely intimate. She touched his hard face, drawing her fingers over his hard mouth.

"It didn't hurt," she said, faintly surprised.

"I didn't rush you," he explained, smiling tenderly. "I would have gotten nothing out of it unless you did, too."

"Really?"

He bent and drew his mouth tenderly over hers. "Really." He started to lift away.

Her hands protested gently.

He settled back over her. He looked into her soft eyes as his hips moved first one way, and then the other. He was still inside her. She was sensitized and he was suddenly capable all over again, probably a result of the long abstinence.

He caught his breath as pleasure tingled up his spine.

"I want very badly to have you again," he whispered. "Will it be uncomfortable? You must be honest."

She shifted under him with new knowledge. "It won't," she said softly. She moved and gasped. "My goodness," she burst out as lights flashed behind her eyes at the jolt of pleasure.

He laughed, deep in his throat. "And now you know a little more about pleasure, yes? Curl those long legs around my hips," he whispered huskily, "and let's see how deep I can go . . ."

She flushed. It was very intimate, not only what he said, but what he did. She watched him watching her. She didn't look away or close her eyes. It was a revelation, being loved physically and watching it happen. She was so gloriously happy that she thought it would be all right if she died.

And then he began to move very quickly, very deliberately, and she thought she had died, when he pushed her over the edge of passion into ecstasy, into climax, into total, absolute orgasm. She cried out helplessly, sobbing as her body throbbed in time to his. She heard him cry out, too, felt his body cord and push down hard as the pleasure took him as well. She looked into his eyes and it was like sharing a soul, for those few faint precious seconds while they transcended earth and space and became one person.

■ ■ ■ ■

Afterward, of course, she cried. She'd done something that her mother had cautioned her about all her life. She'd had sex with a man to whom she wasn't married. She'd committed a sin and her conscience hurt.

He held her tenderly, kissed away the tears. "Listen to me," he said tenderly. "I would never have touched you if I didn't see a shared future. You were a virgin, Sunny," he added. "I'm not the sort of man who looks for a good time with an innocent. Now, am I?"

She looked up at him, vulnerable, hopeful. "No," she said finally.

His hand smoothed down her creamy body. He smiled. "I haven't had it like that in my whole life," he confessed.

She was surprised. "Never?"

He shook his head. "I loved my wife," he said. "But even with her . . ." He made a face. "This was beyond any experience I've ever known."

"It had been a long time," she began.

He chuckled. "That isn't why." He traced her pretty mouth. "My own beautiful little blonde nurse. I adore you."

She relaxed in his arms with a faint, shy

smile. "My very own gorgeous man," she replied.

"We belong to each other now," he said solemnly. "There won't be anyone else. Ever."

She stared at him with a heart that overflowed. She'd never known such belonging.

"You have to say it back, Sunny," he prompted with a wry smile. "No other men, ever."

"There won't ever be another man," she assured him. "But you knew that already."

"I knew."

They dressed. The movie had long gone off. He looked at his watch and grimaced. He pulled her close. "I would have preferred to stay all night, but I have to go home and get my cowboys started first thing in the morning."

"I'd love to see your ranch," she said.

"And you will. Very soon." He wouldn't think about Tonio. Not yet. He was too full of Sunny and joy and . . . love. The thought shocked him. He looked at her and knew, very suddenly, that he loved her. Why hadn't that occurred to him before? He smiled.

"You look very odd," she remarked.

He chuckled. "I'll tell you why, one day. Not now," he added, kissing her nose. "I'll text you." He hesitated at the door. "Don't beat yourself up over what happened," he said.

She bit her lip. "We didn't use anything."

He came back to her and drew her close. "Sunny, I want children. Don't you?"

She flushed. She beamed. He really had meant it, that there wasn't going to be anyone else. "Yes," she said softly. "I want children very much."

"Then we have to do more of what we just did," he replied wickedly. "But not just yet. I have a few problems to work out first. Okay?"

She grinned. "Okay."

"Be safe. I'll text you. Keep the door locked," he added gently.

"You watch your back out there," she countered.

"I will. Good night, *mi alma.*"

"Good night, John."

She heard him drive away. And then the guilt began to grow. Once passion grew cold, reality set in. He'd mentioned a future together. But he hadn't mentioned marriage. Not once.

TWELVE

John drove home in a daze. For the first time in years, he felt whole. Sunny made him feel ten feet tall. She was sweet and kind, and in bed she was his very dream of perfection.

But how to break it to Tonio? That was going to be his biggest headache.

Alongside Sunny, he was worried about the Lopezes. Apparently the policeman Tonio had told him about had found a way to get them into hiding. But Rado had connections all over the city. He could find anybody. If he had a window into the DEA, with that secretive, high-up connection nobody could identify, he could even find a hidden witness.

He didn't want the Lopez boy dead. Perhaps if he'd made better decisions, if he'd been a better father, Tonio would still be in school in Jacobsville and he'd never have met David in the first place. All that led back to John's disastrous date of the year before.

But that woman hadn't been like Sunny. Tonio had reacted badly because John had been belligerent about the boy's attitude. He hadn't told Tonio that he was bringing her home, tried to explain how he felt, how lonely he was. He'd just barged in.

He was like an avalanche when he was on a case. But he was like that in his personal life as well. Cash Grier had said that John needed to live his own life without letting his son make decisions for him. That was true enough. But there had to be some way to compromise. He just didn't know what it was.

The house was quiet when he got home. He showered and went to bed, his body relaxed, satiated. He slept peacefully for the first time in ages, still cocooned in the memory of Sunny's sweet body in his arms.

Two mornings later, he spoke to his foreman, laying out what he needed the man to do. By the time he finished, Adele had breakfast on the table. Tonio was picking at his food, unnaturally quiet and disturbed. The weekend had been solemn. Tonio had avoided him.

"The Lopezes are in hiding," John said as

he poured coffee into a mug.

Tonio's heart jumped. "You did go to see them," he groaned.

"They weren't there," John repeated. He glared at his son. "Apparently your friend the cop had someplace to put them, out of Rado's reach. We can hope so, at least. But Rado has connections, big ones. If it had been up to me, I'd have contacted the US Marshals' service and they'd be in protective custody."

Tonio felt even worse. But there was some possibility that Hollister would have done that himself. Surely a captain of detectives would know a US marshal in the city. He didn't say that. The captain had no idea that John was Tonio's father, and he didn't want him to know. There was too much the captain could tell John, including about Tonio's connection with Sunny, and the gang. He was in enough trouble already.

"Nothing to say, Tonio?" John asked curtly.

"No, sir," Tonio said quietly.

John grimaced. He was just making things worse. He finished his breakfast and poured a second cup of coffee.

"You can't," Tonio said after a minute, and dark eyes lifted to his father's.

"I can't, what?" was the cold reply.

Tonio swallowed. "You can't bring that woman here," he said.

"Like hell I can't," John said icily. "This is my house. You don't tell me what I can do, Tonio."

Tonio heard Rosa drive up outside and honk the horn. He got up and grabbed his book bag. He turned at the door, red-faced and fuming. "Okay, go ahead, bring her here," he told John. "You'll never find me next time! I have friends you don't even know about!"

He took off out the door, threw himself into the car and motioned Rosa ahead before John could catch up.

"Your dad's waving to us," Rosa said, slowing.

"He's just waving goodbye. I have to be early today, Rosa," he said quickly.

"Oh. Okay, then." She threw up a hand in John's direction and accelerated.

Tonio didn't know what to do. His father wasn't going to let it drop. He had a woman in his life and no plans to give her up. Tonio was sick at heart. If it had been Sunny, he wouldn't have minded. But it would be some other hard-faced woman like the one John had already brought home, and Tonio couldn't live with someone like that. Worse, the woman had to mean something to him or he wouldn't be willing to fight Tonio for her.

He knew that if he went to school, his father was likely to come after him. He really was like an avalanche, and Tonio didn't want to fight anymore.

He could skip class and hang out in the city until it was time to go home. By then, maybe his dad would have cooled down. Sunny would be at work later. He could talk to her. That might work. He smiled at Rosa as she drove away, but instead of going into the school, he turned around and walked the other way.

There was a place where gang members hung out, not one where Rado ever went. It was a pool hall, and kids weren't supposed to be there. But the owner was a friend of David's and he knew Tonio, who'd gone there with David once or twice when they cut classes.

The owner just grinned at Tonio's guilty look when he asked why he wasn't in school.

"Okay," he said. "You can stay. But you got to go in the back room and watch TV. I don't want no trouble if your parents come looking around here for you."

"Okay, Bart," Tonio said at once. "Thanks."

The man shrugged. "I was a kid once. You hear anything from David?" he asked, lowering his voice. "He ain't been around."

Tonio shook his head. "I'm worried about him."

"Yeah. Me, too. Go on. You can watch TV." He indicated the back room.

John was frantic. He'd gone to the school, hoping to make up with his son. Tonio wasn't there. He didn't want to put out an APB, but he did talk to a couple of patrol officers he knew and had them watch out for the boy. He told Rosa as well.

"What's going on?" Rosa asked, concerned.

John rammed his hands into his pockets. "There's a woman."

"Oh, dear," she said, because she remembered what had happened.

"Yeah." John drew in a breath.

"He doesn't understand. Maybe if you could introduce them," Rosa suggested.

"That's why he's gone now," he returned. He pulled his hat low over his eyes. "The other one was just a coworker. This one . . ." He ground his teeth together.

"You have to make him understand that you have a life besides being his father," Rosa said.

"I don't know what to do," he said.

"Maybe back off, just a little," she said. "Until you can arrange for them to meet."

"That may be harder than it sounds. What if he's really gone this time?" he asked, in anguish. "It took me two days to find him last time, and that was when Rado wasn't a threat!"

"Rado?" Rosa paled.

His lips made a thin line. "Rado's up to his neck in two murders and Tonio knows it. His friend David told him. Tonio told a cop yesterday. So now I can't find Tonio. I don't know where David Lopez is. Rado's out there —" he gestured toward the street "— and by now he may know that Tonio talked to a cop. What if he finds Tonio before I do?"

"You need to get some help, to find him," Rosa said.

"I've got people looking," John said. "Damn! I just can't find a way to talk to him without turning it into an argument."

"Parenting is hard, so they say," Rosa told him gently. "Go to work. Chances are very good that Tonio will realize that he's putting himself in danger and go back to school. He's not a stupid boy."

John could have debated that. But his phone rang.

■ ■ ■ ■

Banks had been in touch with a friend of his in another agency. "He doesn't know for sure," he told John, "but he thinks the US Marshals are involved in the Lopez case."

"That would make things easier," John said. "But I've got bigger problems than the Lopezes. My son's not in school."

"He cut class?"

John nodded. "We had an argument. I don't know where he is. His friend David Lopez told him that Rado killed the man and woman in our cold case. If Rado knows —"

"Rado knows everything," Banks said coldly. "He has contacts in some high places. The DEA's still trying to finger the one there." His black eyes narrowed. "Does your son have other friends in the city?"

"I don't know," John said curtly. "I wasn't even aware that the David Lopez Tonio knew was related to Tina, or that he had a connection with Los Lobitos," he added harshly. "My son talked to a cop. He wouldn't talk to me. He says I'm like an avalanche. He thought I'd get his friend killed."

Banks cocked his head. "Do you ever sit

down and talk to the boy?"

John hesitated. "No," he said after a minute. "I don't."

"How old is he?"

"Eleven, going on thirty," John replied with a cold laugh.

"That's an awkward age."

"Tell me about it." He finished his coffee and got up. "I'm going back by the school, on the off chance that he had the good sense to show up there."

"Not a bad idea. Good luck."

"Thanks. I'll be in touch."

Tonio had come to the same conclusion, finally, that he'd be safer at his school than hanging out in gang territory, where somebody might rat him out to Rado. He wasn't as afraid for himself as he was for Sunny, though. He was concerned that Rado might know she'd been sitting with him and Hollister when he'd told the man about the murders and David. He couldn't bear it if something happened to her.

If he and his dad had been closer, he'd have told him about Sunny. He'd have asked him to help protect her. But here was his dad, up to his neck in a relationship with some woman, and Tonio hadn't even known. He wished he had a dad who cared about him. It seemed these days that John only wanted to lay down the law with his only child. It was a sad state of affairs.

He eased back onto school property and met the school policeman at the front door. He apologized for being off campus and added that he'd take his lumps for skipping class. The officer, a father of five, just smiled. It would be all right, he said. He wasn't a bad kid, and the principal was a nice guy.

Tonio didn't even get in trouble. He went back to his next class after a heartfelt apology. He hoped he wasn't going to fare worse when his dad found out what he'd done.

John had been almost sick with worry. He stopped by the principal's office at San Felipe, only to be told with a kind smile that the boy had turned up already and was safely in class.

He went back to work with a lighter heart. But it didn't solve his problem. Tonio was going to be watched from now on. He'd arranged for one of Eb Scott's men to shadow the boy in San Antonio, but that wasn't to start until the following day. Meanwhile, he had to decide what to do about Sunny. It was the worst possible time to be hit with his son's opposition. He'd been intimate with her. There could be a child.

How was he going to break the news to her, that he had a son, that there was no immediate future for them? He was devastated. Tonio had threatened to run away. The boy had escaped him for half a day. If he followed through on the threat, and kept running, how would John live with it?

Tonio's steps dragged as he headed toward the children's hospital after school. He knew he was going to catch hell from his dad; the principal had told him his father had come by looking for him.

He thought it couldn't get any worse when Rado and two of his minions were suddenly in front of him. He stopped short, his heart racing.

"Hey, Tonio, where's your buddy David?" the gang leader drawled sarcastically.

"I don't know," Tonio said, and it was the truth.

Rado noticed that. He was good at reading people. He moved a step closer. "If he calls you, you better find me quick and tell me," he said in a threatening tone. "Because I'll know, Tonio. And you'll pay for it. You understand? I got a friend who's a cop," he added. "He'll do anything I tell him. Anything! You remember that."

He turned, motioned to his buddies and brushed past Tonio so hard that he almost toppled him.

Tonio watched him go with cold chills running up his spine. Rado wouldn't hesitate to kill him. But it wasn't himself he was worried about. Sunny was involved. His father had said anybody around him was in danger. What if Rado found out about Sunny talking to Cal Hollister for him?

He brightened just a little when he saw her sitting in the canteen. She smiled as he approached.

"Hi," she said gently. "How's it going?"

"I want to go to Canada," he said on a sigh as he dropped his book bag and sank into a chair.

"Why Canada?"

"I don't think Rado would find me there."

"Oh, dear. What do you want? Hot chocolate?"

"I'll get it."

"My treat," she said softly, and smiled.

"Okay. Hot chocolate."

She bought two cups and put his in front of him as she sat down. "Tell me what's going on."

"My dad and I fought," he said miserably. "I cut class and he came looking for me. If that wasn't bad enough, Rado just stopped me outside and said if I heard from David I'd better tell him or else. He says he's got a cop in his pocket, somebody who'll do anything he tells him to."

"That's bad news," she said. "You can't tell your father?"

He shook his head. "He's mad at me."

"Tonio, you can't cut class and run away. Problems follow you. They're portable," she said gently. "You have to face them. Your dad will get over being mad at you."

"He's got a girlfriend," he said through his teeth. "He brought one of them home before. That's why I ran away. She was cold as ice. This one . . . My dad's got no sense about women."

"That's not true," she contradicted softly. "He married your mother, didn't he? And she sounds as if she was a wonderful person."

"She was."

"This is hard for you to understand," she said. "But grown-up people don't do well alone, especially people who've been married. I know your dad is happy that he has you. But I imagine he's just lonely, Tonio."

"It wouldn't be so bad if I didn't have to see her," he said. "She'll be just like that other one. He never talks to me. He tells me what to do and he goes to work. If I ever try to talk to him, the phone rings. Maybe he'd be happier if I was out of the way."

"Don't you say that," she chided. "Shame on you for even thinking it."

He drew in a breath. He managed a smile. "He did go looking for me today."

"Of course he did. You're his son. If he loved your mother, he must love you, too. You're part of her. You're all he has left of her."

She had a way of making things easier, making him see the good things instead of the bad. "Thanks," he said gruffly.

She smiled. "Sometimes it helps to just take a step back and look at things from a different perspective."

"That's hard."

"Life is hard," she countered. "We get through it one day at a time. But Hollister needs to know what Rado told you, about the policeman he's got in his pocket."

"If he comes here again, people will notice," Tonio said. "I don't want to get you in trouble. Rado's killed two people already."

"More than two," she said. She frowned. "I think I know a way. I'll talk to him myself."

"If you go to his office —"

"Oh, I won't do that," she said, smiling. "I'll come up with something." She checked her watch. "I'll be late. When does your school let out for the holidays?" she added, thinking that he'd probably be safer at home than walking around the city after school to get to the hospital.

"Friday," he said. He sighed. "I won't see you again until after the new year," he added miserably.

"I might have a surprise for you Friday," she said, her eyes brightening.

He laughed. "I might have one for you, too," he returned. He looked at her sadly. "At least I have my dad, even if he gets mad at me. You don't have anybody, Sunny."

"I have you," she teased.

"Yes, but it's going to be Christmas . . ."

"I go to church. There are people I know. And there's this guy." She flushed.

"The special guy, right?" he asked, and tried not to look as disappointed as he felt.

"Very special." She drew in a long sigh and smiled dreamily. "I've been alone so long. I never thought I'd find anybody who'd want me for keeps."

"He has to share you," he said firmly. "I'm not giving up half my family to some strange man." He grinned.

She laughed, delightedly. "I'll be sure and

tell him. I'll be off after today, but I come back to work Friday. So I'll see you then. Don't worry about Rado. I think he's going to be in some serious trouble very soon."

"It won't be soon enough for me. See you."

She smiled. "See you."

Tonio finished supper before his father showed up. He looked as apprehensive as he felt.

John put up his hat and coat and slung his gunbelt over the back of a chair. He glared at his son.

"I apologized to everybody," Tonio said quietly. "I did a dumb thing. I'm sorry."

John didn't reply. He sat down, filled a plate and ate in an icy silence. He'd worried the problem all day. He was no closer to a solution.

"I'm going," Adele called from the hall. "Can I get you anything else?"

"Nothing. Thanks," John added.

She glanced from one set face to the other, grimaced and let herself out.

"No video games for the rest of the week," John said when he'd finished eating.

Tonio swallowed. It was what he'd expected. "Yes, sir."

"And if you leave school again in the

middle of the day, for any reason whatsoever, I'm going to start looking up military
schools."

Tonio's heart stopped. He'd never see
Sunny again. "But, Dad —"

"You know how dangerous Rado is," he
said icily. "Your friend David has put you in
harm's way. I'm not taking any more
chances with your life."

"I'll do better. I will!"

John didn't reply. He sipped coffee instead.

Neither of them was addressing the real
issue, that Tonio had run away because of
John's woman friend. But it was on both
their minds.

"May I be excused?" Tonio asked in a
subdued tone.

"Help yourself. Bed at eight."

Tonio didn't bother to argue. It wouldn't
have done any good. He was in enough
trouble. "Yes, sir."

John watched the boy walk down the hall
with dead eyes. Today had been a near
thing. He couldn't lower his pride enough
to let Tonio see how frightened he'd been
when he couldn't find him. He didn't want
to give up Sunny. He wished there was
another option.

But he couldn't lose his child over a

woman, not even this woman. He'd have to tell her. He just didn't know how. And he had to pray that there would be no consequences from his headlong rush into intimacy. He should never have compromised her. She was innocent. He'd robbed her of courtship, proposal, marriage, all in one fell swoop. He'd made promises he couldn't keep.

He wondered if life could get any harder.

Sunny phoned Hollister after work, once she got home and kicked off her shoes.

"Do you still dance the tango?" she teased.

He chuckled. "Like a pro. Why?"

"I need to talk to you, but I can't do it at work. Rado's watching. I found out something pretty important. I can't come to your office and I really don't want to tell you over the phone."

"How about Friday night, at Fernando's?" he asked. "That's the soonest I'll have any free time. I'm tied up for the next couple of days. Something intense."

"That suits me. I'll see you there about six?"

"I could pick you up."

"Rado might be watching," she said. "Too risky. I'll get a cab."

"Okay. I'll see you Friday."

She hung up. She wondered if John was going to call her at all? Surely he hadn't been lying, about wanting a future with her? He didn't seem the type of man to lie. She hoped she was right.

But the very next day, he was at her door, just after lunch.

"Hi," she said, smiling breathlessly at the unexpected visit.

"Hi." He was quiet. Subdued. He indicated the living room. She winced inwardly at the sofa where they'd been so intimate, but he seemed not to notice. He sat on the edge of her one armchair and leaned forward, his hat in his hand.

"Something's happened," she guessed as she perched on the arm of the sofa.

"Something." He looked up. His face was hard as stone. "I haven't been truthful with you. I'm a widower," he added quickly when he saw her expression. "That part was true. But what I didn't tell you is that I have a son." He averted his eyes. "I was involved with a woman last year. I took her home. He ran away." He looked down at his boots. "I thought if I could just get him to meet you . . . but he took off again. It took me a long time to find him." His lips made a thin line. He couldn't look at her. "I made promises to you that I can't keep. At least, not right now. I have to work things out at home first. I'm sorry."

She hadn't moved. She hadn't breathed. She just sat there. She was a little paler but she didn't speak. She stared at him with such pain that one glimpse was enough to keep his eyes elsewhere.

"I see," she said finally.

"It's only temporary," he said, trying to make the best of it. "I just need to make him understand that I have a life apart from being a father. I need . . . a little time."

She knew what he was saying. He was too kind to blurt it out, but she knew. She got up, forcing a smile. "Okay."

He looked up. "Okay?"

She walked to the door and opened it. "I've got a dentist's appointment," she lied, and the smile stayed. "I know you'll work things out. It's fine."

He hesitated. "Sunny," he began. She was too calm. Far too calm.

"It's all right," she emphasized. She looked up at him. "We'll just back away for a while. No problem. I hope you have a good Christmas."

He hadn't thought about presents. He hadn't thought about much, since Tonio had run away. "I'm not handing you a line," he said quietly. "I meant everything I said."

She nodded. She looked at the clock. "I really have to go . . . I'm sorry!"

He let out a harsh breath. "Okay. But I'll call you in a few days. I was going to take you to the lieutenant's Christmas party, but I can't go. I have to work a double shift Saturday, so that another Ranger can be off with his family."

"I'm working overtime, too," she said. "I'll see you, John."

He went out the door but before he could get another word out, she'd shut it behind her. He heard the lock slide into place. He closed his eyes and shuddered inwardly. He knew what she was thinking. He loved her. He wanted her. If only he could find a way around one stubborn, hardheaded eleven-year-old, there might still be hope. But for now, all he could do was retreat.

Sunny heard the SUV crank up. She threw herself down on her bed and cried until her eyes were red.

She was so miserable Friday that Tonio winced at the sight of her ravaged face.

"Something's gone wrong," he said worriedly.

She managed a smile. "Just another disaster. Nothing to worry about. Hot choco-late?"

He could have groaned. "It's that guy, isn't it? The special one?"

"I'm just stupid, Tonio, that's all it is," she said. "I don't know anything about men. I thought he cared." She laughed. "More fool me."

"I'd punch him for you, if I could," he said with some heat.

"Thanks. But it's nobody's fault." She opened her purse and pulled out a small, wrapped present. "Merry Christmas."

He reached under the table and pulled out a bud vase with a single yellow rose in it, tied with a bright yellow ribbon. "Merry Christmas!"

"Oh, Tonio!" She hugged him and hugged him.

He thought he'd never felt so happy in his life. He hated feeling glad that Sunny's guy hadn't worked out, because now he had a chance to introduce her to his dad. If he could just find some way to do it. First, he thought miserably, he'd have to find a way to get rid of his dad's present heartthrob. But where there was a will . . .

"What is it?" he asked, turning the pack-age over.

"Open it and see."

"I don't have to wait?"

She laughed. "No. Open it!"

It was a game disc for the Xbox One. In fact it was a brand-new space game that he'd read about online.

"I wanted this one so much!" he burst out. "Thanks, Sunny!"

She grinned. "The man at the game store said it was popular and very good. Thank you for mine," she added. "I love yellow roses."

He grinned back. "Merry Christmas."

"Merry Christmas. I wish I could stay, but I'll be late, again."

"I'll see you next year," he said. He smiled sadly. "I'll miss you."

"I'll miss you, too."

"What about Mr. Hollister?" he asked under his breath.

"All arranged. And no danger to either one of us." She smiled. "I'll tell you all about it. Next year. You stay out of trouble."

He crossed his heart.

She laughed as she went off to the elevator.

Friday night, she and Hollister danced the tango.

"Okay, so tell me," he chided at her ear. He looked around. "It looks like we're a normal couple on a date."

"Hopefully if it gets back to Rado, that's just what he'll think. He told my young friend that he has somebody in the police department, a man who'll do anything he tells him to."

Hollister stopped dancing. "What?!" he exclaimed.

"Dance," she said "or we're going to draw attention."

"Of all the damned outrages. My own department," he muttered.

"It explains how he knows so much."

"Hopefully, he doesn't have a line into my office. I'll get some people on it today. People I know I can trust. Thanks, kid," he teased.

"You're welcome." She cocked her head up at him. "It's such a shame that I don't like blond men. You're a great dancer."

He grinned. "Well, I'm partial to blondes."

"Sorry. One broken heart a year is enough," she said.

"Ruiz?"

She nodded. She drew in a breath. "I thought it was getting serious. But he didn't."

"Damn. I'm sorry."

"Me, too. But no harm done," she lied. "None at all."

"If you say so."

He put her into a cab and went back to his office. He had a mole to flush out.

Sunny went back to work the next day, only to have John Ruiz show up on her floor during her break and take her downstairs and out the front door.

"Hollister," he said icily. "You said you didn't have anything going with Hollister. But you were on a date with him!" He didn't add that he'd been near the restaurant on a case. He'd seen her go into Fernando's and followed, just inside the door. She'd been doing the tango with Hollister, dancing close. So much for her lies about not liking blond men! He was livid.

Her eyebrows levered up. He had some nerve! "What if I was?" she asked. "Have you already forgotten that you tossed me out of your life?" she added with a cold smile. "You don't want me. What do you care if someone else does?"

He was good for five minutes of pure, unadulterated fury. He let her have it in two languages. She was nothing but a two-timing, faithless hussy who wouldn't know a serious relationship from a squash. He was well rid of her. He couldn't believe he'd thought of getting serious about her.

"Just as well, under the circumstances,"

320

she bit off, flushed and hurt. "You weren't serious anyway."

"No, I wasn't," he lied, wounded and hitting back. "I got what I wanted from you," he said with a sarcastic smile. "Nice, but not worth giving up my freedom for. Maybe Hollister's more your type."

She forced a smile. "Maybe he is," she said in a haughty tone.

He let out a furious curse, turned on his heel and stormed back to his vehicle. He'd never been so angry in his whole life. And he'd risked his son for that faithless flirt. He couldn't believe it!

She watched him go with dead eyes. She'd saved her pride, at least. That would be cold comfort in the years ahead. But at least now she knew where she stood. It had all been a means to an end. He'd just needed a body. Hers was handy. Nothing could have been more humiliating than what she'd just endured.

Or so she thought, until the next morning, when she started throwing up and couldn't stop.

THIRTEEN

John was so miserable that he didn't even question where Tonio had obtained the new video game he was playing. He kept busy at work, and at home, during the holiday break. He'd sent Adele shopping for Tonio, but mostly what the boy was getting was educational software and a new jacket. He didn't have the heart to go to town himself. He didn't want to go shopping in San Antonio for fear that he might run into Sunny.

His heart was breaking. He'd lied to her about wanting her only out of desire. She'd become such a part of his life that he felt like half a man. He'd deleted her phone number and contact information in the heat of anger. He'd have given a lot to have it back. He might have tried to text her. But he doubted that she'd even answer him.

Apparently she and Hollister had discovered a mutual attraction. The man drew women, but John had been sure that Sunny belonged to him alone. Had he driven her away by not calling after they'd been intimate? Women were sensitive about intimacy, after all, and he'd only hinted of a shared future. In fact, he'd told her that there was no hope of them being together in the near future because of his son. He hadn't meant that it was hopeless; only that he had to get his son to accept her. But she'd taken it for a goodbye and she'd gone out with the only other man in her life. He hated knowing that Hollister was dating her. He didn't know how he was going to live if they got involved.

And still, above all, there was the matter of Tonio and Rado. The gang leader couldn't get to Tonio on the ranch, but after the holidays he'd be back in school, vulnerable. John would have to make sure that he was watched around the clock.

Tonio avoided him, even just after presents were opened on Christmas morning. He stayed in his room. He wouldn't even go out to see the horses, and he loved them. He did sit at the table for Christmas dinner, but he hardly said two words to his father and those had to be dragged out of him. John felt like a castaway. He'd managed to alienate the only two people on earth he loved, and he had no idea how he was going to get them back.

Christmas was lonely. Sunny had hoped she'd be going places with John. But that had been an illusion of love. He'd only wanted a night in her bed, not forever.

She wondered if he even had a son. It was probably a line he used to push women away if they got too close. He was very handsome. He could have any woman he wanted, women much prettier than Sunny. All that talk about the future, about children. Had it really all been just a means to an end? He hadn't called since he'd blown up at her over Cal Hollister.

She grimaced and placed her hand on her flat stomach. The nausea was ongoing. She was tired all the time. She felt and saw changes in her body that she knew all too well meant she was pregnant.

She didn't know what to do. She couldn't go to a clinic. That was impossible. Even if she hadn't been a person of faith, she couldn't step on an ant, much less terminate the tiny life inside her.

She thought of having a child, and she felt warm all over. A child of her own. It was something she'd dreamed of. Of course, the dream had also included a husband and a home together. She looked around at her lonely apartment. This wasn't her dream of happiness.

She walked to the back to do laundry and grimaced at the back window whose screen still hadn't been fixed. The lock was wonky, too. Sometimes it didn't quite catch. She'd have to contact the superintendent again. He was overworked, especially during the record cold snap, so she'd have to wait in line for repairs. He had bigger issues, including a fire in one of the apartments that meant major repairs. Fortunately it was at the other end of Sunny's building and didn't affect her.

She wondered if Hollister had found the bad apple in his department yet. She grimaced as she recalled John's fury that she'd gone dancing with him. If she'd had the chance, she would have told him that she'd only done it because Rado would think it was a date, not that she was imparting confidential information to the captain of detectives. But she hadn't had the chance.

Once, she'd been tempted to text John, just to have any contact with him. But she'd chickened out at the last minute. He'd made his position crystal clear. She'd been a bit of fun and now he was off to new conquests. She had just enough pride not to throw herself at his feet. It wasn't easy. She missed him terribly.

Christmas came and went. So did New Year's. Sunny faced the new year with a home pregnancy test that was decisive. She wasn't showing yet, so there was time to make decisions. She wasn't sure that she was going to stay in San Antonio. There were nursing jobs in Houston, and even Hollister admitted that she might be safer far away from Rado. She didn't tell him why she wanted to leave, however.

But Hollister seemed to understand that her breakup with Ruiz had spoiled things in the city for her. He didn't understand what was going on. Ruiz was obviously crazy about her, and vice versa. But all of a sudden, they were enemies. He hoped they could work it out.

Colter Banks was poring over an arrest report when John walked into his office the second week in January. His fellow Ranger had called and asked him to come over, because he thought they might have a break in the cold case.

"What's new?" John asked.

Colter grimaced. "Something hopeful, something else that's pretty bad. Hollister's got a rogue cop in his department. He doesn't know who it is. Very likely it's one of Rado's men, and he'll do anything he's told."

"How did Hollister find out?" John asked, frowning.

"He has a contact," Banks said. "I don't know who, but somebody who has a friend in Los Diablos Lobitos and is willing to risk his life to betray Rado. Hollister's known about it for a few weeks, but he hasn't been able to track down the informant. He's got an old comrade helping him, from what I hear. They may turn him up."

"Brave so-and-so, whoever gave him the information about the bad cop," John commented.

"Very brave. The word is that he's a kid," he added. "Which makes it an act of very rare courage."

"Considering Rado's reaction to anyone talking about him, yes, it is." He leaned against the wall and crossed his arms. "How about anything connecting Rado to our cold case?"

Banks grinned. "That's the only good news I have. We've had a backlog in the forensics lab because of the holidays and several more gang shootings. But forensics found dog hairs on our female victim's clothing. They were brown. I understand that Rado keeps a brown pit bull chained outside his house to ward off unwelcome visitors. They also processed a partial tread print from a pair of sneakers and a cigarette butt of the type Rado is known to smoke."

John felt lighter. "That's probable cause."

"Yes, it is, although it's largely circumstantial. But I found a judge who was willing to sign a search warrant." He waved it. "I'm waiting for Marquez to send two patrol officers over to go with me to take hair samples from the dog. We're taking Animal Control along as well. The warrant also allows me to obtain biological samples from Rado himself, look for the pair of sneakers that might match the tread pattern and look for samples of the cigarettes Rado smokes."

"That's going to cause some problems," John remarked.

"I hope it's going to cause Rado some," came the dry reply.

"I mean, for anybody Rado suspects of selling him out," John amended, and he was thinking with cold fear about his own son. Rado wouldn't hesitate to kill a child. Only the fact that Tonio was watched made him hopeful that the boy would be safe. He frowned. "Damn! I forgot to get with Longfellow on the note Hayes Carson found!"

"It won't help," Banks said. "I phoned her, just to check. She said it was a telephone number. The victim's."

"Damn."

"Yes. But when we serve this warrant on Rado, we may get all we need. I've put everything but the kitchen sink on the list of things I want to search."

John chuckled. "Wise man. Need backup?"

"Not really." Banks grinned as he stood up. "The two patrol officers are also on the SWAT team." He raised his eyebrows. "It would be totally cool if Rado decided to resist."

"Bad Ranger," John said, shaking his finger at the man.

Banks just chuckled.

John was working on an assault case. A young woman's boyfriend had gone after her at the restaurant where she waitressed after they broke up, argued with her and assaulted her with his fists. Customers broke it up, but she was bruised and broken and terrified. He'd been pulled off her by customers and the manager just in time to save her from being strangled to death. The boyfriend yelled that he'd kill her next time as he ran out the door. The manager had called 911. SAPD, overwhelmed with gang violence, had requested a Ranger to help find the young man.

The boyfriend had fought free from the customers as soon as he heard sirens coming closer. John had interviewed customers, along with the patrol officer who'd responded and a detective assigned to the case. He was tracking the boy down, slowly, through friends and family.

He sat at a traffic light with the engine idling. Out the window, he saw a blonde woman in nursing scrubs walking along the sidewalk toward a clothing store. Blonde, like Sunny. His heart jumped. The light changed and he moved slowly ahead. But when he got even with the woman, it wasn't Sunny. He ground his teeth together and drove on. He'd missed her so much. It was like losing an arm. If only he hadn't jumped to conclusions and shot his mouth off.

He really was the way Tonio had once described him: an avalanche when he got going. Looking back, he knew that Sunny had no real attraction to Hollister. They were friends. He'd been the detective on her case. They'd had years to get involved if there was any interest there. But there wasn't. He'd let jealousy prod him into an unwarranted outburst, and now he'd lost her. Maybe if he'd been less judgmental, maybe if he'd tried to talk to Tonio instead of at him about Sunny, maybe, maybe, maybe . . .

He'd had to go by the children's hospital one night on a case. Sunny had been in the hall when he walked toward the emergency room. She'd seen him and gone straight into the women's restroom to avoid him. His heart had sunk into his boots. The look on her face had been one of shame, embarrassment, anguish. He'd hurt her so badly that she wouldn't go near him anymore. That was when he lost hope.

It could have been so different. He drew in a long breath and drove on to the next witness's house. Looking back would serve no purpose. He had to go on, no matter how much it hurt.

Tonio had noticed that Sunny hardly smiled anymore. She had hot chocolate with him after school most days when she was working. She worried about Rado and gossip that he was about to be interrogated in the murder cases. She didn't want anything to happen to Tonio. But she was sad.

He wished he could do something to cheer her up. His dad had been morose lately, too. He never smiled. He went to work. He came home. He watched the news and went to bed. He made no more overtures toward Tonio. It was as if he lived alone now.

Adele had remarked about the sad change in Tonio's parent. He'd been so happy lately, she remarked, as if he had the world at his feet. Then, so suddenly, he was quiet and somber and dead inside. She wondered what had happened to change him so much.

Tonio knew. His father had loved the woman, whoever she was. Tonio had made a scene and acted like a spoiled brat. He'd run away, scared his dad. Now his father had given up the woman he wanted. Tonio had what he thought he wanted. But he didn't. He and his father were so apart that they hardly spoke to each other. Tonio felt guilt like a brand on him. He could have given the woman a chance. She might not have been like the other one. He'd never know. And he still had no idea how he could introduce Sunny to his father. If he could just meet her, he might find her as fascinating as Tonio did.

"You're very quiet," Sunny remarked.

He grimaced. "I did a stupid thing," he said. "My dad liked this woman. I made threats. I ran away." He made a face. "Now Dad won't even talk to me. He walks around like a zombie. He never smiles. It's like his heart died or something."

Sunny knew exactly how that felt. She was the same. "We hope for things in life," she said quietly. "But sometimes, God has other plans for us." She smiled sadly. "Tonio, I may be moving soon."

"What?" he exclaimed. His expression was one of pure horror. "Sunny, you can't," he said miserably. "You're the only real friend I've got. What will I do if you go away?" he asked, fighting a lump in his throat.

That was very flattering. She managed a smile. "It isn't definite," she said, trying to wipe that horrible expression off his face. She didn't want to hurt him. But she couldn't stay here once she started showing. "It's just an idea . . ."

"Please don't go," he said, and his big brown eyes glimmered with unshed tears. "Please don't."

"Tonio," she began, grinding her teeth together. "Things have happened in my life," she began. "I'm not sure what I'll do. But I have to make some changes. Listen, even if I go, I'll be as close as the telephone. We can text each other. We can talk. I'm not leaving you. Honest."

The panic died down a little with those words. He drew in a breath. It might not be as bad as he feared. "Okay," he said after a minute.

"Don't worry so," she said. "We don't control anything, really. Life just happens, you know?"

He sighed. "I guess it does."

The next day after school, Rado confronted him in the parking lot. The man was raging mad.

"Somebody ratted me out," he said icily. "They took hairs from my dog. They got blood and a pair of my sneakers. If you had anything to do with this, I'll make you pay. I'll make everyone around you pay!"

Tonio's heart raced. "Please, don't hurt Sunny," he pleaded. "Do anything you want to me, but leave her alone!"

"The nurse?" he laughed coldly. "I owe her already, for threatening me. She talked to that cop. Didn't think I'd find out, did you? I got people everywhere! She went on a date with him, but it wasn't a date. She was passing information. Where'd she get it, Tonio? From you? And where the hell are David and Tina Lopez?" he added, moving closer.

"I don't know," he said, flustered.

Rado kept coming. He grabbed Tonio by the front of his jacket and drew back his fist. "I ought to — !"

"Let him alone!" Sunny said, moving toward them. She had her phone out. "I just put in 911," she said, holding it up. "I push the button and you go up for assault! I'll testify! So will Tonio!"

Rado let Tonio go with a jerk of his hand. His eyes danced with fury. "I'll get you," he said harshly. "And nobody will know. I got ways. I can off you and make it look like suicide. I know how!"

"Be my guest," Sunny dared. She even smiled.

He threw off a couple of curses, motioned to his friends in the distance and stalked off.

"He means it," Tonio said worriedly. "Sunny, he'll hurt you!"

"I'll call Cal Hollister," she assured him. She was shaking inside, but she forced a smile. "Now let's have some hot chocolate. It's cold out here!"

Tonio went with her. He worried all the way into the hospital. If anything happened to Sunny, he'd just die.

"Rado did what?" John asked the man he had watching Tonio.

"He was about to hit the kid," Chet Billings, one of Eb Scott's men, said coldly. "I started toward them when the blonde woman pulled out her phone and threatened Rado with the police. He cursed her and Tonio and went off with his gang." He shook his head. "He means it. You watch that boy on the ranch. Rado really does have people everywhere."

"I've got good people on the ranch," John said. "Some were feds. They know how to secure the place. A blonde woman?"

He nodded. "Tonio seems to know her."

"He mentioned a woman to me. She got him in touch with a policeman," John recalled. "He told the cop what he wouldn't tell me, about Rado and his connection to the Lopez boy and his sister," he added coldly.

"Marquez says he's zeroing in on the rogue cop. He thinks he knows who it is." He shook his head. "Sad case, the man's two years away from retirement. He should never have gotten mixed up with Rado."

"Neither should my son," John said heavily. "Well, Banks says he thinks they have enough proof to put Rado away. They're rechecking samples at the forensics lab this evening. Tomorrow Banks plans to make the arrest. If he's right, and he can prove it, they may link Rado to Melinda McCarthy's murder two years ago."

"Rado would look good behind bars," Chet said.

"My thoughts exactly. Don't let Tonio out of your sight tomorrow," he added. "I've got a bad feeling about this. Rado's going to be out for blood."

"Tell me about it," Chet agreed. "I won't let the boy get hurt. I promise you."

John managed a faint smile. "I know you won't."

That night, when Sunny got home, she had an odd feeling that she was being watched. She laughed silently at her own thoughts. It had been a long shift, with several emergencies. She was just tired.

She put up her coat and her purse and went into the bedroom to change clothes. The last thing she remembered was walking through the door . . .

It was odd that Sunny was late for work. Tonio knew that she was supposed to be on duty today, and she hadn't seemed sick the day before. He was worried. Rado had made threats. What if he'd done something to her?

He was concerned enough to go up to the floor where she worked and talk to a nurse that he knew was friendly with her, Merrie York.

Merrie was talking to another nurse. Her eyes were red. Tonio had a very bad feeling.

"Have you seen Sunny?" he asked Merrie, watching the supervisor warily, because he wasn't supposed to be up here.

Merrie tried to smile. "You're her friend," she said. "You're Tonio."

"Yeah," he said. "She's not downstairs. She's always early. She's supposed to work today, isn't she?"

Merrie drew in a breath. "Tonio, they've taken her to the trauma center at Marshall Memorial —"

"What?" he exclaimed, and lowered his voice quickly. He was terrified. "Did Rado do something to her? He threatened her . . . !"

"They say it was a suicide attempt. She's not conscious."

"She wouldn't commit suicide. It was Rado! I know it was! I have to go see her," he said. His brown eyes were tragic. "Please! Please! I have to see her!"

Merrie grimaced. "Wait right there." Merrie spoke to her supervisor and went to get her coat and purse. "Come with me," she told Tonio. "We'll both go. Don't you have a cousin who works in the office?"

"I ride home with her," he said.

"Rosa, right?" Merrie punched in numbers on her cell phone as they got to the elevator. "Rosa, Tonio's going to Marshall Memorial with me. Sunny's just been taken there. No, I don't know how bad it is. I'll call you when we get back, okay? Sure."

She turned to Tonio. "She says she'll wait downstairs for you when she gets off work."

"Will they let me see her?" Tonio asked plaintively, because he knew about hospital rules.

"I know several nurses at the main hospital," she said, smiling reassuringly. "I'll work it out."

As it turned out, the nurse in charge of ICU, where Sunny was now, was a friend of Merrie's who'd worked at the children's hospital for a number of years before transferring over here.

She sighed as she registered Tonio's quiet anguish. "This is highly irregular," she began.

"She's like my mother," Tonio pleaded. "Just let me see her, even just for a minute. Please?" His big brown eyes were poignant.

The nurse grimaced. "Okay, but if anybody finds out they'll hang me with a bedsheet."

"Thanks!" Tonio said huskily.

"From me, too," Merrie added. "How is she?"

"Not good," the nurse said quietly as she led the way down the hall to a cubicle. "They're running blood work, but it looks very much like an overdose."

"A suicide attempt?" Merrie asked, horrified. "But she's the least suicidal person I've ever known!"

"Sunny would never kill herself. She's religious. It was Rado," Tonio said solemnly. "He threatened her. He said he could make it look like suicide if he killed her. She told a detective what he'd done," he added. "She wouldn't kill herself," Tonio said firmly. "I know she wouldn't."

"You should talk to the police," the supervisor said.

"I'll call them right now," Merrie assured her. "Tonio can talk to them later. I'll be in the waiting room. Thanks, Mildred," she added, smiling at the supervisor.

"You owe me," Mildred teased.

Merrie just grinned.

Tonio went inside the cubicle. Sunny was unconscious, hooked up to several machines. There was a drip going in her arm. He went next to the bed, and put his book bag in a chair. He brushed back her tangled blond hair and stifled tears.

"Oh, Sunny," he said, his voice breaking. "I'm so sorry!"

John Ruiz had gone by Hollister's office after he finished tracking down the man who'd assaulted the woman in the restaurant. He wanted answers.

"Why are you dating Sunny?" he asked bluntly.

Hollister just stared at him, surprised. "I'm not."

"You were dancing with her at Fernando's," John said belligerently.

Hollister sighed. "She has a friend, a young boy," he said. "He told her that Rado has someone in my department, a mole, who works for him. She didn't dare meet me at the hospital, because Rado has people watching her. So we danced and she gave me what information she had."

John relaxed. "I see." Now he understood where Banks had gotten his information. And he felt worse than ever.

"You idiot," Hollister said. "She's crazy about you. She and I are friends. That's all it ever was."

John ground his teeth together. He'd really messed up. He drew in a harsh breath. "Banks got a warrant yesterday to get biological samples from Rado. He said the man threatened vengeance on everybody, especially the boy who told."

"A very brave young man," Hollister said.

"I don't even know who he is, but Sunny does. She says he's like family to her."

"Any luck on finding the mole?" he asked.

"Marquez fingered him about an hour ago, through a CI," he added, indicating a Confidential Informant.

"That's one good thing," he said. "How about the Lopez family?"

Hollister's eyes twinkled. "Don't you know Tom Smart, over at the Marshals' office?"

"I know him."

"He might tell you," he said. "I'm not allowed to. Privileged info, and I gave my word."

John's heart lifted. He'd been concerned about the boy and his sister. This indicated that the US Marshals had them hidden, safe from Rado. "State's evidence?"

Hollister chuckled. "I can't say."

John smiled. "Okay."

"I'll see if —" His phone rang. He picked it up. "Yes?" Hollister stood up. "When?" He listened, wincing. "Is your CI sure? That little punk!" he exclaimed. "I'll have him picked up right now. I'll send someone to her apartment to check on her. Yes. Yes.

Okay." He hung up. "Rado threatened Sunny's life," he said. "We've got a witness who heard Rado bragging about offing a nurse. He's being picked up and I'm going to send someone over to check on Sunny right now!"

"I'll go," John said at once. He was out the door before Hollister got another word out.

Rado. John was furious. Sunny and her young friend had stirred up a hornet's nest with what they knew. Rado wouldn't hesitate to kill her. He hoped she had her doors locked and her phone handy.

She might not let him in, but he wanted to know that she was all right. He'd see if Hollister could spare someone to watch her. Alternatively, John could get one of his people to do it. He couldn't bear the thought of anything happening to her. Sunny was the most important person in his life, next to Tonio, even if she hated him.

He pulled up at her apartment building and went to knock on the door. Her neighbor was just coming out of his unit.

"Something going on there," the old man told John, nodding at Sunny's door. "Three boys came running out of there about ten

343

minutes ago. I called 911. You the police?"

"Texas Rangers," John said. "Is she home?" he asked quickly.

He nodded. "Heard the television going earlier."

"Thanks. I may need a statement from you," he added, feeling apprehension like a chill.

"I'm just off to the store. Be back in a few minutes. I'll help if I can."

"Okay." John was banging at the door, but Sunny didn't answer. He tried the door. Locked.

He vaguely remembered her concern about a loose screen on a window in her apartment. On a hunch, he went around back. The screen was torn, the window was wide open.

His heart raced as he climbed in the window. "Sunny!" he called. "Sunny!"

But she didn't answer. As he walked into the living room, he saw why. He whipped out his phone and punched in 911, gave the information and got an ambulance rolling.

He unlocked the front door and opened it, going at once back to Sunny, to kneel beside her prone body. He phoned for a detective and a forensic team to come with the ambulance. There was a syringe still sticking in her arm and she was unconscious. Her heartbeat was weaker than he'd have liked, but she was breathing normally, if a little slowly.

He couldn't rouse her. There was only a trace of liquid in the syringe. He took photos with his cell phone, detailing everything while he waited for help to arrive. It kept him from going crazy as he worried about her condition.

He was remembering two other victims of Rado's wrath, Melinda McCarthy and Harry Lopez. Both had been found exactly as Sunny was now, overdosed from apparent suicide. Except this time, Rado had made threats and bragged about killing a nurse, and a neighbor had seen three men running out of Sunny's apartment. Apparently this had just happened, thank God, which meant Sunny might yet be saved.

If only the damned ambulance would hurry! John had hung up on the 911 operator because he had to take pix of the crime scene — because it was definitely a crime scene. The needle was in Sunny's right arm and she was right-handed. Rado had made a second fatal error by not knowing which hand his victim used. With any luck, he could put him away for life, especially with the evidence Banks had already collected.

But Sunny was in desperate condition. He

couldn't move her. He looked at her face and groaned aloud. If she died, and she could, how would he go on living? The last memory of him she had would be of him raging at her, shouting that she was a two-timing flirt and that he was only playing with her.

The sound of sirens finally came close. He went to the door to motion to the policeman who accompanied the ambulance and assured him that it was safe for the EMTs to come in. But he cautioned the officer about procedure. Only essential personnel inside, keep a record of who came and went and what time and assist detectives when they arrived with canvassing neighbors. It was a crime scene. He especially wanted the neighbor next door questioned, because he'd seen three men running from Sunny's apartment and he'd called 911. There would be a record on file of the call.

An SAPD detective showed up while the EMTs worked on Sunny. They had no idea what drug was used. The detective stood by while the crime unit, quickly responding, collected evidence, including the syringe, which had traces of the drug in it. The detective promised John that it would go to the crime lab at once to be processed, so that they'd know what was used on her.

By the time they loaded Sunny onto the ambulance, John had called his lieutenant and requested a Ranger to relieve him, because he was going to the hospital with Sunny. He added that this would almost certainly tie Rado to attempted murder. Lieutenant Avery said he'd phone Banks and have him go to the crime lab to wait for test results. He knew about John's involvement with Sunny through Banks. He added that he hoped she'd be fine. So did John.

They took her into a cubicle where a doctor worked on getting her stabilized. But not knowing what drug was used, they could do very little for the time being. She was sent to ICU to be observed while the crime lab pinpointed the drug. She was still unconscious.

John went with her to ICU, bypassing staff and security people alike. He was going to make sure that nobody could get to her while they struggled to save her life.

The truth was that he wasn't about to leave her, for any reason. They'd have to take him out feet first, he told the supervisor.

She just sighed and let him into the room.

■ ■ ■ ■

He sat with her, agonizing over her condition. He held the soft hand that wasn't being fed fluids through a drip and turned it over in his big one.

"You have to get well," he said huskily. "I've screwed up everything, but I love you, *rubia.* You have to get better so I can apologize, on my knees if you want me to. I don't want to spend the rest of my life alone." He stared down at her hand. "I've been an idiot, Sunny. You have to live, so you can forgive me." He drew in a long breath. *"Mi alma,"* he whispered, his voice breaking. *"¡Mi vida, mi corazon, sin ti, no tengo nada!"*

He bent over her hand in silent anguish. If only he could go back and unsay the things he'd said. She had to live. She had to!

It was agonizing to see her like this. Sunny, so happy and bright and alive, smiling up at him as they rode in the SUV, lying so soft and sweet in his arms while he loved her.

He touched his mouth to her hand and closed his eyes, praying for all he was worth. The cold fear in his stomach boiled up, almost choking him. He fought the damp-

348

ness in his black eyes as he stared helplessly at her prone body.

One more chance, he thought silently. *I'd give anything for one more chance,* rubia, *to keep you in my life. Because without you,* mi alma, *I have no life!*

FOURTEEN

John left Sunny's cubicle just long enough to use the restroom and call Banks. He was drained of life, almost of hope. She hadn't stirred. He knew that, if he lost her, nothing would ever be right again. The color would spin out of the world forever.

"Anything new?" he asked in a subdued tone.

"Yes," Banks said. "The crime lab just identified the drug used on your friend. It was Propofol, the same as Harry Lopez and Melinda McCarthy. We just gave the information to the doctor on her case. They'll be able to counteract it, hopefully," he added. "All three were found with syringes in their arms, but if Rado did it and used a drip, he might have put the syringe in to cover what he did. And he has a house. He could have done it there, with Lopez and Melinda, and moved the bodies where they'd be found. He had privacy enough with Sunny, in her own apartment."

"Yes, and Melinda McCarthy was found with the needle in the wrong arm. So was Sunny, when they brought her in. Now if we can just connect Rado with a supply of the drug," John said harshly.

"We're working on that. Marquez has a contact at the DEA. He said they've identified their high-level mole, and they think he has ties with a pharmaceutical house. A lot of heads are about to roll."

"Good."

"I hope your friend will be all right," Banks added gently, because he knew how deadly the drug was.

"I'm almost positive that Rado did it," John said. "He threatened her. A witness saw three men running from her apartment and called 911 just before I got there to check on her. I'll bet money one of those men was Rado. SAPD has officers canvassing the neighborhood for witnesses."

"I'll offer assistance."

"Thanks," John said. He drew in a breath. "I asked the lieutenant for another Ranger to take over my cases today. I won't leave her, until we know something."

"Life is hard," Banks said.

"Harder than we'd like it, from time to time. I'll talk to you later."

"Sure."

He started back into the cubicle where they had Sunny when he saw something that stopped him in his tracks at the door.

Inside the cubicle, a young boy was brushing back Sunny's long hair and tears were running down his cheeks. The boy was Tonio, John's son.

He walked into the room, shock on his face.

Tonio looked up and grimaced. "Dad?" he asked, surprised.

"What are you doing in here?" John asked.

"Sunny's friend Merrie got me in," the boy said, dashing away tears. "Rado did this. I know he did this! He threatened her. He was about to punch me and she got between us and called 911 on her phone. He went away, but he said he'd get her. He said he knew how to do it, so it would look like an overdose," he added, tears even in his voice. "She can't die, Dad," he said. His lower lip trembled and tears spilled out. "She's my best friend. She's like . . . Mom was . . ."

His voice broke.

John pulled him into his arms and held him tight, rocking him. "It was you," he said gruffly. "You told Hollister about Rado, about the Lopez boy and his sister!"

"It was me," Tonio said unsteadily. He hugged his dad back. The comfort was new and sweet.

"You brave kid," his father said softly. "You brave boy! I'm so proud of you!"

Tonio forced a smile as he drew away. "I wanted to tell you. But if I had, you'd have known David was in Los Diablos Lobitos, and he was my best friend. I didn't want to get him killed. Rado threatened him, too. He threatened her." He looked at Sunny with his heart in his eyes. "She can't die. She just can't!"

"The crime lab identified the drug that was used on her," John said. "They'll find a way to counteract it. She won't die." He hoped, he prayed, that he was right.

Tonio drew in a deep breath. He felt hopeful again. He turned, and then he frowned. "Dad, why are you in here?" he asked. "Is it because you're working the case?"

"Partially."

"Partially?"

John went to the bed and sat down beside it, holding Sunny's limp hand in his. "But mostly, because I'm in love with her, Tonio," he said quietly.

Tonio's face broke into a huge smile. "With Sunny?" he exclaimed.

John saw the boy's expression and registered it with surprise. "Yes."

"I wanted so much to introduce you to her," Tonio confessed. "I thought, if you knew her like I did, you'd love her like I did. Well, sort of like I did. She's like Mom," he added huskily.

"She's very like your mother," John agreed. "She was the woman I wanted to bring home, to introduce to you."

"I love Sunny," Tonio said. "And I'm sorry. I can't think of anybody I'd rather have as my mother. I mean, if you were thinking you might want to marry her," he blurted out.

"I want to marry her, all right," he said. He grimaced. "If she'll have me. I got jealous because she went dancing with Hollister. I said some mean things to her. I broke up with her." His eyes closed. "I was afraid you'd run away again. I love Sunny very much, but I love you more." He didn't look at the boy as he said it. "I couldn't bear to lose either one of you."

Tonio felt as if he owned the whole world. "Thanks, Dad," he said very gently. "I'm sorry I've been such a pain. I'm going to straighten up. Honest I am. You have to make up with her," he added.

John forced a smile. "I'm going to work very hard at that, when she gets better."

"She will get better. Won't she?" the boy asked worriedly.

"She has to," John replied.

It took a long time to bring Sunny out of the drug-induced unconsciousness. She was groggy and barely lucid when they revived her. By then, Tonio had been run out of the room and was on his way back to the ranch with Rosa. He'd made John promise to tell Sunny he'd been there with her.

But Sunny wouldn't speak to John. The detective working her case, from SAPD, came in to speak with her. She was polite to him. She ignored John. The emotional wounds he'd given her weren't so easily treated.

She was frightened about the baby, but they'd done labs to make sure the fetus wasn't harmed. She'd been lucky. Fortunately, nobody had mentioned the baby to John. She'd asked.

John didn't want to give up on Sunny, but she wouldn't talk to him and he had to go back to work. He gave heartfelt gratitude to the doctor who'd worked on her. At least she was going to live, even if she hated him.

He called the ranch and had one of his men come up and stay in the waiting room, to make sure Rado didn't try to get to her again and finish what he'd started.

But in fact, Rado was running. His high-level DEA contact was now in custody facing multiple charges, and two members of Rado's gang had been picked up. One of them was considering giving state's evidence, because he'd been with Rado in Sunny's apartment. He didn't want to go to prison, so Hollister had a man working on him with promises of a lighter sentence. John also was fairly certain that the Lopez brother and sister were with the US Marshals and likely to testify against Rado as well. If they did, it might even mean the end of the gang, with so many members of it facing attempted murder charges. Only one gang, but a vicious one. It would be good to see it ended.

Beyond that, John could only think of Sunny. He was glad that she would live, but she wouldn't talk to him. He heard from Rosa, who knew Merrie York, that Sunny had no memory whatsoever of anything that happened after she walked into her apartment. She couldn't testify to her assailants because her memory of the incident was wiped clean. That was, John had been told by her doctor, one of the side effects of the drug. She'd been very lucky. If she hadn't been found in time, she'd likely have died.

■ ■ ■ ■

Sunny was back at work two days later. Tonio had brought her another yellow rose in a small vase. He hugged her and hugged her.

"Did they tell you I was there?" he asked. "Miss York went with me and got the supervisor to let me into the room with you. I was so scared!"

She hugged him back, tears running down her cheeks. She was very emotional these days, with the changes in her body that the baby was making. "Merrie told me," she said, laying her cheek on his dark, cool hair. "Thanks for caring so much." Her voice broke.

He hugged her harder. "Dad's got somebody watching you," he said.

She pulled away. "Your father has? Why?" she asked. She didn't even know his father.

"Because Rado's still on the loose," he said. "It's a man who works for Eb Scott. Dad borrowed him to watch you and me. I'm safe with Rosa; she's got a gun and she knows how to shoot. She was a policewoman before she took the job in the office here," he added proudly. "She isn't scared of anything. Like you," he added with a shy smile.

"Well!" she said. "That's very nice of your dad."

"He's not so bad," he said, smiling. "He was proud of me, for telling on Rado."

"So was I," she replied, returning the smile. "You're the bravest young man I've ever known."

"Sunny. I'm the only young man you know," he teased.

She laughed. "Not true. I have patients your age on my ward. Speaking of which," she added, checking her watch and grimacing, "I have to go on duty. I'll see you tomorrow. Thanks for this." She held up the rose. "It was really sweet of you."

"You're very welcome. See you tomorrow."

He watched her go with soft, affectionate eyes. Maybe knowing his dad cared enough to have her watched would help heal the breach between them.

He didn't know, of course, that Sunny had no idea who his father really was, because Tonio hadn't been in the room when she regained consciousness, and she hadn't let John speak to her. She wasn't about to walk into that trap again. He was only playing. He'd said so.

He'd been so angry when she'd gone out with Hollister. She was still steamed that he hadn't even given her a chance to defend herself. But what would it matter? He only wanted a good time. She wasn't in any shape to be a man's midnight snack, in her present condition. And she had plans to make because of that.

It would be a wrench to leave Tonio, but she had to get out of San Antonio before she started showing. John was in and out of the children's hospital on cases, and it was inevitable that eventually he'd see her. She didn't want pity from him, or worse, have to refuse a termination if he decided he didn't want a child. He'd told her he had a son, but she didn't really believe it. He just wanted a reason to drop her. It was an emotional blow like nothing she'd ever known. But she'd get through it. Just as she'd gotten through a murder attempt.

To her credit, nobody believed she'd tried to commit suicide. Hollister called to check on her and told her how John had rushed out of his office to see about her and found her in her apartment. She probably owed John her life. He'd been very jealous of the captain of detectives, Hollister had added with some amusement.

She'd replied that it was more complicated

than that, although she was grateful to him for saving her life. What were they going to do about Rado? she added.

"We're working on that," he assured her. "He's on the defensive now. He's running for his life. I have Father Eduardo watching out for him in his territory. Los Serpientes is giving him a bit of help. He's best friends with the leader of the gang in Houston, and also with the leader here."

"With a gang leader?" she exclaimed.

"He isn't your typical gang leader," Hollister chuckled. "Serpientes are keen on children and senior citizens. They've been known to 'adopt' such people and protect them from other gangs. It's a sad fact of life that many families have no choice but to live in gang territory because they don't have enough money for a less poverty-stricken area of town."

"That's really something," she said. "I didn't know gangs ever did anything except steal and kill."

"Most of them do. There are notable exceptions."

"What about Tonio's friend?" she asked suddenly. "David?"

"He's safe," Hollister replied. "That's all I can say. I'm more worried about you, with Rado running loose."

"This is really strange. I told you about Tonio's dad, the absent father who never pays attention to his son, remember? Well, he's having Tonio watched because of Rado. He's also having me watched, for my own protection, and I've never met the man!"

Hollister laughed. "At least he seems to be taking an interest in his son," he agreed. "I don't even know Tonio's last name."

"Neither do I. I never asked. He's a really good kid," she added softly. "He brings me roses."

"Nice manners."

She grinned to herself. "He says I'm like his late mother. Poor woman, to live with a man like Tonio's dad, who's too busy working to pay him any attention. Well, except now, when he's in danger. I guess it shows that he does care about the child."

"Apparently. You watch your back. I told you about the three suspects running from your apartment after you were drugged. One of them has been positively identified as Rado."

"I don't understand why I don't remember any of it," she said. "The doctor says the drug wipes your mind clean." She shook her head. "Imagine anybody using something like that deliberately. I've never even smoked a marijuana cigarette!"

"Good on you," he said, a smile in his voice. "You know, Ruiz went out my door like a twister when I said you were in danger."

She bit her lower lip. "He yelled at me," she said miserably. "He said he was only playing, that he never meant anything he said to me." She sighed. "He said a lot of things, all of them hurtful."

"Men go a little crazy when they get jealous of another man," he said gently. "Sometimes they lie, to save their pride."

She was certain that John didn't. He wasn't the type. "I think he meant every word of it," she said quietly. "He's gorgeous, you know? He could have any beautiful woman he wanted. Why would he want somebody as plain as me?"

"Sunny," he chided gently, "don't sell yourself short. You're not plain."

"Thanks," she replied, and forced a laugh. "I really did need that."

"You watch your back, until we pick up Rado," he said. "He's going up for capital murder if we can connect him to Melinda McCarthy's murder, and I think we can. We've got some of his people pleading to turn state's evidence in return for lessened sentences, and we've traced the drug he used on you to a pharmaceutical company that had dealings with the rogue DEA agent they just picked up. Things are happening at a pretty fast rate. Rado has nothing to lose now."

"I'll be careful," she promised. "Thanks for the information."

"You're welcome. Tell your young friend I'd be very proud to have a son like him," he added. "My wife was sterile. We never had a child."

"I'm sorry for your loss," she said, recalling that his wife had died some years ago.

"It wasn't that sort of marriage," he said curtly. "I'd just come home from overseas and I was loaded. She loved the money. That's all she wanted from me."

"That must have been a painful thing to live with."

"Painful," he agreed. He drew in a breath. "But I had ulterior motives, too. I married her to get even with a woman who loved me." He bit off the words, as if they were almost painful. "More fool me. You never know people from a distance."

"So they say." She hesitated. "Cal, I may move to Houston," she said. "You don't think Rado would follow me there, do you? Or have somebody try to get to me?"

He hesitated. "Listen, if he knows the effects of the drug, and I'm sure he does, he'll know that you have nothing on him. You'd only be able to testify that he threatened Tonio. He'll be more concerned with any of his gang that might sell him out. We've almost surely got him for Melinda McCarthy's murder. The drug alone would convict him if we can get his DEA contact to sell him out. And I think we can. We can link him to a supply of it and his gang members we arrested will link him to the actual murder. He'll go up for capital murder. Death penalty stuff," he added solemnly.

"Somebody else will just take over the gang," she said sadly.

"I don't really think so. We've got too many of them facing stiff prison sentences. The only ones left are juvies, and we're going to get Father Eduardo involved with them. With any luck at all, we may be able to turn them."

"That would be nice, that something good could come out of all this."

"I believe it will. But just in case, keep your eyes open. Tonio's really in more danger than you are, because he knows more and he's told it to the law. That puts him on the firing line."

"His dad's having him watched," she reminded him.

"Yes, but by whom? If it's just a fellow

businessman, he won't have much protection."

"Could you have someone keep an eye on him?" she asked.

"I don't have the people," he said apologetically. "We're stretched to the limit already. But I can talk to Father Eduardo. I suspect that he'd know someone."

"One of the Serpientes," she mused.

"They're really not so bad," he replied. "In fact, I was much worse, some years ago," he added flatly. "So don't sell them short. They're all human beings. They have families that they love and they protect the helpless."

"Maybe they can change my mind," she said, smiling. "It's just that I see so many children come in here, victims of gang violence."

"I see it, too. One day, we'll wear them down in court."

"I hope so. Thanks for everything."

"Why do you want to move to Houston?" he asked suddenly.

Her heart jumped. She couldn't tell him the truth. "I just want a change," she said.

"Ruiz," he guessed.

Her indrawn breath gave her away.

"Pain is portable, Sunny," he said wisely. "And I'd know. Just FYI."

"I'll consider that. Talk to you soon."
"Sure."

She told Tonio the next day about what Hollister had said.

"Your dad may have somebody good," she said, not wanting to hurt his feelings, "but Hollister says that a priest he knows can have somebody protect you."

"Really?" he asked. "Who?"

She hesitated.

He cocked his head and pursed his lips. "Sunny?" he prodded.

She shifted. "He's best friends with the leader of the Serpientes . . ."

"That gang." He smiled. "David's grandmother lives in their territory. She got mugged. They hunted down the guy that did it, got her money back, tied him up and called the police. The cops found him sitting on a street corner, tied to a telephone pole with a note on him telling what he'd done." He laughed.

She laughed, too. "Well!"

"So they're not so bad. But this guy dad's got, he's pretty good."

"If you say so. I just think the more people watching, the safer you'll be," she added gently. "But it's nice, that your father cares that you're in danger."

"He said he'd let his job obsess him. He never turns off his cell phone. He gets called all hours when there's trouble." He sighed. "But he really cares about me. Things have been different since you got hurt."

Her eyebrows lifted. "How so?"

He frowned. "You don't know who my dad is?"

"Listen —"

The intercom blasted away, calling for Sunny.

"Gosh, I have to run," she said. "That's my case they're referring to," she added, indicating the intercom. "I hope my little patient hasn't gone into cardiac arrest again. He's just out of open heart surgery. I have to run!"

"See you tomorrow," he called after her.

She threw up a hand and kept going.

"Sunny said what?" John asked Tonio at the supper table, smiling.

"She said a priest that Hollister knows was going to have one of the Serpientes watch me, too," he replied, chuckling. "She thinks you're an overworked businessman who doesn't know how to hire protection."

He sighed. "Well, she doesn't know I'm your father, either, right?"

"I started to tell her, but she was called to

367

the ward on an urgent case," he said. He grinned at his father. "She really cares about me."

"I really care about you, too," his father said, and smiled.

Tonio smiled back. It was nice, this new relationship he had with his dad. "She said that I was in more danger than she was, because Rado said things I could testify to in court," he added.

"That's very likely true," John said, picking at his food. "But he's facing much more serious charges in a cold case Banks and I are working on. I don't think you're in a lot of danger." He smiled. "But just in case, Billings has you in sight most of the time."

"Rado is a rat," he said curtly. "I hope they lock him up forever. He threatened Sunny the day before she was brought in with that drug overdose. And he told me that he'd done it before, that he knew how to get away with killing somebody and making it look like suicide."

John, who was hearing this for the first time, was dumbfounded. "You didn't tell me that," he said.

"We didn't talk, Dad," Tonio replied. He smiled. "You're different now. I can tell you stuff that I couldn't, before. I was afraid if I told you about David, and you found out he was in the wolves gang, you'd make me stay away from him. He was the only real friend I had, now that Jake's so involved in stuff at school in Jacobsville."

"We can't go back," John said. "I don't know what I'd have done. But whatever it was, it would have been to protect you."

"David's going to be okay, isn't he? And Tina, too? She was so sweet to me."

"I can't find out much about them," John replied. "But the US Marshals are involved. That pretty much means they're being hidden and protected. If they turn state's evidence, the Marshals can set them up in a whole new life, somewhere else."

"I want them to be safe. I'll miss David." He sighed, moving potatoes around on his plate. "I have Sunny, but she's talking about moving to Houston."

John caught his breath. "She's what?" he asked, horrified.

"She says she wants to move away. I wish she'd change her mind. She's the only real friend I have left, Dad. I really love her."

John felt worse than ever. Sunny was so hurt that she didn't even want to stay in the same city with him. His pride was so low that it was even with his boots. He'd wounded her with his stupid outburst. He hadn't even given her a chance to explain what really happened between her and Hollister. Then he'd compounded his sins by lying and telling her he just wanted a night in her bed, that he wasn't serious.

"I thought she was dating Hollister," John said miserably. "They went to a nightclub together."

"It was just so she could tell him about that crooked cop Rado knew at SAPD," Tonio replied. "She said they couldn't do it anywhere else without Rado suspecting. But he knew anyway, so it was a waste of time."

John was miserable. "Hollister told me that."

"You ought to talk to Sunny," Tonio said. "Maybe if you did, she wouldn't want to go away."

"She won't talk to me, Tonio," John replied sadly. "I tried. If she even sees me, she goes the other way."

"She's so sad lately," the boy said. "She almost never smiles. It wasn't like that before. She was so happy that she almost glowed. Like you," he added. "I'm sorry I messed things up. If I'd known it was Sunny you were seeing, I'd have been over the moon. It's all my fault."

"It's not," John said gently. "You didn't know. And it wasn't your fault, it was mine. I jumped to conclusions and said a lot of hurtful things that she can't forget."

"She thinks she's plain," Tonio replied. "But she's not. She's beautiful. I take her roses," he added with a grin. "She loves yellow ones." His eyebrows arched. "Maybe if you took her roses, she'd forgive you."

"Think so?" He laughed. "I'm afraid it will take more than roses. But I'll try. I promise. I'll try."

"Okay, Dad." Tonio finished his milk. "I'd better get on my homework."

That was surprising. He usually had to be nagged about it.

Tonio saw his father's expression and a mischievous look flared on his face. "I really want to get on the soccer team. Remember what you promised? I get my grades up and you buy me a nice uniform."

John laughed heartily. "I meant it, too." He cocked his head. "Someday you and I will have a talk about how things really are here."

"What things?"

"Not now. Later."

"Okay."

John thought about what Tonio had said. Roses. It might work. On the other hand, Sunny was just as likely to throw them at him.

He wondered why she wanted to leave town. It made no sense. And she was still in some danger from Rado. It wouldn't be safe for her to get out of San Antonio. She'd listen to Hollister. Maybe he could persuade her. When time permitted, John was going to go and ask him to. He no longer had bad feelings toward the captain of detectives. As long as he didn't want Sunny, John didn't mind asking him for help.

Banks was grinning from ear to ear when John walked into his office. "We did it."

"Did what?"

"We tied Rado to the DEA mole, tied him to the pharmaceutical company where the drug was produced and even convinced an eyewitness to the McCarthy murder to testify in court for a reduced sentence!"

"Nice work," John said heartily.

"Yes, and he can thank me for all the extra hours I put in that I was barely compensated for," Clancey called from the room she worked in, peering around the doorway at him.

"I did thank you," Banks shot back. "I let you leave five minutes early."

"Oh, gee, thanks, that's so helpful on my poverty-level budget!"

Banks made a face and waved her off. She

372

made a face back before she closed the door.

"Pest," Banks muttered. "I asked for a male assistant. The lieutenant hates me."

"Any word about Rado's whereabouts?" John added. "My son's on the firing line. Rado told him things that he repeated to Hollister."

Banks was recalling what he knew, about the kid who'd ratted out Rado. "Tonio. He's your son?" he asked, surprised.

John nodded. "He's my son. I'm very proud of him."

"So would I be," was the reply. "You've got somebody watching him, I hope?"

"One of Eb Scott's men," he said. "Chet Billings."

"Good shot," Banks said. "We had a hostage case years ago. We borrowed Billings. He took out the perp with one bullet."

"He trained as a sniper in the Army. He still does jobs for Eb Scott," John replied. "He's good at surveillance as well. I feel safer having him on the payroll, even temporarily."

"I don't think Rado will do much, to be honest," Banks said. "He's too busy trying to save himself from the needle. Ironic, isn't it? If we can convict him for Melinda's murder, he's likely to get the death penalty.

I know the DA plans to ask for it. Senator McCarthy is very pleased with our investigation. He said it will give him the first peace he's known since she was killed. And it will certainly prove that she didn't commit suicide."

"I'm happy for him," John said. He sighed. "Now if things would just work out for me."

"You saved her life," Banks reminded him. "That has to count for something."

He shrugged. "It won't even get her to talk to me," he said. "I smarted off when I thought she was dating Hollister and said some things she can't forgive."

"So, life goes on," Banks said philosophically.

"So it does."

John went back to work, downhearted and miserable. He loved his job, but it was no longer enough. He and Tonio were rebuilding their relationship. That was sweet. But he wanted Sunny. He needed her. He wished he could find some way to get back into her life. But it seemed hopeless. He'd never been so unhappy, not since Maria died.

FIFTEEN

Sunny was so sick that she didn't think she could make it to work. She really had to see an obstetrician pretty soon. Hiding her head in the sand wasn't going to make the baby go away. In fact, she didn't want him to go away. She was fascinated with the changes in her body, the knowledge that she had a tiny baby growing inside her. It was wondrous. She was so grateful that the drug Rado had given her hadn't caused her to lose it. That was a blessing. Probably a minor miracle as well.

But she couldn't stay in San Antonio. She'd filled out an online application for a children's hospital in Houston and she'd given references. It was a sad thing, but necessary. She was going to miss Tonio. She'd miss John, too, the playboy rat. She'd only been another conquest. She wondered if he'd settled his attentions on some new woman. Probably. Well, it didn't matter to

Sunny. She was going to start over, in a new city, with her baby. She'd been on her own for a long time. She could manage.

She went into work and there was Tonio, in the canteen.

"Hi," she said.

"Hi." He frowned. "Sunny, you look awful!"

She swallowed. "Some bug I caught, I guess. Oh, dear . . ." She left her coat and purse on the table and ran for the restroom.

Tonio waited, worried, until she reappeared, wiping her mouth with a paper towel from the bathroom. She sat down, but she looked like death warmed over.

"Sunny, you need to see a doctor," he said gently.

She swallowed down another bout of nausea. "I guess I do," she replied. She smiled, but it was an effort. "How's the hot chocolate?"

"It's not bad."

"I think I need something fizzy." She got a dollar bill and went to the machine, fed it in and got a ginger ale. She sipped it slowly as she sat back down. It did help the nausea, just a little.

Tonio was watching her closely. He was adding things up in his mind. His father had been with Sunny a lot. Tonio knew about pregnant women, because Adele had three children, all born since Tonio was in grammar school. Adele had thrown up a lot, and she'd look washed out like Sunny. What if Sunny was pregnant?

His eyes widened as he stared at her. "Sunny," he said gently, "is there a reason you're throwing up? Is that why you want to move to Houston, so that nobody here will know you're pregnant?"

As a wild shot, it was genius. Sunny flushed and then she burst into tears. "Oh, Tonio, it's such a mess," she wept. She wiped at her eyes with the paper towel. "I did a stupid thing. Stupid! He didn't want me. He was just out for a good time, he even said so. And here I am, like this, and I don't know what to do . . . I hate him!" she added harshly.

Tonio was grinning from ear to ear. He had to hide that smile, quickly, because she looked at him suspiciously.

"Why are you smiling?" she wanted to know.

"Sorry. I'm sorry about you. But I was thinking that I'm going to get to go out for soccer," he said suddenly. "Just a stray thought."

"Oh." She wiped her eyes. "You don't tell anybody, okay?"

"Don't go to Houston," he said.

"I have to. I sent in an application already." She wiped her eyes one last time and took one more sip of the ginger ale. "My mother would be so ashamed of me," she said, and started crying again.

"No, she wouldn't," Tonio said firmly. "People make mistakes."

"This is going to be one very large one, I'm afraid."

"Do you want it?"

"More than anything in the world, despite everything," she confessed. She managed a smile. "I'll get through it somehow. But I have to leave San Antonio. I can't explain. It's just . . . complicated."

"Well, you're not going right now, today, right?" he asked.

"Not today," she agreed.

"So, I'll see you tomorrow?"

She smiled. "You bet. You watch out for Rado," she added gently.

"You, too."

"I'm safe enough here. See you."

"See you."

She went to work and he pulled out his cell phone.

John was just finishing a report on a robbery he'd helped solve when he heard the tone for a text alert on his phone.

He took it out of the holder, read the message and burst out with such a cry of joy that his coworkers gaped at him.

He didn't say a word. He grabbed his hat and coat and ran out the door.

Sunny was just going on break when a tall man in a shepherd's coat and a Stetson suddenly came up to her, picked her up gently and started kissing her madly.

"What do you think you're — ?!" was all she got out.

He couldn't stop. He'd never been so happy in his life. She belonged to him. He was never letting her go again.

"Why didn't you tell me?" he asked against her soft mouth. "Never mind, I know now. It doesn't matter. I'm sorry." He kissed her again, aware of curious, amused stares all around them from her coworkers. "I'm sorry, I'm so sorry. Where do you want to get married? I'd prefer San Fernando, but I'll compromise. Just so long as we get married."

She was certain that she'd gone mad and she was hearing voices. She held on tight, afraid that he might drop her. But of course he didn't. He was so overjoyed that she was shocked. He didn't seem like a man who was just playing with her.

"I don't understand," she tried again.

His mouth settled tenderly on her lips. "You're pregnant," he whispered. "I'm so happy. Oh, God, it's like a miracle! You and a baby . . . !" He kissed her harder.

She kissed him back. She was beginning to realize that he actually meant it. He was happy about the baby. He wasn't going to push her away. "You want the baby?" she whispered softly, searching his black eyes.

"Of course I want it!" he said huskily. He studied her hungrily. "I want you. I'm sorry I was so stupid. I was jealous of Hollister. I didn't understand." He kissed her again. "God, I've missed you! *¡Mi vida, mi alma, te quiero!*"

"You love me?" she faltered.

"With all my heart. With all I am," he breathed into her mouth. "You have to marry me."

She started to speak when the elevator opened and a tall man came into the room. He was a Texas Ranger, like the man beside him.

"Sergeant?" Lieutenant Avery asked, because his subordinate was acting in a very odd manner. He was carrying a pretty blonde nurse and he looked . . . spellbound.

John stared at him blankly for a minute,

then he grinned. "We're pregnant," he said. "She's going to marry me. You are, right?" he asked Sunny, who nodded, stunned.

"Well!" the lieutenant replied.

"We'll need somebody to give her away," John said, eyeing his boss. "Would you?"

Avery chuckled at Sunny's expression. "Sure. Just tell me where and when. But for the moment, Ruiz, you might put her down. We've got some people to interview. One of them's here, in the ER. Your son said you were headed this way."

"My son. Oh, God, I have to text him back," he said. He put Sunny down. "I'll pick you up after work, okay? We can make plans. You can come down to the ranch with me."

"Plans. The ranch. Your son." She just stared up at him blankly, her mind whirling.

"Plans." He kissed her one last time. "I'll be here when you get off duty."

She watched him go blankly.

"I suppose congratulations are in order," Merrie York teased. "I'm so happy for you! For two reasons!" she added with a pointed glance at Sunny's stomach.

Sunny burst out laughing. "I guess congratulations are in order," she said. She hugged Merrie, with tears of utter joy rolling down her flushed cheeks. "And I thought he was just playing, that he didn't really want me! Oh, I'm so happy!"

"I'm happy for you, sweetie," Merrie replied. "He's gorgeous."

"He truly is."

"But right now, we'd better get to work. Mayes is growling in our direction." She indicated the stoic supervisor at her desk.

Sunny made a face. "I'll explain it all to her."

"Take her a cup of coffee before you do. It works wonders," Merrie teased.

Sunny wondered who'd told John that she was pregnant. Merrie knew Ruiz, and she'd known about the morning sickness that didn't seem to happen just in the morning. But Merrie only knew Ruiz as a Ranger. Besides, she didn't think Merrie would sell her out. And Tonio didn't even know Ruiz.

She gnawed on the question all through her shift, until she went downstairs with her coat and purse and found a radiant John waiting for her.

He helped her into the coat, kissing her soft hair. "Let's go home, sweetheart," he whispered, and he led her out to the SUV.

She felt like treasure. He held her hand the whole way to Jacobsville and filled her in on

Rado's case. They'd tracked him down to Victoria, where he was hiding out with a cousin. Law enforcement officers from several agencies had surrounded the house and arrested him for capital murder.

It was like a dream come true. With Rado and most of his gang out of the way, Sunny and especially Tonio would be safe. She'd have to tell John about her young friend. He'd like him, too.

John pulled up in front of the massive house and Sunny just stared as he lifted her down to the ground.

"It's magnificent," she said.

"An old Spanish land grant," he told her, holding her hand as he led her to the front door. "I also own property in Argentina. A lot of property. A thriving thoroughbred stud farm and thousands of acres surrounding it."

"My gosh!"

He bent and kissed her tenderly. "One more surprise left," he whispered. He opened the door.

"Sunny!" Tonio exclaimed. He ran forward to hug her and hug her. "Is she going to marry you?" he asked his dad excitedly. "She likes yellow roses, I told you. If you bring her a big bouquet and a pint of hot chocolate, I know she'll say yes!"

Sunny was shell-shocked. "Tonio?" she exclaimed. "What are you doing here?"

"It's my home," he said with a smug grin. "That's my dad," he added, indicating the man beside her, who was also grinning.

She felt her face going numb. "I need to . . ." she began, and fainted dead away.

When she came to, Tonio was holding her hand and John was sitting on the sofa beside her, bathing her face with a cold, wet cloth.

"You have to see a doctor," John said firmly. "You need special vitamins and checkups and things so we can have a healthy baby."

"Gosh, that's so cool," Tonio exclaimed. "I won't be an only child anymore!"

Sunny smiled at him. "I'm so happy," she said, and choked up.

"It's the baby," John said indulgently. "Hormones."

"I read about hormones in school," Tonio volunteered. His eyebrows arched. "Would you like some ice cream and dill pickles?"

Sunny burst out laughing. "No, but I wouldn't say no to a nice cup of black coffee."

"Decaf," John said. "Not the strong stuff. I'll make it . . ."

"You will not. I'll make it," Adele said from the kitchen. She'd been eavesdropping. She came in, leaned over and hugged Sunny. "A baby in the house! I can hardly wait! My sons are too big to be hugged, they say. I'm Adele."

"I'm Sunny," she replied, returning the hug. "You can hold the baby any time you like," she added with a tearful smile.

"If you can get around me," John teased. "I love babies. I used to give him his bottle when his mama was sick. He was a sweet baby. He grew into a brave boy," he added, and Tonio beamed.

"I am so dumbfounded," Sunny said, breathless as she looked around her. "Tonio told me his father was always working."

"I am," John confessed sheepishly. "I get called out all hours. I'd always go, because we had married Rangers with babies and I covered for them. Not anymore," he chuckled. "Now I'll have one of my own and somebody can cover for me!"

"All this time," Sunny said as she sat up and Adele went to work in the kitchen. She looked from Tonio to John. "I never knew you two were related."

"I couldn't tell you," Tonio said sadly. "I was afraid you'd tell him about David if you knew who he was. And I couldn't tell him about David because I was afraid he'd make me stay away from him."

"Secrets," Sunny said, shaking her head. "How's the video game?" she asked suddenly.

"It's great! I play it all the time."

"That new one?" John wondered. He sat down beside Sunny and linked his fingers with hers. "I wondered where you got it."

"Admit it. You thought I'd lifted it from a shop," Tonio teased.

"No," John said, smiling indulgently. "My son wouldn't steal. He's above such things."

Tonio flushed with pride. "Thanks, Dad." He plopped down on the other side of Sunny. "So when are we getting married?"

John chuckled. "We'll get the license first thing in the morning. There's a seventy-two-hour waiting period, but I can get a judge to waive that," he said easily. "So day after tomorrow. That will give us time to outfit your new mother in a spiffy wedding gown. We'll get one from our local designer, Marcella. She does couture stuff for a design house that belongs to one of Tippy Grier's friends in New York City."

"A designer gown? But, John," Sunny protested, worried about the expense.

"We own a thoroughbred horse stud in Argentina," he said, surprising his son. "I used to drive a new Jaguar sports car, every year, before I married your mother," he told the boy. "We both agreed that you should grow up as normally as possible, so we dressed you out of department stores and never put you in private schools."

"Jaguars," Tonio said, with wide eyes. "Horse stud. Argentina." He was spellbound.

"You're not to let it go to your head," John said firmly.

Tonio crossed his heart. "Sure. But you have to promise me a Jaguar sports car when I graduate from college," he added mischievously.

"Done," John chuckled.

Dinner was a boisterous affair. Sunny had never felt so much a part of a family, not since she lost her own.

"It's magic here," she told John while they sat in the living room, after Adele had gone home and Tonio was immersed in the video game Sunny had given him for Christmas. "I love this house. And Adele's so sweet!"

"Her husband is just as nice as she is." He kissed her softly, his black eyes full of love. "I hope you don't want to stop at one child," he teased.

She smiled under his mouth. "No, I don't," she whispered back.

He drew her across his lap and kissed her

hungrily. But suddenly she caught her breath and looked green. "I'm so sorry, but . . . !"

He anticipated what was coming. He carried her quickly down the hall to his bedroom and put her down inside the bathroom. She barely made it in time. He stayed with her, brushing back her long hair, whispering soft words. When she was finished, he gave her mouthwash in a cup and helped her rinse out her mouth. Then he carried her to bed and laid her on the coverlet.

"No way are you going back to your apartment," he said firmly. "Not in this condition."

"But, John," she began.

"He's right," Tonio said, coming into the room. "Sorry," he said with a smile. "I heard the commotion and came to see if I could help. You have to stay here, Sunny, where we can take care of you when you're sick."

"See?" John added with a smile toward his son. "You're outvoted. Majority wins."

"But I don't even have a nightgown," she protested.

"I can fix that." John pulled out his cell phone and punched in numbers. "Adele? Sunny's too sick to go back to a lonely apartment, can you loan her a gown? Yes.

Sure. Thanks!"

John hung up. "She'll bring you one. Luckily you're about the same size," he teased.

She bit her lip and tears ran down her cheeks at the affection she saw on her men's faces. "You're so sweet . . . Oh, dear . . ." She was up and running for the bathroom.

John turned to Tonio as he started to follow her. "Pregnant women 101," he said. "An educational experience."

Tonio burst out laughing as he followed his father to the bathroom. "It's okay, Sunny, we're here! We'll save you!"

She made a reply but it was lost in a burst of nausea.

Nausea notwithstanding, they went the next morning early to get a marriage license. John had taken a day off work, and notified his lieutenant that as soon as he could talk to a judge about waiving the waiting period, they were en route to Jacobsville, where Marcella had a wedding gown in Sunny's size. Father Eduardo was going to marry them. Sunny had taken two sick days as well.

"You'll love Father Eduardo," he told Sunny after they obtained the license, and got a judge to waive the seventy-two-hour waiting period. They were on the way to Ja-cobsville, to Marcella's Boutique. "He's got a big heart. He and Hollister used to run together, in the old days."

"He was a mercenary?" Sunny asked, shocked.

"A good one, from what I hear. He's even better at handling gang violence." And then he related the story he'd been told about the priest who was attacked by seven of Los Diablos Lobitos and put several of them in the hospital.

"Wow," she said softly.

He chuckled. "Not your usual priest." He glanced at her hungrily. "My own nurse, with my own little cowboy right under her heart," he whispered. "You can't imagine how that excites me."

Her hand tightened in his. "I'm sorry I'm such a sick mess right now."

"You'll get better," he promised. "Morning sickness doesn't last forever. Honest."

"I do hope you're right."

"You'll see," he said easily.

The gown Marcella had in stock was one she'd designed for another client, who backed out of her wedding at the last minute and ran off with another man. It was a symphony of white lace with delicate pastel embroidery in the hem and the fingertip veil. It fit Sunny like a glove, and when she stared, spellbound into the mirror, she saw a pretty woman who looked as if she owned the world. It was a shame that she couldn't let John see her in it, but she was just superstitious enough not to.

"You'll be the most beautiful bride ever," Marcella teased as she put the gown delicately into a carrier.

"She already is," John said huskily, as he joined them and handed Marcella his credit card.

Sunny was lost for words. She pressed close against John's side, so much in love and so happy that she couldn't even express it in words. But he knew. He was feeling the same things she was, the wonder of being in love and being loved in return.

They drove back to her apartment. She changed into her gown and he left to go to the church. By the time she was dressed, Colter Banks was in the living room, ready to drive Sunny to Father Eduardo's church. That had been agreed on earlier, since Sunny wouldn't let John see her in the dress before the wedding. Lieutenant Avery, who was giving her away, was also en route. Banks would serve as best man. But at the last minute, John caved in and phoned Hollister to invite him to the wedding. Hollister was amused, because he could still hear traces of jealousy in John's deep voice. But he agreed to come. He'd always been fond of Sunny. He was happy that things had worked out for the two of them.

He was surprised to find Tonio in the seats on the groom's side of the interior. Several nurses, including Merrie York, and a few off-duty residents and interns, were also sitting together on Sunny's side.

Hollister slid into the pew beside Tonio. "What are you doing here?" he teased. "I thought you'd be on the bride's side over there."

"I'm on my dad's side," Tonio replied, grinning.

"Your dad?"

Tonio nodded and pointed to John, who was standing at the altar, waiting for the music to begin. "My dad."

"Oh, good lord," Hollister said, remembering his conversations with Tonio. "I never knew who your dad was. Well, you come from good people."

"Thanks. Sunny's going to be my mom. It's like a dream come true," he added, beaming.

"I can imagine."

The music interrupted any further comments. The "Wedding March" played on the pipe organ, while Sunny came down the aisle on Lieutenant Avery's arm. As Tonio looked back, he noticed some burly, unsmiling men in expensive suits, including one big one who had a little blonde woman and a toddler with him, and, across from them, some boys in gang colors. Serpientes! Friends of the priest, Tonio imagined, who were there just in case any of the wolves showed up to cause trouble. What a mixture, Tonio thought, laughing inwardly.

Father Eduardo smiled as the lieutenant turned Sunny over to John and sat down. Colter Banks stood beside John, as best man. Merrie York joined Sunny as maid of honor. The ceremony began.

Tonio watched with delight, as his father married the nicest woman he'd ever known, besides his own mother.

The priest pronounced them man and wife. John raised her veil solemnly and kissed Sunny with aching tenderness. They smiled at each other as if they were the only two people who'd ever been in love. In the audience, Tonio beamed. So did Hollister.

As they made their way to the back of the church, the big man in the expensive suit stepped out into the aisle.

Sunny, who recognized him, stopped to introduce her husband to the big man, who was her landlord.

"John, this is Marcus Carrera," she said. "His wife, Delia, is from Jacobsville."

"It's an honor," John said, shaking the big man's hand. "Thank you for being so kind to Sunny."

"She's easy to be kind to," came the reply. Carrera smiled. "Money's no good if you can't do useful things with it."

"My thought exactly," John said, without elaborating. Later, his wife and son would discover that he funded scholarships at several colleges and helped fund many outreach programs at local hospitals and churches.

"I hope you'll be as happy as we are," Delia said, smiling as she jostled her son on her hip. "You just need one of these to make your marriage perfect," she added teasingly.

"Oh, we're already there," John said, pulling Sunny close. "Just a few more months," he added. "It's like Christmas already."

"I know the feeling," Marcus said. "Be happy. If you ever need help, I'll be around."

"Thanks," John said, and Sunny echoed the sentiment.

Merrie York came up to hug them both

on her way out, standing beside Colter Banks. "Congratulations. I know you're going to be happy."

"Yes, we are," Sunny said. "We're going to wait on our honeymoon, so I'll see you day after tomorrow," she added.

"I'll see you," Merrie replied with a smile.

Banks watched her go. "She's nice," he said.

"Her whole family's nice," Sunny replied. "Her brother has a ranch in Jacobsville."

"Well, Mrs. Ruiz, ready to go home?" John asked with a grin.

She pressed against his side. "More than ready. Tonio, I wish you could come, too."

"I'll be along after school," Tonio replied, hugging Sunny. "It was nice of the principal to let me out for the wedding."

"It was, indeed. We'll drop you by on the way home. Maybe we can talk to the principal in Jacobsville about getting you reinstated next year," he added.

"Not until after soccer season's over," Tonio protested. "I'm going to be a star!"

"He is pretty good," John said.

"I imagine he's good at anything he wants to do," Sunny said with an affectionate smile. "I love having a son of my very own," she added softly.

Tonio fought a lump in his throat. "I love

having a mom of my very own," he replied after a second.

"Will you two stop before I start bawling?" John grumbled. "Imagine that, if anybody sees me, a grown Texas Ranger with tears rolling down his face? We'd be disgraced!"

"Sorry, Dad," Tonio said.

"Sorry, John," Sunny added. But she grinned from ear to ear. She knew that John was fighting some strong emotions of his own.

"That's all right, then," he said. He smiled indulgently.

They dropped Tonio off at school and went home to a blessedly empty house. An hour later, they were draped over each other in a damp, spent tangle.

"Better than ever," he whispered huskily.

"Much better than ever," she agreed, stretching and wincing. It had been a rather overly enthusiastic coming together, and she was sore. She laughed. "It just gets better and better."

"Yes, it does." He pulled her over and kissed her softly. He brushed back her tangled hair. "Have I mentioned that I'm crazy about you?"

"Several times. Did I mention that I'm

also crazy about you?"

He nodded. "Several times."

She drew in a long breath. "I feel like I've come home."

"Me, too." He wrapped her up tight. "I'm sleepy."

"I'm sleepy, too."

They dozed off.

"Mom? Dad?"

There was knocking on the locked bedroom door. Loud knocking.

John came awake at once, attuned to sudden interruptions. "Tonio?"

"Can you come out?" Tonio called. "I have a surprise!"

John kissed Sunny awake. "Our son has a surprise," he teased.

"Oh. Of course." She got up, nude, looked around at her beautiful wedding dress and her underthings draped over a chair and made a sudden realization. "John, I have no clothes!"

He looked at her with sated passion. "I suppose we have to dress you in something. Okay. I have an idea."

He pulled out a pair of jeans that were too small for him and a thick flannel shirt. His eyebrows arched as he handed them to her hesitantly.

She burst out laughing. "They'll do. But we have to go back to San Antonio and get my clothes tomorrow, okay?"

He had some shopping in mind, but he didn't tell her. "Okay."

She dressed quickly and they went out into the living room. Tonio called from the kitchen. They went in, and their faces brightened. Adele had made a wedding cake. An elegant, beautiful cake, with a bride and groom on top. Beside the cake, there were covered dishes of every sort.

"People have been bringing food for the past hour," Adele said, grinning at them. "But I made the cake. There are cards and flowers from so many people," she added, shaking her head. "You'd think the President just got married here!"

Sunny and John exchanged delighted looks. "I don't think we even know this many people," he said when he saw the stack of cards on the table.

"How sweet of them!" Sunny exclaimed.

"We could take wedding pictures, but," John said worried, noting how poor Sunny was dressed.

She hugged him. "I'll have real clothes tomorrow. We can take them then. It's okay. Honest."

He shook his head. "Adele, thank you."

"You're most welcome." She had a mischievous look. "You need something borrowed and blue for the wedding, even if I missed it because of my doctor's appointment. You come with me and I'll provide both," she told Sunny.

And she did. Sunny had her wedding photos with John taken in a beautiful borrowed blue shirtwaist dress with all the appropriate underthings, while her new son stood by and watched with loving eyes.

Their new baby, Rafael Wesley Ruiz, was born several months later. A daughter, Angelica, followed the next year. And they did live, all of them, happily ever after.

ABOUT THE AUTHOR

The prolific author of two hundred books, **Diana Palmer** got her start as a newspaper reporter. A *New York Times* bestselling author and voted one of the top ten romance writers in America, she has a gift for telling the most sensual tales with charm and humor. Diana lives with her family in Cornelia, Georgia.